WITHDRAWN

CONTENTS

WITHDRAWN
WESTERN ISLES LIBRARIES
F9060225
MACGILL

INTRODUCTION

Moleskin Joe is a navvy, an itinerant construction worker.

> He is an outcast of society, a children's bogey, the shunned of civilisation – of which he is the pioneer. It is he who goes out into the deserted ways of the world, who works and dies in combat with Nature, the rude uncultured labourer under whose feet railways, bridges, cities and castles spring into being.

The novel that bears his name is the story of his love for Sheila Cannon. The action of the novel starts in 1915 at the building of a Yorkshire waterworks and ends in the 1920s at a construction camp in the Highlands of Scotland.

It is an unlikely setting for a love story; the world of navvies' bothies and model lodging houses – a world that the author, Patrick MacGill, knew well from first-hand, youthful experience. It is also an account of the emotions, instincts and way of life of a underclass of society written by an author who understood the navvy, the tramp, the poor and ragged of the earth because he had been one of them.

MacGill was born into poverty on a subsistence farm in Glenties, Donegal, around March 1890. After a rudimentary education at the local school, which ended at the age of ten, he did casual work on local farms before going off, aged twelve, to the hiring fair at Strabane, in County Tyrone. He had a variety of jobs on farms, under good masters and bad, before going, like so many of his fellow countrymen, to Scotland to find work at the potato-picking. The story of MacGill's early life and hardships is told in his first novel, *Children of the Dead End*, published in 1914. Patrick MacGill appears in this novel as its central character Dermod Flynn and the autobiographical nature of the novel was freely admitted by the author in his Foreword to the first edition:

Most of my story is autobiographical. Moleskin Joe and Carroty Dan are true to life; they live now, and for all I know to the contrary may be met with on some precarious job, in some evil-smelling lodging-house, or, as suits these gipsies of labour, on the open road.

Dermod Flynn/Patrick MacGill meets Moleskin Joe when Dermod has lost, through gambling, all the money he earned from the season's potato-picking. He cannot face the shame of returning home to Donegal without any money to support his family and, with the end of the harvest season, has to take to the life of the tramp. Moleskin's homespun philosophy, 'There's a good time comin', though we may never live to see it', sustains Dermod, and the two men become friends and share many experiences together, including a spell labouring at the Kinlochleven Hydroelectric construction site in Argyll. The novel *Moleskin Joe*, published in 1923, takes up the life of its title character a few years after the incidents related in *Children of the Dead End*, although Moleskin, who was about forty in the first novel set around 1909, is only thirty-three in 1915. However as MacGill was intending to portray a love affair, long frustrated although eventually happily concluded, between Moleskin and Sheila, who is just eighteen at the start of the story, he doubtless wished to reduce the age differential between the two central characters.

MacGill's first novel, and its interlinked sequel *The Rat-Pit* (1915), which tells the story of Dermod Flynn's doomed love, Norah Ryan, burst on the literary world with remarkable force. There had been nothing quite like this before in its depiction of Irish immigrants struggling to survive in a hostile Scotland, in what one of his characters called 'the black country with the cold heart'. This was popular literature written with unusual power, driven by a palpable anger at the injustices and inequalities of society, enlivened by passages of memorably vivid description created from hard-won, first hand experience. A silent, despised, and indeed, feared class of society had been for the first time given a voice, and a voice which came authentically from within that class.

As novels of proletarian life MacGill's early works can be compared with such classics of the genre as Robert Tressell's *The Ragged Trousered Philanthropists*, which was also published in 1914. MacGill's debt to the novels of Zola, which he discovered while working in Glasgow as a railway labourer, is clear.

> I lived with Hugo's characters, I suffered with them and wept for them in their troubles.

MacGill escaped from the life of the navvy through his self-taught literary skills. While still a worker at the Kinlochleven construction camp he had successfully submitted descriptive sketches to the *Daily Express.* When the contract at Kinlochleven ended he came south and found employment on the Caledonian Railway, as a permanent-way worker on the line from Greenock to Wemyss Bay. He arranged for an Irish printer to bring out a collection of the poems he had written during his navvying days and sold them as *Gleanings from a Navvy's Scrapbook* from door to door round Greenock. One house he called on was that of the novelist and journalist, Neil Munro, who wrote generously in his weekly column in the *Glasgow Evening News* about MacGill:

> He has done even better than the majority of modern poets who venture upon the publication of their own works under more favourable circumstances than his, for he has induced a good many people to buy his poetry who never indulged in any such extravagance before, and he is likely to have a modest profit left after meeting with his printer . . . MacGill is a native of Ulster, as his tongue betrays. 'The fact that everything has been said about everything does not naturally suggest that everything has been sung about everything,' he remarks in the Introduction to his booklet. 'Some day – when I become famous – I will take immense pleasure in reminding the world, like Mr Carnegie, that I started on the lowest run of the ladder, or, as is more correct, in looking for the spot where the ladder was placed.'

MacGill acknowledged in an interview with the Glasgow labour leader Patrick Dollan (later to become Lord Provost of Glasgow) in the Scottish socialist journal *Forward* in June 1914, that this article of Munro's was to be instrumental in the development of his career. Munro's praise was valuable enough, the author of *Para Handy* and *John Splendid* was at the time one of Scotland's most influential critics, but his column was seen by Andrew Lang, then perhaps the pre-eminent British literary critic, who reviewed MacGill's collection of poetry:

> . . . with the result that orders came to me from all parts of England. Altogether, I sold 8000 copies . . . in that way. Shortly afterwards I was offered a post as descriptive writer on the

> *Daily Express*, which I took for three months, thereafter going to the library at Windsor Castle, where I am now located.

MacGill does not seem to have been entirely happy in Fleet Street but was rescued from it by a job offer from the most unlikely of quarters. Canon John Neale Dalton, who had been tutor to King George V and domestic chaplain to three successive sovereigns, was Treasurer and Steward of St George's Chapel, Windsor, and took the young MacGill off to Windsor to work with him as secretary and librarian. MacGill's formal education, a few years at a village school in Donegal, was hardly designed to fit him for his duties at Windsor, working on ancient manuscripts with Canon Dalton. However MacGill seems to have been an auto-didact of quite prodigious proportions – his course of reading while navvying on the Caledonian Railway embraced not only Zola but Thomas Carlyle's *Sartor Resartus*. Montaigne's *Essays* and John Ruskin's *Sesame and the Lilies* as well as Marx's *Das Kapital*. Neil Munro, in his article, noted that the young MacGill had translated Goethe's *Erl-King* and La Fontaine's *Fables* – his knowledge of German and French being 'mainly derived from dictionaries'.

MacGill lived at Windsor until he enlisted in the Army on the outbreak of war, and his Foreword to *Children of the Dead End* is written from 'The Garden House, Windsor' – an address and a world far removed from the navvies' bothies of the story. Dalton remained a friend and MacGill's 1917 war novel *The Brown Brethren* was dedicated to 'my friend JND'.

Patrick MacGill's political views were formed during his early years and moulded by his reading. As he told Patrick Dollan:

> I suppose I must have been a Socialist always, and I did not require much conversion.

While working on the Caledonian Railway he organised a strike over pay and working conditions. He describes this strike in very similar terms in his interview with Patrick Dollan and in *Children of the Dead End* and the two accounts are of some interest in providing a degree of cross-checking on the autobiographical nature of the novel. He told Dollan:

> We were working in an ashpit which was the nearest approach to hell I have known. Into this pit were emptied the ashes, still hot, from the engines which passed over it. We had to go

> down into this pit and throw the ashes up into the wagon – a feat by no means easy to perform. Sometimes we would throw the ashes up, only to catch the brim, and back would come the hot ashes, to tumble all over us, burning our clothing and scorching our skin.

The strike having failed, his fictional *alter ego* Dermod Flynn:

> sent a letter to the railway company stating our grievance. No one except myself would sign it, but all the men said that my letter was a real good one. It must have been too good. A few days later a clerk was sent from the head of the house to inform me that I would get sacked if I wrote another letter of the same kind.

That day MacGill left the railway and went off on the tramp with Moleskin Joe. Later, in his pre-literary career, he was a member of the Social Democratic party in Greenock. The Social Democratic Federation, founded in 1881, was Britain's first Marxist party. MacGill found its members 'too Marxian in speech – but fine fellows for all that' and thought that their talk of the 'Marxian analysis of Capitalism' was not the best way of recruiting socialists.

MacGill's socialist politics were not essentially a matter of book learning or theory but rather a human response to the sufferings of his fellow men. Perhaps this is why his reaction to the question of Irish independence was never particularly strong – the form of government was of less concern to him than the relationship between the weak and the powerful, the worker and the master.

His concern for the experiences of the ordinary man carried forward seamlessly into his series of war-time novels – three of them, *The Amateur Army*, *The Red Horizon* and *The Great Push* are every bit as autobiographical as *Children of the Dead End* or *The Rat-Pit*. In these books he gave the experiences, thoughts, fears and emotions of the private soldier a lively and authentic voice.

After the war MacGill continued to write but without ever quite recapturing the striking success of his early novels. *Moleskin Joe*, with its roots in his early formative experiences, is the only one of the later novels which has consistently found a readership. The figure of Joe and setting of the novel in the world of the navvy was seen by a reviewer in the *Times Literary Supplement* as 'the best part of it' but he clearly found much of the novel, particularly the scenes involving Sheila's four-year-old son, the curiously named 'Cunning Isaacs', to be over-sentimental. Indeed the depiction of the good influence of little Isaacs on the dwellers in the navvies' shack does perhaps strain credibility and verges on the mawkish.

MacGill married in November 1915, while on home leave recuperating from a wound sustained during the Battle of Loos in October 1915. He and his wife, the novelist Margaret Gibbons, settled in Queen's Road, Hendon, where they stayed until they emigrated with their three daughters to the United States around 1930.

A play based on a wartime incident in the trenches, *Suspense*, was produced in London in 1930 and another play, *So Said the Woman*, was later staged in Hollywood and Broadway. Suspense was filmed in 1930.

MacGill's move to America, which seems to have been both an attempt to find work in the film industry and a search for a better climate (a wartime gas attack had left him with chest problems), was not a great success. *Helen Spenser* published in 1937, when he was only forty-seven, proved to be his last work. No novels appeared during the remaining twenty-six years of his life. While ill-health doubtless played a major part in this long silence, there must also be the suspicion that the further MacGill was removed from his early experiences, the vivid sources of inspiration for *Children of the Dead End*, *The Rat-Pit*, *The Great Push* and *Moleskin Joe*, the less convincing was his work and the thinner the vein of inspiration.

His best work, however, has abundant strength, vitality and energy – like Moleskin Joe himself.

Brian D. Osborne
January 2000

CHAPTER I

MOLESKIN JOE

Remote from mansion and from mart,
Beyond the outer furrowed fields –
One with the rock he cleaves apart,
One with the weary pick he wields –
Bowed with his weight of discontent,
Beneath the heavens sagging grey –
His steaming shoulders stark and bent
He drags his joyless years away.

– *From* The Navvy.

Moleskin Joe was in a strange mood on the day that the Hermiston Reservoir burst. But the mood was his not on that day alone, but on several preceding it. Seven in all, perhaps. If counted on his fingers, as he generally counted, he would have found that tally to be correct.

It had all started – the mood had come into being – a week previously. He was on the road from Liverpool, tramping to Hermiston. At Liverpool he was paid off a boat newly in from Australia. At Hermiston, on the Yorkshire moors, his mates of the olden days were building a reservoir. Moleskin wanted to see them and set out on foot, after spending all his money in a seaport boozing den.

The season was summer. Cows grazed nightly in the rich fields, and Moleskin was a good milker. Though a steady walker, he was apt to stumble now and again across farmyard fowls in the darkness, which, as he often vowed, was unlucky – for the fowls. These things, recorded without comment, may explain how a man without a penny may fare well on the highways of England.

One evening, at ten o'clock, Moleskin housed himself in a wayside barn, stretched out his limbs in the straw and was presently half-asleep. The building was a large and roomy apartment, and Moleskin being considerate and thoughtful had shut the door behind him. This was a very wise precaution, as he had found from long experience. The opening of the door always gave time for defence.

Not more than five minutes after his entry the door opened again, and a man and woman came in. Silhouetted against the night the male showed himself to be dressed in the appointments of a soldier, but in the darkness the faces of both were invisible. Coming in a few yards, they halted and embraced. Moleskin stiffened on the straw and waited. The woman was sobbing.

'Now, you silly, don't cry!' mumbled the man.

'But, Dick, it's so awful!'

'It's only as how you think of it,' said the soldier. 'It'll all be over 'fore Christmas, and I'll be back with the brass band playin' in front –'

'But I'm afraid, Dick,' she sobbed in a choking voice that was hardly audible.

'Afraid, you silly!' laughed the man with affected carelessness. 'Now, tell me, what are you afraid of?'

He caught her in his arms and kissed her.

'I don't know,' she said helplessly. 'You'll maybe get killed!'

'Killed!' was his answer. 'Only good folk get killed. Anyway, we'll never go near the trenches. I heard today that the war will be over in a fortnight. Garrison duty, that's what we're going for, Nan.'

'I don't believe it, Dick. I don't believe it!' sobbed the girl. 'They'll kill you, that's what they'll do. And if that happens –'

''Twon't happen,' he interrupted. 'I'll see to it.'

'If anything happens to you, I'll die!' she said, as if not hearing his remark. She sank on his breast, crying as if her heart would break.

'Now, you're not to cry like that, you silly wee dear,' said the man, kissing her. 'I cannot stand it! I want you to laugh, just as I am doing.' His voice was strangely broken, even as he strove to cheer her, and it was evident to Moleskin that the soldier himself was almost on the point of tears.

'But I'm afraid,' she responded dejectedly.

'Tomorrow will see you away and then night and day will be lonely till you come back again. If you ever come back,' she added, gulping down her tears with an effort.

'I'll come back!' was his lame reassurance. 'Garrison duty, that's what they are sending our regiment on.'

For half-an-hour Moleskin lay there listening, at times angry with 'they', whoever 'they' were, who were responsible for the sad parting, at times on the point of tears, brought on by the helpless, hopeless passion of the young girl, Nan, and deeper than all these emotions and sensations was his own feeling of loneliness, and not being wanted. No woman ever wept when he departed, nor laughed with joy when he returned. For the first time this fact struck against his consciousness, giving him a feeling that was almost awe. He realised that he had no woman friend, that he never had one, that, in fact, he had hardly ever spoken to a woman. And his age was thirty-three!

A giant in build, handsome, and not at all stupid, Moleskin Joe was a superman among his navvy brethren. In a manner he was a noteworthy individual, and his fame as a fighter, a worker and even a drinker, was known to most inmates of shacks and doss-houses up and down the country, and varied incidents of his life were common gossip amongst the migratory peoples of the road. These stories were, of course, distorted and magnified until the narrative spun in a Manchester 'model' had little semblance to the actuality which had footing in a Glasgow doss-house.

This, as far as can be ascertained, is the story of Moleskin's early years.

History had no report of his birth. He had been found in a roadside barn one morning, thirty-three years ago, his layette a threadbare petticoat, and attached to the petticoat was a simple message scrawled on brown paper: 'Jos his naim don be crule to him His mother.' The probable age of the child was fourteen days.

Joe was discovered, the matter reported to the police, whereupon the parish in which the human atom was found took the said atom in charge, and it was entered upon the list of resident inmates of the parish workhouse.

Here he remained until he reached the age of eleven, then was transferred into the keeping of a farmer. In this vocation, Joe did various jobs, herded and foddered cattle, gathered potatoes and washed them, shoo'd crows away from the seedfields, and engaged in the many varied operations of farm life.

He got up at five in the morning. ('Lie-abeds never get

anywhere,' said the farmer.) He was fed sparingly. ('Full sacks cannot bend to work,' said the farmer, though the sack, which was Joe, being empty could hardly stand upright.) He was paid no wages. ('Money would get the like of him into mischief.') He was given no holidays. ('Holidays for him, the base-begotten!')

The rod was applied to him without stint or sparing. ('I'll never spoil him by sparing the switch!' The farmer was a respectable Christian).

Joe went to bed early, as soon as he had finished his day's work. Ten o'clock was the hour. The rule of the house was strict on this matter. Staying up late might lead the youngster into mischief. But Joe, humble and docile, never showed any particular bent towards mischief, though on several occasions it was discovered that he went to bed and really fell asleep without taking off his clothes. Possibly, with base-begotten impertinence, Joe was too weary to remove his raiment.

This not being exactly Christian, the farmer, when he discovered it, was constrained to waken the sleeper, make him remove his clothes and chastise him with vigour.

But despite the farmer's care, Joe was guilty of a serious transgression when he reached the age of fourteen, and might have really been useful as a servant. He went away. Where he had gone to was unknown, but six years later a man dressed in the garb of a sailor came to the farmhouse and asked if the farmer were about.

'I'm the farmer,' said the man to whom he addressed the question.

'And where's him that was here six years ago?' asked the sailor.

'Dead,' was the answer.

'Chancin' my arm on a loser,' said the sailor, sorrowfully.

'You look upset,' said the farmer. 'What did you want him for?'

'To make him die violent,' was the sailor's admission. The sailor was Moleskin Joe, who had just returned from a long sea-voyage in which he had been 'an A.B. before the mast,' which modernly understood, meant that he had been a coal-trimmer in a stokehole.

But the life of the open sea did not attract Moleskin; the open road was more to his liking. He fell in with the fraternity of the roving casual workers, the buck-navvies.

The buck-navvy is a type of workman in whom are the qualities (or lack of them) of the hobo, sundowner, vagrant and tramp. He is an outcast of society, a children's bogey, the shunned of civilisation – of which he is the pioneer. It is he who goes out into the deserted ways of the world, who works and dies in combat with Nature, the rude uncultured labourer under whose feet railways, bridges, cities and castles spring into being.

Joe was his name and the soubriquet 'Moleskin' was acquired, the why and when of this acquirement being untabulated in the recollection of the possessor.

His career from the age of twenty, though varied, had in it many recurrent episodes. When working he wrought hard, never at so much the hour, but so much the task. 'Not by the time, but by the piece,' was his motto. Change was the breath of life to the man and all transitions in space were performed on Shank's Mare. Today he worked on a new railway in the South of England, next week he blasted slag in the Scottish Highlands. He slept easily out of doors in the summer, the lee of a hedge his shelter, a stone his pillow, the moon his lamp.

In winter when work was scarce and storm-swept hedgerows were poor sanctuary, Moleskin went on holiday. His manner of obtaining a holiday was very novel and quite effective. In some crowded thoroughfare he would walk up to a plate-glass window, shove his foot or fist through it and wait until the ubiquitous policeman appeared. Then, under another name, he would become a guest of His Majesty the King and have his winter residence in a hostel where food and clothing were supplied free.

Although his history made sorry reading Moleskin Joe was a man of kindly attributes. If strength and courage are cardinal virtues Joe had both, 'but not worth a tinker's damn, either of them,' as he indirectly remarked in after years when he tried to raise the price of a 'wet' on two medals, Distinguished Conduct and Military, which he had won in France.

His life was one without scope or aim. His immediate needs were his constant reckoning. A thirty-six-hour shift never came amiss to him. There was money to burst at the end. But a year's labour of ten-hour days, labour continuous and cohesive, never entered into his scheme of things. For him, as for so many others, there was no objective, no end which was worth attainment.

Moleskin was fundamentally a courteous individual. He was civil, even in argument, which was not a property of his mates, who mostly mistook civility for servility. This sometimes gave a false impression to those who knew him but slightly. In the most heated moment, impulse with him did not always lead to immediate action. Although he knew that the opinions of a man who argues with his fists are always respected, he would continue arguing the point even when fists were uplifted.

Moleskin was never, as he often vowed when the fair sex was a subject for discussion, much of a hand with the wenches. He saw further than the courtship, he saw the marriage. The whole story of love and matrimony was to him a month of slop and a lifetime of saltpetre. 'Wenches are always nice, but the nicest are them you're not buckled to!' was his pet aphorism.

But life is a series of constant changes, fresh angles of observation, and new sense of values. Such a change had come to Moleskin Joe now in the late summer of 1915, and a conversation overheard in a wayside barn was responsible. He had just returned from a voyage to the Antipodes. How he had started on that voyage was a mystery to himself. All that he remembered was a visit to a pal, a coal-trimmer in an outgoing vessel, which stood in the Mersey.

Moleskin had a drink in the fo'c'sle and a smoke of some queer Eastern mixture which might have been opium. He fell asleep and on the noon of the following day he awoke to find the vessel out at sea. A coal-trimmer who should have reported had not turned up and Moleskin, being versed in the art of trimming, got the job.

He was still in the barn. The lovers had long since taken their departure, one to prepare for war, the other to weep for the soldier who was to leave her. When Moleskin fell asleep he dreamt of Nan, a beautiful supplicating Nan who asked him not to go away, not to get killed. He awoke from the dream feeling mystified and very unhappy. It seemed to him that in one night he had suddenly changed, or had been forced to change, his angle of vision, that life opened out a wider prospect, showing an objective worth striving for. The objective as yet lay beyond the field of his experience, but it existed. In it was a woman, a woman's sympathy, a woman's caresses. But what did he want with a woman? he argued. He never cared much for them, and now he was too hard in the horn to have any truck with the sex.

'Me, tied to a petticoat!' he snorted, as he took to the road again.

In the late afternoon of the next day he arrived at Hermiston, a lonely stretch of Yorkshire moor where a large reservoir, on which the navvies had been working for two years, was almost completed. The process of clearing up the place was now in progress, derricks were being dismantled, light railways broken, rails unscrewed, sleepers stacked, and tool-sheds crammed with implements of labour.

But Joe took no notice of these things. His mind was heavy with the mood born in the wayside barn, that vague sensation of loneliness, sterility, incompleteness, which had never been his before. Life was passing by, its days thrown off one by one like the decade beads of a rosary. And for it there was nothing to show, nothing of those little things that pin man's mortal existence within limits, a home, wife and children, a seat by the fireside at night, a lighted lamp and, perhaps, a gramophone.

He was passing by a huddle of discarded wood, empty barrels, tins, wire and rusty iron, when he met Sheila Cannon.

'Here you are again, Moleskin Joe?' was her exclamation when she met him. He looked at her in surprise. He remembered seeing her two years before, while she was yet a child, little more than sixteen, a rather shy creature, endowed with that grace which betokens the delicate transition of girlhood into womanhood. Now the transition had taken place. The child was no more and Moleskin found himself looking at a young woman, who in face and figure was ravishingly beautiful.

Her eyes of deep blue, curtained with heavy lashes, gazed on the man with a look of welcome. Her chin, charmingly chiselled, was held at a piquant angle, unconscious and unstudied. The delicate profile, the firm and supple neck, the lithe body which the bright sunshine lighted in a hundred subtle gleams of colour, brought forth in a mysterious way that borrowed nothing from pose or artificiality, the hidden curves of her body, the style and harmony which is youth's and woman's.

'Sheila Cannon!' Moleskin stammered in confusion, feeling for some reason pleased and uncomfortable at the same moment. 'If I met you in the street I wouldn't know you!'

'And why wouldn't you?' she inquired.

'Because you've changed so much!'

'Not for the worse, I hope?' she asked with a blush.

'No,' Moleskin stammered. 'You are good-looking. I mean, you are very good-looking. I mean, I never saw –' He came to an abrupt clumsy stop and gazed helplessly at the girl. 'And your dad, where is he now?' he asked desperately, treading safer ground.

'He's got a job here as night watchman,' Sheila remarked. 'He was in bad health for a while and had two months' holiday at the sea. Now he's here and much better. Where have you come from now, Joe?'

'Australia,' was his answer.

'I suppose you will be going for a soldier now?' she inquired. 'Just the same wild Moleskin always!'

'Who said I was wild?' he inquired.

'Everyone says it,' the girl confessed, looking at him. 'But I'd rather have a wild Moleskin than a tame one. And I would be sorry if you went away and got killed.'

'Do you mean that?' he asked, a startled look showing on his face.

'Well, who does want anybody to get killed?' was her inquiry. 'Now I must go and get my father his dinner. Goodbye, Joe.'

Moleskin made his way to the huddle of shacks occupied by the navvies. Three times on his journey he looked back at the girl. On the first occasion she did not see him; on the second occasion she glanced sideways at Joe, then turned her head quickly away as if caught in an action of which she was ashamed. The third time she waved her hand to him, to which action Joe responded. But he was too late for her to see. She had already disappeared within the hut where she and her father dwelt.

After a while Moleskin found himself in a shack owned by the ganger, Billy Davis. Billy was a time-bitten worthy, who had been a works' foreman since the very beginning of things. But something of greater import was filling the old man's life at that moment. A son of his had been gazetted an officer in the army.

Many whom Moleskin knew off and on for years were in the shack: Ganger Macready, Digger Marley, Carroty Sclatterguff, Horse Roche, Tom the Moocher and Sid the Slogger, and most of these, good fellows all, either in a fight or a drinking bout, were on the point of joining the army to have a whack at the Germans.

Tom the Moocher, to whom pugilism and pyorrhoea had scarcely left a tooth, was going, not from any sense of patriotism it must be confessed, but because there was a man, a mate of his own, who made a fortune in the South African War 'by pickin' up things.'

Sid the Slogger was also joining up. He had been in the army before, in the Holmshire Regiment, and was drummed out for some misdemeanour. A sergeant was responsible for this happening, and Sid was joining the old regiment to get even with the sergeant.

'When there's a scrap on, it's easy pluggin' a bloke unbeknowin'!' he said. 'Simple as winkin'!'

'And what are you goin' to do, Moleskin?' asked Ganger Macready, a six-foot giant who was on the point of donning khaki, because he felt that there might be a chance of becoming a quartermaster-sergeant, a post with possibilities.

'Lyin' doggo,' was Moleskin's answer. 'I don't want to get killed.'

'Afraid?' asked Macready in a voice half-taunting and half-timorous. 'Cold steel's not to your likin', eh?'

Moleskin pulled up a sleeve, showing a red scar on his forearm, pulled his shirt neck apart and disclosed a somewhat similar scar across his shoulder.

'Met with an accident?' asked Macready.

'Knifed,' was Moleskin's rejoinder. 'I have three like these on the thick o' my leg, a Lascar's doin's at Port Said. That's only one leg! You should see the other! If I'd a pound for every stab of cold steel on my carcass, I wouldn't fight in this damned war. I'd run it! So, shurrup, Macready; I'm not goin'.'

Moleskin was not going! He was not particularly averse to fighting. In fact, his history, if mere physical events were recorded, would have shown a certain tendency towards that type of self-expression. He did not fear hardships. His life was an annal of hardships.

But to salute an unlicked cub, because that cub had pips on his shoulder straps, was something that Moleskin could not do. Therefore he was not going to join up!

The catchword: 'Come and Lick the Germans', had no effect on the man. He had seen Germans, some good, some bad, and so entirely like any other race, that the desire to lick them was no sufficient urge to Moleskin.

Come and Fight for Your Country! That stared at him from every hoarding, but was not sufficient to allure a man whose country consisted of all that was under his fingernails.

And then there was Sheila Cannon.

His thoughts were filled with Sheila Cannon. Her eyes, her soft neck and white arms twinkled across the tablet of his mind, rushing into shape, glimmering, dissolving. A great unreasoned happiness had taken possession of the man. Even the dark hut seemed very light, comfortable and filled with hope. The inmates looked very strange, more brotherly in some way, of different nature from the men he had known before. More homely. That was it. And somehow he felt sorry for them and sorry for himself.

That evening he was absent from the shack for a long time. None knew where he had gone and on his return he would give no explanation to anyone. He simply had a stroll round the moors, and a navvy who strolls round is unknown. It meant doing something without purpose. Strolling round a farmhouse in the darkness, or round a public house, could be explained. The first would mean a stolen fowl for the next meal, the latter a free drink. But simply strolling round! Moleskin, who did the strolling, could hardly explain the phenomenon. But, of course, there was Sheila!

Moleskin had taken a sudden interest in the shack which held her. It was a place of beauty as shacks go. There were a few roses attached to the walls, a pot of geraniums in the window, a lamp with a pink shade, a dainty dresser and a clock. Not much else, but in outward show and inward comfort it far surpassed the other habitations of the encampment. There were in all three women in the shack, Susan Saunders, Sally Jaup, and Sheila. They did washing for the men, darned, sewed, and sold tea and cocoa to the workers. Susan and Sally were old and withered, but were, despite their years, members of the most ancient profession in the world.

Though Moleskin went as far as the door of the shack he did not enter. In fact, when he neared the door he edged off at an oblique angle, walked for some fifty yards, then lay down in the heather and fixed his eyes on the window. When Sheila came out in the starlit night bearing a little basket which contained her father's supper, Moleskin did not alter his position in space, or if altered, it was done so slightly that a mere twist of the neck was sufficient for the change. This movement was sufficient for the time being, and the man could see Sheila passing and his eyes could follow her down into the pocket where the earthen breastworks held the water in place, and where her father occupied his post as watchman.

When the girl's figure was a mere blurred outline in the night mists, Moleskin rose and followed her for a distance, then lay down again and waited for her return. She passed, he followed her back to the shack and lay on the ground outside until the pink-shaded oil-lamp was turned down. Afterwards he went back to his sleeping quarters.

For some nights his movements were the same. He settled himself on the same part of the moor at the same time, waited until Sheila came out, followed her to the breastworks and followed her back again, but careful not to let her know of his proximity.

Something strange had crept into his life, something that was almost ridiculous, but uncommonly sweet and radiant. Never in his life had he felt anything like it, never had he known the fairy-like power of enchantment such as the girl possessed. The other men were unaffected, they spoke casually to the girl, and did not seem to feel her magical influence.

When Moleskin met her by daylight, she spoke to him, always shyly, half in a whisper as if afraid. He stammered his replies, wishing two things at the same moment, one that he had not met her, the other that she should not leave him. And always deeper than any other feeling was the desire that she should be his, not for a passing moment, but for years, forever.

Never had Moleskin felt like this before; never had the man's being surged to such an excess of emotion. Prior to this he had shunned the company of women. They had been as nothing to the man. And now his previous ideas and prejudices had all vanished. A woman had entered his life and he desired her above anything that he had known or dreamed of. The man's heart was in a turmoil, he found himself living in an atmosphere of pain, jealousy, fear. She was to him the apple of Tantalus, within sight and out of grip. Her presence quieted him, but did not make him happy.

The fourth night saw him follow the girl when she was bringing supper to her father. He came to the point where the moor dipped sharply to a dene across which was built the breastworks that dammed a river fresh from the gathering grounds of the moor. The water lay a sheet of sullen darkness in its confinement, borrowing light neither from the stars overhead, nor from the frail moon that sat on the far horizon.

But Moleskin had no eyes for the sombre beauty of the night. His soul was filled with thoughts of the girl who was with her father. Below him lay the little valley, its thalweg steeped in a grey mistiness, out of which the watchman's hut showed like a black rock.

Presently Sheila could be discerned making her way up the incline, her little basket in her hand. Moleskin stretched himself out, becoming one with his hiding-place, and waited. 'I am going to speak to her tonight,' was his thought.

At that moment he heard something creak like a steel girder being strained. Then came a sound as if a giant boulder were being drawn along the masonry, followed by a dull rumble as of hollow thunder. Moleskin sprang to his feet, realising and terribly afraid. A moment's silence followed and from the other end of the valley came a voice, no louder than the squeak of a harried rabbit. 'Run, Sheila. It's goin'! Run!'

The tone of the night changed and was filled with portent.

Movement for a moment stood still, suspended as if the gods waited the signal to destroy the world. A faint gurgle reached Moleskin's ears, something that seemed a sluggish intake of breath. His body and soul parted company for the moment, clamped together again and he found himself striding gigantically down the hill, in the direction of the girl who was now running towards him. At that moment the breastworks broke, withered, and the water bulked out solidly and swept through the channel beneath, firm and substantial as a frozen, cocoa-coloured river. Moleskin had a vague impression of a dumb animal crawling in silence.

A white face looked up at him. He reached for a hand, found it, drew the owner of the face towards him, and pulled her free, lost foothold, tried to regain it, and suddenly felt himself swept along at a nightmare speed, spinning dizzily. His mouth filled with water, he swallowed, choked and swept on into an illimitable eternity.

He had a sudden vision of a woman, Nan, Nan's face and figure bending over him, tenderly, radiantly, looking into his eyes, saying something, whispering something sweet and comforting that he could not understand. He was going to bed, to a bed, soft and warm, with a pink-shaded lamp, a chair, a gramophone, and a fire. And it was not Nan! It was Sheila. He fell asleep.

He awoke drenched, cold and shivering. Something painful, a red-hot iron, was stuck down in his throat. His head had swollen, was on the point of bursting, something moved round on the drum of his ear, something sharp and pointed. It came to a stop, was shoved in, pulled out again and restarted on its circular crawl, going round and round. He got to his feet on hard ground, looked blindly into space, tottered a few steps, then sank to the earth again. The pointed thing, whatever it was, still crawled on the drum of his ear, going round and round with slow disciplined speed.

Suddenly he realised what the thing was. A gramophone needle! Playing a tune on the drum of his ear. He leant forward, hit his occiput with a heavy hand, in an effort to throw the needle from its bearing. But this only intensified the agony: the needle now ripped into the flesh, tearing as it ran, and without losing pace as it tore.

Again he was on his feet, running he knew not whither. All that he wanted was to escape from the terrible pain. But it was impossible to get away from it. Something heavy was holding him. He tried to throw it off and fell. With the fall came relief. The needle had been jerked off and the pain was no more.

He found himself on his back, looking upwards at a sky bright with stars. From a distance, vaguely remote, and having little to do with the man's present plight, came the sound of running water. A woman was looking down at him.

'You're all right now, Joe, aren't you?' she asked.

'Where am I?' he asked, looking up at Sheila.

'I thought you were lost,' she said, stroking the man's wet head. 'You pulled me out of the water, and then you missed your footing and fell in. I followed you on the bank and you were swept back again. And now you're safe!'

Her voice was filled with heartfelt joy and a warm wave of tenderness swept through Moleskin. He wanted to speak, but could find nothing to say. He shut his eyes. From near at hand came the sound of voices.

'It's the men comin' now,' said the girl. Moleskin was still lying on the ground. A piece of grit had got into his eye and he was rubbing it out.

'You're wet through?' he asked.

'I'll soon get dry,' was her answer.

'But your father?' asked Moleskin.

'He's all right. I could hear him shoutin' from the other side a minute ago. The men will take you in and I will have tea ready for you at the shack.'

Her voice was very near him. He could feel her breath on his face. He pulled his hand away from the troublesome eye, and felt her lips rest on his.

'Moleskin Joe,' she mumbled, kissing him, 'you saved my life and – and you're the best man in the world.'

She kissed him a second time and then hurried away as the rescue party bore down upon Moleskin.

Escorted by Ganger Billy and Carroty Sclatterguff he made his way back to the shack. On the journey he felt something crawl from his ear down his neck. It was a daphnid, one of the minute aquatic crustaceans known as water-fleas. Moleskin held it in his hand and looked at it for a moment.

'I thought it was a gramophone needle,' he said.

The Ganger glanced at Carroty; Carroty returned the glance, and the looks exchanged were filled with understanding.

'A brother of my own, sailor he was, got washed overboard in the Bay of Biscay,' said the Ganger. 'Pulled out half-dead he was, and for a month after he thought that a bell was in his head.'

'Loosinations,' was Carroty's comment.

CHAPTER 2

OFF TO THE WARS

When rugged rungs stand up to fight, stark naked to the buff –
Each taken blow but gives them zest – they cannot have enough!
For they are out to see red blood and curse and club and clout,
And few men know and no one cares what brings the fuss about!

– *From* Hard Knuckles.

Next day Macready, Digger Marley, Horse Roche, the Moocher and Sid the Slogger packed up their few belongings, gathered in their wages, and bade goodbye to their old mates. They were going to change uniform, khaki for moleskin, and puttees for knee-straps, supplant the shovels with the sword, the pick-axe with the rifle.

The workers came out to cheer them off and when the contractor made a speech, filled with the usual flowers of oratory, then the common stock of every patriotic tub-thumper in the country, and gave to each man a sovereign in gold, another dozen men joined the party.

Even Ganger Billy Davis, infected by the emotional epidemic which then affected the country, could not resist speaking a few words. He had a son, an educated scholar, a gentleman, and this son, when the call came, was one of the first to step forward and offer his services. He had been wounded already, but was now on the point of going out again to fight for his country. And him an officer! And if he was willing to go, why should they not be willing? was the Ganger's question. He has everything to lose.

'And we have nothing to gain,' was the thought of Moleskin who was a listener.

Father Nolan, middle-aged and grey-haired, was there, dressed in khaki. He was the Catholic priest, who attended to the spiritual needs of his migratory flock, and as the colloquial phrase had it, 'followed the waterworks all round the country.' He spoke to the men, dwelt at some length on the cruelty of the Germans, the desecration of churches, monasteries and convents.

The priest's address struck no emotional spark in Moleskin. Of convents he had the vaguest ideas. He knew, of course, that priests married nuns and that one escaped nun was a 'hot piece of goods.'

Two women were in attendance, Susan Saunders and Sally Jaup, the former old and wiry, who cried all the time, the latter all skin and bones, and more bones than skin, who could drink like a fish, swear like a trooper and work like an ant. Sheila was not in the crowd, and Moleskin felt a chill fear take possession of him. Suppose she were ill, dying. Women are not as strong as men. And last night she got wet when the dam broke. An overwhelming feeling of passion, of love and fear caught him. He went towards Saunders. The tears were streaming from the old woman's eyes, eyes which could hardly take in the form of the priest who was declaiming against the injustice of the Germans.

'Susan Saunders.'

'What's wrong with you, Joe?' she asked, looking at him. 'The poor nuns, God bless them! Raped. Ah, the dirty faggot, that Kaiser!'

'Where's Sheila Cannon?' Joe inquired.

'Is that all that's troublin' you, Moleskin!' Susan cried. 'Sheila Cannon; and the young boys, God bless them, the dears, givin' up their blood behind the parry-pits. But wait till the steam-roller gets the dirty Huns!'

'Sheila Cannon?' asked Sally Jaup, looking at Moleskin.

'Is she not up yet?' asked the man.

'Up hours ago,' was the woman's answer. She had been drunk the night before and was not yet sober.

'But she's not out here.'

'She's gone to Halifax with her old man,' said the woman, giggling. Her blood-threaded skin lay taut across her cheekbones, and one solitary tooth, that resembled a rusty nail, stuck out from her upper gum.

'Desecration!' Saunders echoed a word that had fallen from

the priest's lips. 'Gawr! If I had one o' them here, I'd skin him!'

'Why have they gone?' Moleskin asked Jaup.

'The old feller has got a bad turn. 'Eart,' the woman explained. 'The two o' them went on a motor lorry.'

'The fight for freedom!' Saunders was saying, obviously repeating one of the stock phrases then so common. 'If I had kids o' my own, the wee dearies, off they would go, every man jack of them – and you,' she turned to Moleskin, 'why are you not doin' your bit?'

'Where are they goin' to 'list?' Moleskin asked Susan.

'The contractor is giving them a trolley to take them into Halifax,' the old woman explained. 'And a sovereign too, for nothin', before they start. He's a good man, a man and a half. If he gave me a sovereign I'd go myself.'

'I'm on the shift,' said Joe, who had come to a sudden decision, and therewith become one of the assembly who were ready to dare and do for the sake of their country.

Nineteen in all set off on the four-wheeled wagon three hours later, bound for the town of Halifax. The contractor accompanied them. He was brimming over with good nature, kindliness, fellowship. If he weren't such an old man himself, he would have joined up, demned if he wouldn't! (Forty was the man's age. He was compelled to join up later.) Even his choice cigars, Coronas at two shillings each, were dished out to the navvies on the journey. They were instructed in the art of lighting them. Not that end, but the other end, you know. Horse Roche, who preferred chewing to smoking, chewed his. All pocketed the coloured bands. First souvenirs of the war!

The day was unspeakably hot, and a hot day for a navvy spells thirst and delicious longing, which longing is not to be denied when the pocket is not empty. The vehicle was passing a wayside public house when Horse Roche clasped the driver in a brotherly embrace which, when performed by Roche, was the embrace of a bear.

'Stop!' was his order.

'Ah, a drink!' said the genial contractor. 'Stop, driver. I'll stand a drink all round. Now, whatever you like,' he said, when the motley assemblage stood at the bar. 'I pay!'

This was an unwise admission even for those hysterical days. Sid the Slogger called for a bottle of Scotch; the Moocher, not to be outdone, went one better.

'I pay for what you can drink here,' the contractor hastened to add.

'How long will we get to put it down?' asked Macready, with a look which told of infinite capacity that would show its power if allowed infinite time.

'Five minutes,' said the contractor, looking at his watch.

When they set forth again, the men were much merrier. Germans! Wait till they got a whack at them! Who said there were no guns? The navvies would finish it with pick-shafts! Horse Roche started 'The Bold Navvy Man', and all took up the chorus:

'Tis wenches, fights and blurry booze in barrel, mug and can
That makes the life of stress and strife as suits the navvy man!
Then hurrah, every one
For the bold navvy man!
Safe in a ditch with heels cocked up, so dies the navvy man!

They reached a second public house.

'Stop!' yelled the navvies.

'Drive on!' shouted the contractor.

But driving was an impossibility. Horse Roche saw to that. The wagon came to a halt and immediately was bereft of all occupants save Moleskin Joe and the contractor. Presently loud noises could be heard from the public house, thumping of tables and chairs, singing and swearing. The Slogger, bare-headed and in shirt sleeves, was in the street in a pugilistic attitude challenging anyone who desired such a vital method of amusement to come out and 'put up his fives' to him. Half a dozen were willing to oblige and presently there was a scrimmage, none of the combatants knowing why it started, nor caring when it would end.

'Now, men, come on!' shouted the contractor. 'You'll have plenty of opportunity for fighting when you get over there!'

'There's no hurry!' said Ganger Macready with a benign smile, holding a glass to his mouth.

'It's getting late,' said the contractor.

'Well, why the hell don't you join up yourself?' asked the Slogger, landing, even as he spoke, a smashing right on the Moocher's ear and knocking the man into momentary repose.

'We had better go, boys,' Digger Marley, who had just emerged from the four-ale bar, advised.

'Yes, we'll be late,' said the contractor. His smile was tolerant.

The navvies were just big children, that was all they were!

'If you were goin' to risk your life you wouldn't be in such a damned hurry,' said the Slogger, and stopped dead – for which stoppage the Moocher's fist was responsible.

It took ten minutes to get the live cargo aboard. Two men had to be escorted from the public house and helped up on the vehicle. Slogger was carried on and dumped on the floor of the wagon, where he lay stretched like a stricken bullock.

'Turn to the left at the first crossroads,' the contractor advised the driver. The advice was unwise. At the crossroads the order was obeyed, but Horse Roche countermanded it in his ordinary way. He gripped the driver and ordered him to stop.

'Take the turning to the right!' he roared. 'There ain't no pubs this way.'

'But he's got to go as he's ordered,' demurred the contractor.

'Ordered!' shouted Ganger Macready. 'Up there' – he waved his hand towards Hermiston – 'you're boss, but here one man's as good as another. We're going to fight for our country – but what are you goin' to do?'

'Shove on the damned brake and turn about!' Horse Roche was advising the driver.

'I think he's a Hun,' suggested the Moocher pointing to the contractor. The Moocher's ear had the appearance of a trampled cutlet.

'I'm goin' to have a whack at the Hun!' said an ancient navvy who up till that moment had kept silence. 'Forty-five I am, and older than 'im.' He pointed a calloused finger at the contractor.

'Course he's a Hun,' grumbled Horse Roche. The wagon was now going back to the crossroads. 'A spy – that's what he is. Look! He's goin' pale!'

Which was true. The contractor had suddenly become afraid. The men were getting out of hand. Another drink and he would lose part of the consignment. But there were more than one public house on the road. There were seven at least. Each public house would claim a few, men who would not mount again. Already there were four lying asleep on the floor of the wagon.

Even if he brought all to Halifax, there was the difficulty of getting them to the recruiting station to be considered. An armed battalion would be needed. And at present those near him were discussing, in no subdued voices, the advisability of tipping the contractor overboard. A German! That's what he was! A big-bellied Hun trying to spy on the British working man! If he was in the army he would be shot, strike them stiff if he wouldn't!

'Now, men, if you just get off for a minute till we get to the crossroads, then we can start afresh,' said the contractor. 'It's too heavy a pull up the hill for the engine!'

A few of the unwary scrambled off.

'Where the hell are you fools goin'?' Macready shouted. 'If you go off he'll leave you behind. That's his game, the damned spy. Come on the wagon again!'

Before leaving Hermiston, Moleskin Joe had procured himself a stick, or to be more exact, a knobbed cudgel. That he had such a weapon at this moment was nothing novel. When on tramp he always carried a stick, which served the man in various ways, as a support in walking, a weapon of defence, and a food provider. Moleskin had been known to hit a scurrying rabbit at thirty yards, a chicken at ten, the latter blow so apt that the fowl dropped without a squeak.

Holding the cudgel in his hand he went to the back of the wagon, stepping over the recumbent Slogger, placed one hand on the side of the vehicle, and looked at the contractor.

'Tell the driver not to come back any further, but go straight to Halifax,' he said.

'What damned game is this, Moleskin?' asked Roche, glowering at Moleskin from the upper end of the wagon, which had now come to a dead halt.

'I'm goin' to Halifax,' said the big man, his knuckles tightening white on the cudgel. 'All that want to walk there, get off and pad it. But the wagon's going the way I want it to go. I've just elbow room here in case any of you want to show dirty like!'

Moleskin was in a perfect position, his back against the rear door and a clear space in front. He gave a few deft turns of his cudgel to show the means in hand were his position rushed. At that moment a number of fingers showed on the lip of the wagon, telling of those who wanted to get back again. Moleskin rubbed his stick along the knuckles and they disappeared.

'On like hell, driver!' he commanded, and the wagon set off again.

Most of the men were asleep when they arrived at Halifax.

Roche was feeling extremely unwell, 'had come over all of a sudden,' as he expressed it. He had never felt like that before.

'Probably it is because you chewed the cigar,' the contractor suggested.

'That's the blurry thing,' Roche agreed in a tempest of fury. 'The cigar. You've poisoned it, that's what you did, you elephant-stomached sack of German cat's-meat. Tryin' to poison me, that's what it was. I'll give you poison, I'll give you seegar! I'll . . .'

Seizing the opportunity, Moleskin Joe descended from the wagon and was presently lost in the smoky streets of Halifax. Only one of the party went to the recruiting station that night. He was the ancient navvy of forty-five. The medical officer turned him down.

That night Joe paced up and down the streets of the Yorkshire town, looking everywhere, knowing in his heart that the job was futile. In daylight his search might be rewarded, but at night all effort was fruitless. The only thing to do was to get shelter for the night and resume his search in the morning.

Ten o'clock came, eleven, and still he was prowling from corner to corner. He had not eaten all day, and even now he did not feel the pangs of hunger. He had not even drunk, and an untouched sovereign lay in his pocket. The thought of Sheila was in his mind, her kiss was still on his lips, the look of the girl's eyes as she bent over him on the previous night was still before him.

When he stopped for a moment, pondering, he could revive the whole scene, not alone revive it in the spoken word and the soft pressure of her face against his, but in something that was even greater than all this – the commingling of two natures, the warmth and ethereal radiance of love.

An essence, new, fresh, unexpected – like rain in a season of drought – had entered the man's being. Never before had he loved anything. His life had been solitary, nobody's child, nobody's lover, nobody's friend. No vague, distant impression of anything sweet, homely, was his. A youth that had given rise to no tender emotions was followed by days devoid of pleasing memories. There was not one moment of these years that the man would live over again. Now, having met Sheila, he felt his heart moved, opened up to something fresh and wonderful. An inward yearning had taken possession of the man, an emotion incomprehensible and sweet, of first love, primitive in its intensity, the emotion of Adam, when he saw the first woman, and knew her as the handiwork of God.

The life that he had led seemed suddenly hateful to the man. He detested it: the aimless wandering, the drinking and fighting. All was without purpose, he realised. And it would go on and on in this way to the very end of his life, to the end of the days of drink and drought, famine and feasting, work and idleness, freedom and confinement. He thought of the job which meant nothing except the pay, the pay which meant nothing except the pub, which, in its turn, meant the prison. He looked upon his life now as a dyspeptic programme seller in a music-hall views the comic turn performing to the Wood family in the last house on Friday night. All repetition of the same stale outworn joke which had been performed a hundred times before.

But against all this nausea and heartsickness was the dream of Sheila. He was agitated and enthralled. He longed to see her again, and a vague internal voice, deep down in his being, told him that he would. But, possibly, she had already forgotten her admission of the previous evening. She was only eighteen, and one does not want to die at that age. If he had saved her life it was certainly worth a kiss. The circumstance was an excuse for any action, any impulse.

Five days later he was still in the town, and still unsuccessful in his search. Then he went back to Hermiston to make inquiries there. The place was deserted. The reservoir was a mere puddle. Where the torrent rioted on the night that he almost lost his life, a mere stream was now flowing. The shack in which Sheila dwelt was now pulled down; the navvies had disappeared.

A week later Moleskin was a soldier of the King; the early part of the following year saw him in France.

CHAPTER 3

SEARCHING

There's a good time coming, though we may never live to see it.

Five years had passed and the world was swinging on in its accustomed way. The war was won, but by whom was still a matter of grave doubt. A few kings had been shoved out of work, without much harm to themselves or hurt to others. The war-babies who were honoured in 1915 were now reaching the age when they would become subject to jibes and jeers at school and play. The war profiteers were being accepted by society, that society which found grace in the fact that its days of profiteering started in ancient times unpolluted by eaves-dropping journalists. The men who did so much (not in the hazard of the field, of course) to win the great war were dying off, doing time, or holding on to the public favour by the hair of their eyelids; and the men who had really taken part in the war, who had suffered, but had not died, were in a bulky measure starving in a land fit for heroes to inhabit.

In fact, things were going on much the same as ever. The eternal verities of Nature were unchanged, the world still stood on the three thin things on which it will stand for ever: the thin stream of milk from the breast, the thin blade of corn on the holm, and the thin thread through the hands of the spinner. The emotional epidemic which infected the more civilised races in 1914 was now dulled, and the world had rested for a while to lick its sores and prepare for a second upheaval greater than the first.

Moleskin Joe had escaped from the mêlée, somewhat scratched, but still hearty. He had gone to France, a man with a purpose and an ideal. To kill did not enter into his scheme of things. His whole object was to make money, and he threw himself heart and soul into the business, and thought of nothing else. One clear aim stood before him: to reappear in the country of his birth, to lay siege to Sheila's heart and make her his own.

All the time the girl's sweet and beautiful face was in the man's mind. At the end of six months he was a sergeant and attributed his success to her. She was his talisman. He had done this to please her, to obtain grace in her eyes when he returned. He was a fighter by instinct, but it took a newly-formed sense of duty to make him a disciplined soldier. Such and such a thing had to be done: if it were not done the Germans would overthrow France, overrun England, and what had happened in the first country would certainly happen in the second. Children would be massacred, women violated.

Though Joe had seen nothing to prove that such incidents had taken place in France, he believed it, and this belief was strengthened with fear, fear when he thought that the girl whom he loved might come in for such treatment. Each German he saw, when in direct action, was a potential persecutor of Sheila, and he strove to put an end to the man's activities.

The Distinguished Conduct Medal was given him and the Military Medal thrice. When the war came to an end, he wore three gold stripes (these signified wounds in those days) and had a sum of money exceeding two hundred pounds in his pocket. This was in the summer of 1919.

Then he set out to look for the girl. He never had word from her in all those years. He knew not where she lived, if she were married or single, if she had forgotten him, or remembered him still.

Demobilised, he obtained a free railway ticket to Halifax, and went there, because it was as good as anywhere else. If it had nothing to offer the man, it was, at least, the playground of a happy memory and a dream. He stopped one day in the town and on the next tramped to Hermiston. Grass grew in the bed of the ancient reservoir, which had never been rebuilt. A solitary bullock grazed in the valley where he had rescued Sheila Cannon. Beyond a broken wall, out of which stuck a rust-bitten girder, the place had the aspect which might have been its own on the sixth day of God's handiwork.

Joe, striving towards his happiness, and looking on the desolate prospect, had a sudden feeling that the few faint hopes which he had nursed so desperately were failing him, that from now on he was what he had always been, an outcast, an

Ishmaelite. Today, tomorrow, the whole future was without discipline. He could go where he wished, stay where he desired, and all the prospect offered no hope, no solace.

Love profits little by a severance that is too long drawn out. It lives by giving and taking, a communion of souls, each soul making that given by the other its own. Like the body, the soul needs continual sustenance and neither will live for ever on a chance scrap picked up in a lucky moment. But the soul can maintain itself for a longer period, being gifted with that inherent faculty for digesting the same tit-bit over and over again and always finding in it something palatable. But weariness will eventually come and Joe was becoming weary.

His money became suddenly distasteful to him. It was a means to an end, but how to reach that end was not quite clear to the man. Sheila might be anywhere at that moment. Her father was possibly dead, then she would have no further need to 'follow the waterworks.' She had no address when he left her; she did not know his address; there was no bond between them whatever, except a kiss given years ago at the spot where he now stood.

'However, I'll try and find out old Ganger Billy,' was his thought.

A few days later he found himself in a Leeds model lodging house, one that he had often visited years before. The place was newly done up, the proprietor was not the proprietor of the old days, the lodgers were not those whom he had known. Instead of fustian jackets, moleskin trousers, velvet waistcoats with ivory buttons, the time-honoured garb of the hard-bitten navvy, they wore second-hand khaki and smoked cigarettes. Moleskin, chewing a quid, looked them over and saw not one whom he had known in his old days.

Bradford, Newcastle and Carlisle were just as useless. He met no one whom he knew. His ancient world had fallen and a new world had sprung into being. He was even told that these lodging houses, which were much more stylish than they had been when he knew them before, were inspected by sanitary inspectors nightly. And some of the inspectors were women!

'And I suppose they give you baby soothers to put you to doss!' was the comment of Moleskin.

One day, in the early morning, he came to a crossroads, some miles distant from the town of Wigan. At the point of intersection he saw a two-pronged fork scored in the gravel, its haft towards one road that branched off at right angles to the town. He followed the direction indicated by the haft. Other roads were dangerous. It was the old cadger symbol of the days that were no more. Half a mile along the roadway he came across another symbol of the road. A circle fashioned with pebbles, with one in the centre, was fashioned on the highway. 'Beware police and slide', was the message.

But Moleskin at that moment had no fear of the police. He was still a rover of independent means and had money to the value of one hundred and fifty pounds in his pocket. Two months before the sum was a bigger one, but now it was wearing down and would go on wearing until not a penny remained. But perhaps something will turn up before it is all gone, he told himself.

The person who had written on the road was on in front and there was a possibility of overtaking him. He was not far in advance, for neither wheel nor foot had disturbed the circle or fork and the roadway was not devoid of traffic.

His eyes took in the road in front, a long yellow streak, and as he looked Moleskin became conscious of a little black moving speck half a league ahead. This gave him pleasure – it was somebody, possibly a buck-navvy whom he knew.

Moleskin accelerated his pace and gained on the object that moved rather slowly and lengthened as the pursuer gained on it. At the end of an hour he was on the heels of the figure, which turned out to be that of a man well past middle age, ill-shod, unshaven, and in rags. Round his face was a large poultice bag, which told of toothache. Only the man's eyes were visible.

'Paddin' it?' was Moleskin's question as he came abreast of the man.

'Paddin' it, matey,' was the man's answer in a dry, cracked voice. 'A bit of baccy to spare?' He held a much-burned cherrywood pipe in the cup of his hand, and looked sideways at Moleskin.

'Any luck?' asked Moleskin as he handed the ancient a plug of tobacco.

'Flat on the dead-end,' was the man's answer. ''Aven't seen bread for two days, nor that what buys it for weeks.'

He cut several slices off the tobacco, curled the slices in his hand, and still retained the plug. He shoved that which he had twirled into the bowl of the pipe and re-started cutting again.

Meanwhile, Moleskin was eyeing the man narrowly. He had seen him before, but where, he could not determine.

'What do you work on?' Moleskin inquired.

'Navvyin',' was the answer of the man. He was helping the bowl a second time, but the more he put in the further it sank into the cavity.

'Where were you working last?' asked Moleskin.

'Wales,' said the man, restarting slicing. 'The first piece of baccy I've seen for days.'

'Aye, cully,' said Moleskin. 'And by the look of it, it's the last time I'll ever see that damned plug again.'

'But the pipe doesn't hold a lot,' the man remonstrated, handing all the tobacco that remained back to Moleskin.

'No, the pipe doesn't hold much,' was Moleskin's retort, gripping the pipe and taking it from the man. 'This is the game, is it?' he asked, looking at the bowl, which had two openings, one at the top and one at the bottom. The man had passed part of the tobacco through the bowl and this was now resting on the palm of his hand. 'But you haven't got the hang o't yet. Your hand shook and showed you were up to some dodge. That never does. You've got to look innocent and you looked like a nipper when the apples fall from his pouch as he legs down the garden with the farmer waitin' at the bottom. Here's your pipe, here's the plug, and now spit out all. Where have I rumbled against you before?'

The tramp looked at Moleskin.

'You're Moleskin Joe?' he inquired.

'The board is yours. You've turned up the ace first go,' Moleskin admitted. 'And you're Carroty Sclatterguff? I'd know your skin on a bush. God was tired of his work the day He made you, Carroty.'

The two men shook hands.

'And where have you come from, Joe? I'm trudging laboriously on foot. I've jaw's ache and a corn on every toe of my foot. Abombibble things, corns. I've a pain in my lummar regions too, and a vacooity in my stomach, and I'm getting old, Moleskin.' The old man sighed and shook his head.

'Were you ever spliced?' Moleskin inquired, keeping pace with Carroty, who had trudged off while speaking.

'Three times I was party in the nup-ti-al ceremony,' said the old man.

'Chew them long words, Carroty!' Moleskin advised. 'Speak

good English like me. Were you spliced, or weren't you?'

'Three times,' said the old man, filling a second pipe from the overflow of the first.

'Any luck the three goes?' asked Moleskin.

'There's never any luck in the business,' was the admission of the ancient. 'The first woman left me, because she couldn't live with me. I parted company with the second because I couldn't live with her.'

'And the third?' Moleskin inquired. 'The third time is always lucky.'

'H'm!' was the moody ejaculation of the ancient. 'I'm goin' to see her now. She's quartered 'cross there, if she's still livin'.' With a turn of his thumb he indicated the chimney stacks of Wigan.

'Takin' it for all and all it ain't what you might call a bad shuffle, is it?' asked Moleskin.

'What?'

'Gettin' spliced,' said Moleskin. 'After the parson has jawed his bit, it's straight sailin' from then on!'

'The parson!' Carroty pulled his bandages aside and eyed Moleskin. 'The "parson" were yer words, Moleskin?'

'What's wrong with it?' asked the big man.

'Nothin' wrong with it, for it all depends on the way as you look at it,' said Carroty. 'If you haven't the parson at the start, it means that you're a free man whenever the fancy takes you. And the one woman, Moleskin, day and night, when you go to doss, when you wake up, when you have a crock and when you haven't it, is more than mortal man can bear.'

'And you skedaddled when you got sick o' them?' asked Moleskin, biting a piece of plug and chewing thoughtfully. Marriage was a queer contrivance, certainly! But up to the present he had not realised that three wives were a necessity for married happiness.

'The first was Nelly Grimes of Liverpool, and she scooted –'

'Showed her good taste,' was Moleskin's thought, but he forbore to give it words.

'– and the next was Maggie. I forget her other name. Maybe she 'adn't one, and we got tired of one the other simultanissly.' Carroty put a match to his pipe and pressed the lighted tobacco down with his finger. 'And her that lives at Wigan, Beth Smithers, I'm goin' to now. Left her six years ago.'

They reached a crossroad. Carroty came to a stop.

'And if you don't run across her, what then?' Moleskin asked.

'If I don't run across her, it will be plain sailing,' was Carroty's reply. 'If I do run across her I don't know how it will turn out. I'm a bit old on it, with pains in the lummar regions, and gettin' a bit on in years.' He was silent for a moment. 'A bit on!' he sighed, as if realising the natural outcome of life for the first time.

'But what the devil has that to do with it?' Moleskin inquired.

'She maybe is married again,' Carroty informed him.

'But if she's married to you once she's your wife and there's an end on't,' Moleskin argued. 'All you've to do is to go to her and say, "Here I am," and it'll be all right.'

'But if 'e's a young bucko, what can I do agen him with pains rackin' my lummar regions? Once I was able to stand up to the best o' them, crook an elbow when them as didn't take quarter's much as me were flat in the sawdust of the four-ale.' The old man's eye gleamed as he thought of his ancient prowess. 'Did I ever tell you how –?'

'A thousand times,' said Moleskin, knowing not what story the man was going to narrate, but knowing that it would be one which he had heard a thousand times in the old days. 'Now tell me what you were workin' at in Wales.'

'Light railway near Newport.'

'Is Ganger Billy there?'

'Him. Tom the Moocher, Sid the Slogger, Ganger Macready –'

'Mick Cannon?' Moleskin inquired.

'Five years a stiff,' was the answer.

'And hadn't he a daughter?' questioned Moleskin. 'Her name was . . . was . . .'

'Sheila's her name, and a soncy wench,' said the old man. 'She's gone. I haven't seen her since God Almighty knows when. Hermiston that was it? Hermiston it was. But if I was a youngster at the time I'd have her in hand. Just to get my arms round her . . . '

He saw Moleskin's face darken and he stopped.

'You've escaped a whalin' because you're old!' growled the younger man, turning on his heel and walking back the way he had come. A fortnight later he crossed the marches of Wales.

Here he found a number of the compeers of old days, Ganger Billy, somewhat balder, but wearing a longer and more venerable beard; Sid the Slogger, who had altered little, who could swear as forcibly as of old, and had added a few French words to his vocabulary; Tom the Moocher, resplendent in a set of false teeth which he washed every day, though he washed nothing else; Macready, a man of means (he had become a quartermaster-sergeant); Digger Marley and many others known to Moleskin Joe. Horse Roche had gone to lift his lying-time (which in navvy parlance means unpaid wages) on the Somme battlefield, but the moiety due to him in the High Court must have been very small, for Roche never banked on an Hereafter.

Moleskin made shift to gather information concerning Sheila Cannon, but made inquiries in such a roundabout manner, that it took him days to get to the kernel of the matter. His thoughts were of Sheila all the time, but he spoke of everyone except the girl, of Susan Saunders, Sally Jaup, Father Nolan and others, but never of the girl, not even of her father, the night watchman.

The Hermiston Waterworks never came into conversation on Joe's urging. Even that was too personal, it was something that he could not dissociate with the great event of his life. If he spoke of it the navvies might guess, and the one thing he sedulously avoided was the showing of his hand.

He approached Ganger Billy one day while the old man sat apart at meal time, chewing a crust, and entered into conversation.

'Ganger, how the hell can you keep so young lookin'?' Moleskin inquired. 'You're younger lookin' now than you were five years ago.'

The old man spat out a particle of gristle which his teeth could not master and looked at Moleskin.

'What are you comin' to cadge now?' To the Ganger's mind compliment and cadging were seldom dissociate.

Moleskin pulled a piece of paper from the heel of his boot and spread it out on his hand. It was a five-pound note.

'Blokes that stuff their boots with paper like these has no cause to cadge,' was the mild rebuke of Moleskin.

'Well, I'm feeling as young as ever I did,' said the Ganger, speaking warily as yet. He still suspected the snare. 'But times are not what they were. Trade Union and no piece-work.'

'And the old buck-navvies are off the map,' said Moleskin. 'I was at the old kip-shops in Newcastle, Manchester, Bradford, and they're not there. And there ain't so many o' them at this skinny job.'

'Under the clay most o' them!' said the Ganger, struggling with a second piece of gristle. 'But when it's only so much the hour whether you slack or shove, what the hell's the use o' livin'? I saw Horse Roche and his gang do a straight thirty-six hour shift at Kinlochleven in the old days, and it was ten quid a man when the job was at an end. And they were drunk for a whole week after.'

'And all the time you kept sober and made a little on the deal, selling them tipple,' Moleskin remarked, filling his pipe.

'And why shouldn't I?' was the Ganger's unblushing admission. 'Barrin' yourself, the only man that cares for your pocket is the man that picks it. And then I had my laddie to educate and that cost hard money. Did you see him when you were at the war?'

'I never saw him in all my natural,' was Moleskin's answer. 'Has he a job now?'

'A job!' said the old man with some asperity, as he wiped a greasy palm on the leg of his trousers. 'He never has a job. He has what is called a profession!'

'Good screw?' asked Moleskin who, like his brethren, could never think of work apart from its wage.

'Thunderin' good screw,' said the old man, with a flourish of his pipe. 'Two thousand a year. Can wear a collar at his business and never has to wash his hands – if he doesn't want to.'

'Some come into the world on a lucky deal,' Moleskin remarked.

'But it has to be here.' The Ganger winked and tapped his head with the bowl of his pipe. 'Not, if the truth must out, that I hadn't somethin' to do with it. It cost me hard money to get him started. Did I ever tell you how –'

'You did,' said Moleskin, cutting across the old man's remarks. Ever since he remembered his son had been the principal topic of the Ganger's conversation. In the father's estimation the boy had been a prodigy. A son of a navvy he was to be sure, but at a very early age gave promise of being a cut above the ordinary, and had in him the makings of a gentleman. How he was made a gentleman, the father's efforts to help in the matter, the years of scraping and saving, the gathering of penny on penny for months on end, the paying out of cash for education, lodgment, tailoring and as 'incidental expenses', which general expression was never sobered down to a detailed statement, was a subject of which the father never wearied, but which, if truth is to be told, wearied many of his listeners.

'But you didn't hear about the time when he was in the war – a lieutenant he was, but if he had his rights he'd be a capen – when the General rose up –'

'The last time I heard about your boy was when I was at Hermiston,' Moleskin cut in. 'That was where the dam burst and where old Cannon, the night watchman –'

'And the General says, "The Holmshires are the tidiest –" '

'You knew old Cannon, didn't you, Ganger?'

' "– the tidiest soldiers!" Course, I mind old Cannon. A stiff five years. "The tidiest soldiers in the whole damned brigade, and number ten platoon the best of the whole damned lot!" '

'And Mick Cannon's daughter, you mind the girl, Ganger? Where is she now?' Moleskin inquired.

'How the hell am I to know?' asked the old man. 'And what are you wantin' with the wench? And you're gettin' red in the face, too.'

'Red be damned!' Moleskin blurted. 'Can a man not ask a straight question without gettin' red in the face, eh?'

'Well, you did get red, Joe,' laughed the Ganger. 'Like a blood red rose, my bucko.'

Moleskin tapped his pipe on the leaf of his hand, blew the ash into the air, and put the pipe in his pocket.

'I'm goin' into Newport,' he remarked, moving off a few steps.

'I can give you a job,' said the Ganger, 'if you care to squat here. One and tuppence an hour.'

'I'm too hard-horned to slave by the hour,' was Moleskin's answer. He turned and looked at the old man, then came back a step. 'I don't mean that it's a shame for a man to slave,' he said in a voice that was strangely subdued, 'if he has anything to slave for. You have something to sweat for, but I haven't anything. They've dealt you out a hand, Ganger, and it's now lyin' face down on the board and you've backed it with every brass penny you've got and you've liked backin' it. I was dished out a hand and 'twas swiped off the board as soon as 'twas set down – and I'm backin' it yet, Ganger, backin' a hand I haven't got –'

'Here, Moleskin! what the hell's comin' over you?' asked the Ganger.

'Nothin' wrong with me,' was Moleskin's answer. He took a step towards the Ganger and the Ganger took a step backwards. 'Do you know why I've shipped myself here?'

'I'm broke,' the Ganger professed hurriedly. The old man could not dissociate Moleskin's present mood from an ancient time-rooted cadging proclivity. But Moleskin was not going to cadge. All that he wanted was news of Sheila Cannon.

'I don't want any of your tin,' he growled, tightening his fists and priming himself for the questions. 'What I want to know is this. I've been wantin' to know for years, since the time I left Hermiston . . . And that is, where has She – Sally Jaup got to?'

'Sally Jaup! Old Draggle-tails, you mean?'

'Not her,' said Moleskin. 'The one I mean is Sheila Cannon.'

'That's it, is it?' asked the Ganger. He looked at his watch as he spoke. 'Aye, Joe, she was a comely wench, but where she is or what she's up to, I don't know . . . Time to settle to't!' he yelled to a crowd seated round a fire which burned brightly in an adjacent cutting. 'You love work so much that you would lie beside it all day and look at it! . . . Aye, a comely wench, Joe, a comely wench. But I've not set eyes on her since Hermiston, but Digger Marley saw her two months back at Newcastle. 'Twas a Saturday night and he was lookin' out o' the winder o' Sam Lighter's doss-house in Sholto Street and he saw her on the other side o' the street. But he couldn't run across and have a talk with the wench cos someone had pinched his overcoat the night afore.'

'But what the devil did he want with his overcoat?' asked Moleskin.

'Well, his trousers were up the spout.'

'When did the Digger leave here?' Moleskin inquired.

'A fortnight ago,' said the Ganger. 'He's a spoilt man, Moleskin, and stinkin' with pride. In the war he got a bit o' lead through his belly, and he gets a pension and he gets a dole and Lord Almighty knows what else, and he has no need to work. I don't blame him for that, but what I do blame him for is his snotty conceit . . . And my boy that has got it there' – the Ganger tapped his head – 'has no more conceit than a child of two . . . Come on, you uncircumcised poultice-faced muck-wallopers and grease to't!'

Three minutes unsobered invective got the men to work, and when the Ganger, tongue-weary and out of breath, looked round Moleskin was not to be seen. That night he was not at the encampment, and the next day and the next passed and he did not make his appearance.

'Wonder where he's slid to?' Ganger Billy asked Macready. 'He's in love, you know. And he's such a damned funny cuss!'

'God look sideways on the wench that gets him,' was Macready's comment. 'He'll strangle her. He's a stallion, a steam-navvy!'

Meanwhile, the 'steam-navvy', powerful and gigantic, with a stick in his hand, fire in his heart and fortune hidden in his socks, was eagerly and persistently stepping the highroad towards Newcastle. He was hurrying on without looking round, one thought in his heart, one form in front of his eyes, hurrying towards the place that held the one who was so dear to him.

In the man's stride there was something joyous, invincible and determined. His shoulders were thrown back, his chest expanded to the winds of the country, his eyes fixed greedily on the road in front. Houses, hamlets, towns, stretches of green country slipped by like moving pictures on a screen. Hereford, Shropshire, Cheshire were passed, then came the smoke and chimney stacks of Lancashire, Halifax of ancient memories and afterwards the moorland across to Durham. When weary, he lay and slept, indifferent in choice of hour, but in choice of place careful.

The journey, some two hundred and sixty miles as the crow flies, and with a hundred added as the navvy pads, was completed in fourteen days, and Moleskin Joe found himself a resident in Sam Lighter's model lodging house, Sholto Lane, Newcastle.

CHAPTER 4

TRIALS

From the start you've striven; you're striving still –
No road runs straight to the top of the hill!
Bitter the buffet, the stress and strain,
Yet threshing removes the chaff from the grain!
And God, for the work, when judging the same,
Gives much for the job, but more for the aim.

– *From* Wayside Wisdom.

Two years had almost passed, and we find Moleskin on the road again, a Moleskin without a penny in his pocket and without a dottle in his pipe. He had grown somewhat thinner, a little grimmer, and his step had not that same dynamic energy it possessed when he tramped the highroad to Newcastle two years before.

For the first three months in Lighter's doss-house, he spent the evenings by the window overlooking the lane outside, hoping by some fortuitous chance to see Sheila as Digger Marley was reported to have seen her. But in this he was unlucky. By day he walked through the streets, scrutinising every alley, every corner. Some streets took his fancy and he felt that if she were living anywhere in the place she would be living in that street. And he would walk up and down, up and down, watching every window, every door opening and closing, but all to no purpose.

Often in the half-light of dusk he would take a form to be hers, follow it, to find out he was mistaken. Sometimes he almost ventured to ask kindly-faced women if they ever had seen a girl like Sheila, but when on the point of addressing them he would turn about, leave the street and probably not go near it for days afterwards.

At the end of three months he left Lighter's. The withdrawal was the result of a tragedy. Moleskin Joe rose from his bunk one early morning, turned down the blankets, which bore the inscription written in tar, Stolen from Sam Lighter, and felt his throat. The little tweed purse that contained his money was missing. He had worn it suspended from his neck with a string, worn it in this manner for months.

Moleskin turned chill all over. Motionless he surveyed the bed, fearing to make a thorough examination. He held his breath – if only his eyes could see it! The string was a good thick one, but perhaps the knot became unloosened while he slept. All the lodgers were still steeped in slumber. The one next him lay, with mouth open to the ceiling, snoring heavily. Moleskin felt the straw mattress, rubbed his fingers along its crinkly surface, looked under the bed, went down on his knees and brushed the floor with his hand. There was nothing. Moleskin's head became dizzy, a bell seemed to be booming in his brain. He stood upright, his knees shaking, and stared vacantly at the bunks.

'They've pinched it, the swine!' he suddenly yelled, and gripping the snoring sleeper he pulled him out of the bed. ''Twas you! What the hell were you up to?'

'What the hell're you grousin' about!' grumbled the sleeper, knowing not what had happened, but thinking it must be something terrible. He was out of bed, wearing nothing but his shirt.

'Pinched it!' Moleskin was roaring, his one hand gripping the man's shoulder, while the other was examining the clothes, the pillows, the blankets. 'A hundred and thirty quid and it's gone. I'll search every man here, every damned lag, and find who's pinched it! Ah! where're you slidin' to? You're the bloke that's done it!'

This was addressed to one who had awoke, and hearing the noise Moleskin was making thought that the big navvy had gone mad. A certain timidity prompted the man to withdraw quietly and nakedly, for he had slept without his shirt. Moleskin saw him get to the door with his clothes under his arms. In a bound he was upon the timid man and flew to his throat.

'Ah! he's got it and he's givin' me the slip,' Moleskin yelled hoarsely. 'Cut the string and took it away. But your game's up!'

'I don't know what the hell!' gurgled the naked man. 'I – I –'

'I'll give you hell! I'll gouge your guts out! Thievin', you skunk, thievin'. You came to the wrong shop this time, I'm telling you!'

The poor man had ceased groaning; his face was turning green; his eyes stared from his head as if they were going to spring from their sockets. In Moleskin's grip he swung backwards and forwards like a sodden, superannuated scarecrow in a January gale.

'Wanted to slide off, did you!' Moleskin roared. 'But you weren't quick enough, were you? I'll strangle you – like a chicken!'

'You've done that five minutes ago!' someone remarked. The whole room was up now, and a few were armed with bed boards.

Moleskin came to his senses, and loosened his grip on the man's throat; the latter fell heavily to the floor. Sam Lighter, hairy and unshaven, in shirt-sleeves, appeared at the door.

'Vhat is thees?' groaned the proprietor, waving his arms helplessly.

'Come in!' shouted Moleskin, gripping the proprietor's shirt front, pulling him into the room and shutting the door behind him. 'I've lost a hundred and thirty quid. 'Twas tied round my neck when I went to doss. I woke up and 'twas gone. Where is it?'

'I don't know,' was the proprietor's answer.

'It's in the room!' said Moleskin. 'Nobody's gone out since I woke up. I'll search every damned lag in the place.'

'Two men vent out early this morning,' said Lighter.

'Who were they?'

'I don't know,' said the proprietor. 'They came here the day before yesterday and now they've skedaddled. And if they've took your tin it's ten to one that they'll not come back again!'

And they did not come back. Moleskin had some thirty shillings left and that night he spent it in a carouse which ended, as such nights often did, in a police station.

Then followed troubled times and peace was the last thing he enjoyed. Perhaps he did not desire it. Still, he did not leave Newcastle. He worked in the town in various odd jobs, as a casual labourer. But he saved nothing. As soon as money was made he spent it in the public house. But why should he save? The old hopes, the old illusions were shattered. Life stretched round him, a hopeless vista in which he moved without motive, incentive or stimulant.

And thus passed eighteen months.

At the end of this period he found himself out of work and made his way to Carlisle. The Newcastle police had got to know him and it was time to slide. He knew not where he was going when he started. He knew where he was leaving and that was sufficient. The toss of a button, the fall of a cudgel at the crossroads determined his way, and he took it, accepting his fate with the equanimity of a wanderer who knew that one road was as good as another.

Life was a very simple matter now. In little things – a hen roost quietly raided, a cow milked secretly, a crust begged here and there – he fared well. He struck up against Carlisle one morning and inquired the name of the town.

'I'll get out o' the place as soon as I can,' he said, when the name was told him.

Going through the streets at noon he saw a tramcar passing and noticed one of the passengers, a girl, and knew the girl as Sheila Cannon.

The recognition came as a shock to Moleskin. All that morning she had not entered his mind. Possibly he had thought of her on the day before, but had he? He suddenly felt guilty of committing a terrible wrong against the girl. He had almost begun to forget her. The keenness of the first days had gone. His love had grown less, was filled with intervals of forgetfulness and callousness. Was his passion of years ago a reality? Had he known Sheila Cannon? Had she kissed him? Was it not all a myth?

He saw the car turn a corner. He followed it, walking briskly. In a moment he started running. When he reached the corner the car had disappeared.

'Where did it go?' he asked an old gentleman.

'Where did what?' As he spoke the old man looked down at Moleskin's clothes. A hole showed in the knee of his trousers; one sock showed through the toe of his boot.

'The tramcar,' said Moleskin.

'Where do you want to go?' asked the old gentleman.

'Don't want to go nowhere –'

'But what car do you want?'

That night Moleskin met an old friend, a navvy with whom he had wrought before the war. His nickname was Twister, and Twister had lost a leg in the Great War.

'Help me to crook an elbow, Joe?' he asked.

'Don't mind,' said Moleskin.

'Any o' the old swaddies about here?' asked Moleskin, when he and his friend stood in the four-ale bar.

'All 'ave 'ooked it,' said Twister.

'Where've they gone?'

'A waterworks in Scotland, in a place called Glencorrie,' said Twister.

'Not comin' with me to't?' asked Moleskin.

'No blurry fear, matey.'

'Why?'

'Pension for this.' He tapped his wooden member. 'Dole and an old woman.'

'Buckled?' asked Moleskin.

'Aye,' said the man.

'All right?'

'Not so bad. Does chars, she does, and I keep to bed till one. Then she comes in and dishes me up a meal. Then out to chars again. She's a good worker, Joe. I never say a cross word to her, and that's the best way to treat a woman. And where are you off to, now?' he asked Moleskin.

'Glencorrie,' said Joe.

'Tomorrow?'

'Tonight.'

He had decided to go on the spur of the moment. Attired as he was, he decided not to show himself to Sheila. Thank God, she had not seen him! He would go to Glencorrie, work hard for six months, make money and come back to Carlisle. Then –

He knew that he loved Sheila Cannon as madly and foolishly as he had loved her years ago.

Now he was on the road to the Highlands of Scotland, where the big waterworks were being built. Various navvies were on their way there when Joe had decided to go. It was now the latter part of August, the weather good, hot by day and mild by night. But the road was a lean one; too many unemployed had begged and stolen from the homes that fringed the highway. Game-keepers were awake all night in the plantations, a poached pheasant meant many days' hard labour. Farm servants were alert and armed. Hen roosts were death-traps, the pastures where the milk cows grazed by night were often fields of bloody adventure.

Still Moleskin plodded on. He was now well in the Highlands, far north of Glasgow, and bound for Glencorrie where the big job was in progress. This was the fourteenth day of his journey. The time was near the sunset hour, and the sun, which had scorched his body all day, rested on a mountain ridge, having one last look at the world before sinking in the sea. In the distance could be seen the hills, clothed in a light grey vapour, and resting shoulder on shoulder as if cuddling for the night.

The sun disappeared, the stars slipped out and took their accustomed places in the heavens, the smell of ripening corn and new cut hay filled his nostrils, corncrakes railed across the meadows, the whispering trees settled to repose, sorting their leaves, tucking in their branches; far away a light showed in a home, then another; a startled bird shot across the roadway chattering volubly . . .

'Where are you padding to, matey?'

A figure rose from the roadside and standing erect showed itself to Moleskin as that of a man well over middle height, clean-shaven and dressed in the clothes of a working man, but more the appointments of an artisan than those of a casual labourer. A rucksack was strapped to his shoulders.

'Glencorrie, matey,' was Moleskin's answer. 'You're paddin' it there as well?'

'Yes, my friend, I am going there,' was the answer, given with studied slowness. He looked sideways at Moleskin, and swung into his stride. 'You haven't been up there before.'

'Not me,' said Moleskin. 'Have you?'

'I haven't, matey,' was the reply of the stranger.

'You're maybe not used to the work?'

'Maybe not.'

'Close,' thought Moleskin to himself, 'and if he's not a swell down on his hobnails, ask me another. On the dead-end and lookin' for a job, likely?' he inquired aloud.

'Very likely.' This was given in a tone suggesting that the one who gave it was not in a mood for confidences. 'But the damned work leads nowhere,' he continued. 'The job will last for some fourteen months, or maybe more. Then it comes to an end and one is as poor as when one started.'

'Aye, there's sense in that,' said Joe. 'But all the same, the belly has to be filled, and it can always make a good argument for itself. I've done a short tucker stretch for three weeks, and so I'm chancin' my arm on Glencorrie, for a wee while anyway.'

'And after that?' the stranger inquired.

'Aye, after that, what?' said Moleskin with the air of one who was not willing to prophesy. 'As I say, there is a good time comin', though we may never live to see it.'

'Perfectly correct, my dear fellow,' was the stranger's remark, and having spoken, he pulled a cigarette case from his pocket and held it towards Joe. 'Have one of these. Only gaspers, but I find that I like them just as well as any other. Don't you?'

'I do,' Joe hazarded in answer. The man's air and remarks, half-cynical and half-tolerant, nonplussed Moleskin. He did not know whether to hate him or like him. 'You haven't a match on you?'

'A match? Oh, certainly,' said the man. 'Not a match though, but a flint gadget; one of those used in the great war, daddy . . . Were you in the trenches?' he inquired when the cigarette was lit.

'Had a bit o' a whack at Jerry,' said Joe.

'Simply a bit,' laughed the man. 'You are quite modest in your admission. Ever had the wind up, had you?'

'Well, I wouldn't say as I hadn't sometimes,' was Moleskin's answer. He spoke as if viewing the emotional feeling of fear from a distance.

'Yes, my friend,' laughed the stranger, coming to a sudden halt and stretching an arm towards Moleskin. The fist was shut and stretching out from the angle where the forefinger forked from the thumb was a nozzle of steel that reflected the night light in a dull metallic lustre.

Moleskin, considerably surprised, came to an involuntary halt and looked at the man. 'Now shoot up your hands over your head!' was the sharp order of the stranger. 'This is a revolver!'

Moleskin complied, holding his stick in one mighty paw, the cigarette which he had taken from his mouth in the other.

'What's the game?' he asked.

'Have you any money?'

'Two quid!' said Joe in a shaky voice.

His hands shook: one lost purchase of the cigarette, which fell to the ground; the other tightened on his cudgel. 'The dough's in my boot. That's where I always keep it. You can have it – the whole damned lot. But don't keep that pointed at me!'

'Wind up!' laughed the man sarcastically, still keeping Moleskin covered with the revolver.

'Had the wind up,' mumbled Moleskin. 'But not no more!' he yelled, giving the man a sudden jab on the wrist with his stick. The stricken one gave a yell of pain, the revolver dropped to the roadway, and Moleskin had the stranger by the throat.

'Don't choke me, my dear f-f-friend!' spluttered the stranger, making a vain effort to loosen the grip.

'I'll give you dear, bloody friend,' was Joe's casual comment, holding the man at arm's length and looking into his face. 'What was the game? Are you off your napper, trying to make your fortune by pinchin' from buck-navvies? Back there and let's have it out!'

He shoved the stranger back against the highway dyke, lifted the revolver from the road, made a cursory examination and found that the weapon was not loaded.

'What was the game?' he again inquired.

'It's not a game I would like to play every night,' the stranger admitted, rubbing his neck. 'You almost choked me. And I wanted to frighten you – for your own good.'

'And now it's all off?' Moleskin remarked.

'All on,' was the answer. The stranger drew his cigarette case from his pocket, put a cigarette in his mouth, then handed the case to Moleskin, with the remark, 'You dropped yours on the road. We'll light up and talk of business as we walk.'

For a few minutes they paced together in silence, Moleskin wary and watching his fellow traveller from the corner of his eye, the latter silent as if deep in thought.

'I don't know much about this Glencorrie job,' said the stranger, breaking silence. 'How many navvies are working there, do you know?'

'I dunno, but I've heard that there are about four hundred.'

'How much have they to spend after they've paid for their board and lodging?'

'Not as much now as they had in the old times,' was Moleskin's answer. 'So much an hour is the ticket now; but once it was so much the job.'

'We'll take it that each man gets two pounds a week as an average. What does he pay for sleeping quarters?'

'Ninepence a night blanket doss, thruppence the cold kip,' said Joe.

'What is the cold kip?'

'Sleepin' on the floor of the shack.'

'Well, we may take it that they pay seven shillings a week

for lodgings,' the stranger resumed. 'That will leave thirty shillings or more for clothes and food.'

'Clothes doesn't cost much,' said Moleskin. 'We don't often buy them.'

'But shirts, for example,' asked the stranger.

'No man has more'n one shirt –'

'And wears it always?'

'Aye, till, like the old soldiers, it fades away.'

'What do they do with their money, then?'

'They want it all for feeding.'

'For feeding?'

'Aye, on the bottle.'

The stranger smiled, eased his sack on his shoulder, and blew a puff of smoke into the air.

'If somebody made whisky for them, made it cheap, say at two shillings a pint, would they buy it?' he inquired, after a short silence.

'If they've the money they'll buy it; if they haven't, they'll pinch it. Are you goin' to make it?' asked Joe.

'I did not say so,' was the man's answer.

'One man cannot run the job on his own. It takes two at least, the distiller and the salesman. The distiller must work in a quiet place where nobody can see him. Glencorrie is wild enough; the nearest village is sixteen miles distant. But the question is: would the men tell the police?'

'Not them!' said Joe with emphasis. 'We know nothin' in the favour of the cops.'

'You don't like the police?' asked the man.

'Here, whoever the hell you are, what's the game?' asked Joe coming to a dead stop. 'By the way you speak you weren't brought up on a shovel. You're askin' me this and askin' me that, wantin' to find out somethin'. What are you wantin' to find out?'

'Don't get excited,' said the stranger in a voice, calm, equable and without guile. 'I want to make mountain dew for the navvies. I want somebody to help me, one that I can rely on, one that doesn't get the wind up when he sees a gun pointed at his head. It means money. You can make more in one night than the other men make in a week. If I offered you the job would you be afraid to take it?'

'Afraid!' exclaimed Moleskin with the sublime confidence of a giant whose strength is disputed by a child in arms. 'I don't think I'll funk anything that you will face. I'll take the job, but if I find you up to anything dirty or underboard, I'll – I'll skin you alive!'

'That's the spirit!' laughed the stranger, gripping Moleskin by the hand and squeezing it heartily. 'We'll get along like a house on fire. My name is Tom Jones, the name of a foundling famous in fiction.'

Moleskin paused for a moment before replying. He was not certain of his new acquaintance. Might he not be a spy? Possibly he wanted to find out Moleskin's name, and get him into trouble. He looked round at the wild deserted country, looking for the gin. But there was no trick, no pitfall, and one man was as good as another, or a little better if Moleskin were the one man.

'My name's Moleskin Joe,' he said. 'Reckon ye've never heard o' me. I'm what is called a come-by-chance, meanin' that I'd one mother too many to be decent. I've been a lag, a crook, an A.B. before the mast, a joint as can keep puttin' down tipple in the four-ale when my butties are on the sawdust and a bloke as knows that an inch of steel is as good as a foot of tallow. You've to take my word for some of what I say; other things you'll know to be true when you know me better, and the truth of what I say about steel and tallow my fists will bear me out in any hour of the day or night.'

'Now we know one another,' laughed the stranger. 'And if we pull together we'll be able to make our fortune.'

'Aye, aye,' said Moleskin Joe. 'There's a good time comin', though we may never live to see it!'

CHAPTER 5

NAVVIES

Down on creation's muckpile where the toil-scarred swelter and sweat,
Where the rough of the earth foregather, crude and untutored yet;
Where they swear in the six-foot spaces, or toil in the rubble drift –
The men of unshaven faces who hash on the piece-work shift,
Where the brute is more than the human, the muscle more than the mind,
Driven by loud-voiced gangers, rugged, uncouth, unkind –
There have we met in the ditchway, there have we plighted our trust.
Wonderful navvy shovel, last of tools and the first!

– *From* The Shovel.

Darkness had just fallen over Glencorrie, a wet grey darkness, devoid of shadings and painfully monotonous. All that day the glen had been filled with fog, rising high enough to cover the crests of the surrounding hills and hanging low enough to blot out the objective of scurrying rabbits. Night coming brought little pronounced change, the obscurity changed colour, but became no more intense. The fingers of an outstretched hand were invisible by day or night.

Though darkness had fallen, the glen was filled with the muffled sounds of labour. Those who wrought at the new waterworks were busy with their toil.

Here and there where naphtha lamps lent their red diffused lustre to small patches of gloominess, ghostly figures, ghouls of the solitude, could be seen digging the sloughy ground, hammering piles and laying pipes.

Glencorrie, at any time and in any mood, was solitary. Up

to a very recent date humanity had done little to disfigure the imprint set there on the day that the Master Architect rested from His labour. Civilisation had not touched it unless, perhaps, in the hunting season, when it appeared in the form of Man, with implements of destruction, barbed hooks and metal firearms to levy toll on fin and feather.

When, however, came one, an engineer, bearing chain, cross-staff and field-book, who determined three elements of a triangle, took stock of the valley area which this triangle contained, and calculated the amount of water which could be held upon its surface, the ancient peace of Glencorrie was broken.

Hundreds followed on the engineer's track, and started damming the lower contraction of the glen, until the Glencorrie Waterworks were well under way. Six months more and the job would be completed.

Among the workers the buck-navvies predominated. Some four hundred were employed there. They lived in rudely built shacks, run up from spare wood props, discarded girders, half-rotted joists and rails, and roofed with canvas purchased for a song from the Government Disposal Board. Astute gang foremen were generally the proprietors of these shacks.

The few amenities desired by the navvies were not within easy reach. The nearest hamlet, which to the workers meant the nearest public house, was some sixteen miles away. No woman was ever seen in the place; a postman came twice weekly and was always accompanied by two policemen fully armed.

Despite its situation, however, Glencorrie had a certain rude orderliness of its own. The strongest man, or body of men, was boss, and all disputes were settled with the fists. Men died from violence and privation, and when they died they were shoved into the 'tipper' and covered up with the merciful clay. Glencorrie was a place primitively savage, having neither a God, Church nor a Gallows.

At the present moment the men were badly out of hand. Order was maintained up to a point, up to the day when the first illicit whisky was distilled and supplied to the workers. To get drunk often in the ordinary way was out of the question. The nearest public house was too far away. In the beginning, it was a case of drought without the drink, demand without the supply.

But this altered when there came upon the scene a certain individual, name unknown, history uncertain and credentials unsavoury, who started an illicit distillery in the hills and supplied mountain dew, duty free, to the navvies. The reputable Moleskin Joe, whose first article of conduct was impeding the police in execution of duty, who vowed that the opinions of a man who argued with his fists were always respected, and who knew more of the conduct of His Majesty's prisons than was good for any human being, was fellow in practice to the distiller.

And so the navvies, getting too much of that which was not good for them, fought and drank and earned and spent and lived lives of mad, undisciplined devilry.

This state of unquiet did not appeal to Ganger Billy Davis, although the wrinkle-rutted ancient, inured to hardship, used to things mad and murderous, sordid and sad, was afraid of nothing that did not affect his pocket. But the old dog, who never stuffed his nostrils against smell, shut his eyes against sight, nor plugged his ears against sound, was the proprietor of Windy Corner. This, a shack, was once an army hut. It housed twenty-four human beings when under military jurisdiction, but now by skilful ordering and delicate handling, it housed five, where only one was housed before.

Though not the acme of comfort, it had a certain rude orderliness of its own. A bunk therein cost fourpence a night, sleeping rights on the floor with a blanket cost threepence, and without a blanket, twopence. The inscription: Pinched from Ganger Davis, written with a brush dipped in tar, showed on the blankets. This, not being worth the trouble of washing out, was sufficient security against theft.

Two men were appointed to watch over the well-being of the furniture. They would be designated 'hut orderlies' in the army; in navvydom they were known as 'chuckers out'. They were experienced in the handling of boot and belt, and were the strongest men in the shack. One was Sid the Slogger, the other Tom the Moocher. The latter had his false teeth still, which fact was almost as remarkable as having ever had them. He was the first and only navvy known to have worn false teeth.

Of course, he did not pay for them in the ordinary way. A dentist gave him the set, top and bottom, in exchange for a number of gold-plated sets that Tom had picked up on the Somme battlefield.

Sid and Tom had their work cut out for them, keeping order in Windy Corner. Two men trying to keep four score in control was, to say the least of it, too much of a good thing. Sid was the first to come to this conclusion and told Ganger Billy.

'But I'm payin' you, Sid,' said the old man.

'But what's the damned good of money if I haven't time to spend it?' blurted the Slogger.

'See them that's spendin' it!' pleaded the old man. 'It's all right for them when they're full up – but their heads the next mornin'!'

'But to hell with it! what about me?' cried the Slogger. 'My two eyes are blacked, cos I've only two, my two ears thickened, cos they're all as I've got. Strike me stiff if I put up with it any more!'

He went out, returned at midnight, and spoke in a voice thick with liquor, that he could stand, stand, blamed if he couldn't! stand up to any white-livered tyke in the shack, with one hand behind his back, tied if you like, and knock his double blinking eyes out!

Tom the Moocher (twelve shillings, hard silver, his weekly screw as orderly) endeavoured to knock sense into the Slogger's head, but in this knocking, started by two and taken up by the whole shack, three bunks were smashed to smithereens and several blankets torn. The stove overturned almost set the place on fire.

'Too damned thick is what I calls it!' Tom the Moocher told the Ganger on the following afternoon. 'Gettin' bashed about like this for twelve shillin's a week!'

'I'll make it a pound a week,' said the Ganger.

'Blimey! I should smile!' groaned the Moocher. 'Not if you make it a pound a minute! This evenin' won't see me at the job!'

The evening came.

Ganger Billy sat in the shack, puffing a coloured clay, his red beard sticking out from his chin at an obtuse angle. In the dim apartment he looked his sixty winters, for at that age the life of one who has endured much and bears in many wrinkles the striae of arduous grind, is never counted in summers.

In the shack, hanging from the roof on a chain, was a naphtha lamp, under which, and at the only table in the apartment, sat a man in shirt sleeves counting money. This was Carroty Sclatterguff, back again to his old grind and now nipper to Ganger Billy's gang. Carroty did all the odd jobs, cooking, running messages, and tool repairing.

'Six fives are thirty-five and four are thirty-nine, and that's two quid all but a bob. Doesn't seem right nohow!'

Carroty scratched his head, and looked at the money which lay on the table in front of him.

'Well, I'll have another try,' he muttered thickly. 'Six fives are thirty-five and four is thirty-nine. That's two quid, less a bob and – that's not right neither.'

'Not able to make the tally, Carroty?' the Ganger inquired. As he spoke he drew a match along the leg of his trousers and applied it to his pipe.

'I thought I had it all, but somehow I haven't,' said the puzzled Carroty. 'Six fives are thirty-five, and –'

'Let me give you a hand,' volunteered the Ganger, getting to his feet and approaching the table. Carroty drew the money in.

'No, Ganger, I've lost things in that way before. Six fives are –'

'Are not thirty-five. You're not sober. An old cadger like you, with one foot in the grave and the other in hell, should be ashamed of what you're doin'.'

The Ganger spat to the ground, put his coloured clay in his mouth and fixed a scornful eye on the man with the money.

'Are you not afraid of carryin' on in this way?' he asked.

'In what way, Ganger?'

'Gettin' us this duty-free whisky,' the Ganger explained. 'It has been goin' on now for four months, ever since Moleskin Joe came here. It's a shame, a crying shame. No sooner do the men get their pay than they go and spend it on this devil distillery.'

'They'd spend it, anyway,' Carroty remarked. 'If they didn't get it here, they'd hop to the towns, spend it in the boozer, and what they'd have left the smart women would get, and nine times out o' ten they'd finish up in broad arrows.'

'The men that are makin' this will soon have broad arrows,' said the Ganger grimly. 'Nine months on a plank – the same as many better men got afore 'em.'

'One dollar short,' muttered Carroty, again mucking into his financial problem. 'There are two more as have to pay, Pig-iron Burke and the Digger. I'll get what they owe, and add it to the credit side. They're always slow, payin' their just debts.

Honesty! there ain't any here; and Moleskin will be in any minute!'

Rising to his feet he ambled towards the door in the rear. There were two in the shack.

'Carroty!'

'Aye, Ganger?' said the man looking back across his shoulder.

'Have you heard about the notice that the polis put up outside Dunrobin courthouse this mornin'?'

'I've heard.'

'Fifty pounds it is that's offered for information that will lead to the conviction of the party that's makin' this tipple.'

'It's not a party,' said Carroty. 'There are only two in it, Moleskin Joe and Tom Jones.'

'Have you put eyes on this cadger, Jones?' asked the Ganger.

'I have, and I haven't, so to speak,' was the answer of Carroty. 'I saw only the back of him and it in the dark, and only twice. That's next to nothin' to go by. Ah, Ganger, whoever he is he's a close one. Nobody's seen his face, barrin' Moleskin, and Moleskin's a quiet individual and never says much any time.'

'Everybody has got a tight mouth these days,' the Ganger grunted. 'How much do they pay you to collect the money for them?'

'Can I speak as man to man?' Carroty inquired.

'Man to man be hanged!' roared the Ganger. 'When you speak to me, you've got to speak as if you are talkin' to the Lord Almighty. Man to man! And a damned nipper too!'

'Human bean, I am, Ganger, for all you say!' Carroty struck a heroic attitude.

'Human louse!' jeered the Ganger. 'How much do they give you?'

'Two shillin's per diem.'

''Twill take a long time to make fifty pounds that way,' said the Ganger meaningly.

'Well, I'm not goin' to make fifty in the way that you mean!' shouted Carroty from the doorway. 'I'd be struck stiff 'fore I'd turn on 'em! They've troubles enough as it is, with the sword of Dam-o-cockles over their head. I'm not the man to get 'em into trouble!' he said emphatically.

'Well, think o't, Carroty, think o't,' persuaded the Ganger. 'If they're caught, you'll be caught, because you're helpin' them. You're the one that collects the money. That'll mean two years' hard at least, and you'll have the same chance of weatherin' that as a wax cat in hell!'

'Couldn't be worse off there than here,' said Carroty, ambling out into the fog. 'Couldn't be worse off, no, nor half as bad. Woo! A collusion with a muck barrow!'

There was a sound as if a bullock dropped amidst hurdles and Carroty was silent for a moment, then suddenly his voice mumbled into song:

I gripped him tight by his hairy thrapple
And swiped his nose with a heavy clout!
I gouged the juice from his Adam's apple
And with a pickshaft I knocked him out.

Other voices from the near and far distance joined in with the singer:

So it's fare ye well to the brick and mortar
And fare ye well to the hod and lime –
For it's fifteen hard upon bread and water
For the pore old navvy that's doin' time!

Ganger Davis sat himself on a wood-stump which served purpose as a chair, and stirred up the fire in the stove. Outside he could hear the Moocher hail somebody in a thick voice which was evidence that the man was already drunk. The shift would end in another hour, then it would be a repetition of last night's scene, when a row that started at the card-table at ten o'clock finished out of doors at two in the morning.

Ganger Davis did not know what to do. The police were scouring the countryside for the illicit distillers, and a reward was offered. Fifty pounds! Enough to make a heart yearn, and quake. There were dangers to be feared if the Ganger got the practice stopped. The man who went between the navvies and their liquor was running into grave risks. Sober, the men of his gang were dangerous; drunk, they would stop at nothing.

'Two nights like last night,' he muttered, grinding his teeth, 'and the shack will be pulled to the ground. It must be stopped somehow or another!'

'All by yourself, Mr Davis! Just passing; got lost in the fog. Didn't know where I was – and here I am!'

The Ganger turned round on his seat and looked at the speaker, Father Nolan, who had come to see his flock. The priest was, perhaps, a little over fifty years old, but smooth-shaven and without wrinkles he looked younger. In repose his lips closed tightly over his even teeth and gave the impression of harshness, which impression was strengthened by the sharp intentness of his gaze, and his rather abrupt manner of speech.

'Didn't think you'd come in this night, Father,' said the Ganger. 'Won't you sit and warm yourself?' He shoved the wood-stump towards the stove and brushed it with his sleeve. 'A mucky night, ain't it?'

'Mucky,' said the priest sitting down, and taking a snuff-box from his pocket.

'Not much o' a night to be out in, is it?' asked the Ganger.

'Not so bad, not so bad at all.' The priest took a pinch and handed the box to the Ganger. 'I got a car a bit of the way, but the fog got so very soft that I had to come off and walk the rest of the journey. And how is everything here?'

'Not so bad, Father, if the men would only stop drinking. Hishoo.' The Ganger held himself stiff against a second sneeze. 'This duty-free whisky is the curse of the place,' he resumed. 'Broken heads at night, thick heads in the mornin'. Hishoo! It puts the devil into the men. Hishoo!'

'Always does, Ganger, always does,' the priest remarked, putting the snuff-box in his pocket.

'Before they got this they were natural. When they had a fight they always started with the fists, and maybe, when they got hot at it they would go in for a bit o' bootin'. But now,' sighed the Ganger, rubbing his nose on his waistcoat sleeve, 'a fight always starts with pick-handles.'

'You've seen the reward the police are offering?' inquired Father Nolan.

'Only heard o't,' said the Ganger. 'But to get grip of a man in this out o' the way place takes some doin', and when it's a man like Moleskin Joe, it will take the devil out o' the black pit to collar him. He's not the man to take kindly to life inside quod.'

'Still, it keeps him out of worse mischief,' laughed the priest. '*He's* often been in before, hasn't he?'

'Aye, but never in the summer!' said the Ganger. 'Some will go in summer and winter, but not Joe. He's particular in that way. And always was from the time I first knew him. If he only got started in the right way when he was a nipper, he'd be somethin' better than a navvy this day. If he had the education that my son had –'

'Oh, by the way, how is your son?' inquired the priest. 'Have you had any word from him of late?'

The face of the Ganger lighted up at the question.

'Not for a good while now,' he said. 'But he's so busy, and his studies never come to an end. That's what he told me in his last letter. And the books he has to get!'

'They cost a lot?' asked the priest.

'Big money,' said the Ganger. 'Seventy-five pounds he wanted the last time he wrote to me, and fifty pounds the time before. And 'twas sent him the minute I got his letters. I've a good job here. I own this shack.' He swept his hands with the assurance of a man of property. 'He's my only child, and a gentleman, Father, a gentleman with education!'

'And when did you see him last?' Father Nolan seemed to be particularly interested in the old man's confidences.

'Two years and six months now, come Monday week.' The Ganger placed his pipe on the table. 'I went to his office in Glasgow and he was glad to see me. He had a nice snug room, with pictures on the walls, and a fire, Father, that lit up when he turned a knob. I never saw anything like it before. He was just the same as ever. "I have only ten minutes to spare," he said, and we sat there and began talkin', and before I knew, fifteen minutes were up. That was a long time to give me and him so busy, wasn't it?'

'Yes, it was.' Father Nolan's lips twitched ever so slightly and he fixed a queer, searching look on the old man. 'You're fond of your laddie, are you not, Mr Davis?'

'Aye, that I am.'

'Very fond?'

'Very, very fond,' said the Ganger. 'Never can know how it is that I have a boy like him, such a gentleman –'

'A gentleman!' said the priest. His tone seemed to question the assertion. 'Yes, yes, of course,' he smiled, rising to his feet. 'I've got to go along now to the engineer's place, to see if I can get a shakedown for the night. Tell the Catholics that I'm here, and that Mass will be tomorrow morning at seven in the usual place. And for Heaven's sake try and keep them from the drink for once in a time. There are a hundred or more of my flock here and last month only a score came to their duties and half of them were drunk. I think you're the only man here that never drinks.'

'If I spent my money like some of them when I was a young

man, what would my boy be this day?' asked the Ganger. 'Nothin' better than the rest o' them.'

The priest was silent for a moment as if he did not want to make any comment on the Ganger's statement.

'You haven't thought of becoming one of us, Mr Davis?' he asked, looking at the Ganger.

'A Roman!' laughed the Ganger. Nolan had put the question to him many times and the foreman had treated it as a joke on all occasions. 'To tell you the truth, I might as well be that as any other thing if it wasn't for the confession.'

'Possibly you'll see better one day, and possibly you'll not,' said the priest good-humouredly. He brought a cigar case from his pocket and held it towards the Ganger. 'Somebody gave me these. But I don't smoke. I thought you might like one, however.'

'For me it's the old clay always, thank you all the same. The tooth that's used to clay bogs in one of them. But if you don't mind, I'll take one and keep it for my laddie,' said the old man, catching one of the proffered cigars gingerly. 'He likes one and it good like this. I saw him smokin' one long ago, and the price of it, guess.'

'I'm sure I don't know,' the priest replied.

'Two shillin's,' said the Ganger, wrapping the priest's cigar in a red handkerchief, and putting it in his pocket. 'Ah! he'll like this'n. Thank you very much for givin' it to me, Father Nolan.'

I am a navvy bold,
Tiddy fol-lol; tiddy fol-lee!
I'm full as I can hold,
Tiddy fol-lol; tiddy fol-lee!
I'm full up to the neck –

'Is that the state I find you in, Moleskin Joe?' asked Father Nolan, as the singer heaved in through the door. The singer was Moleskin, Moleskin with a month's growth on his jaw, a day's distillation, three two-gallon jars, in a sack on his back, Moleskin sublime, resplendent, unconcerned, recking not of State nor Church, of the police who were reported on the point of making excursions into Glencorrie for the purpose of bringing the bodies of the distillers to justice, of the priest who had come to bring peace to the souls of such sinners as Moleskin Joe! Moleskin, however, was glad to see Father Nolan, who for a time had been chaplain to Joe's battalion in France.

'Holy hell! Father Nolan and is it you?' Moleskin exclaimed, dropping his sack of booze and gripping the priest's hand.

'Moleskin Joe!' the Ganger reprimanded.

'Well, what the devil am I to say?' asked Joe, pump-handling the priest's arm. 'Me and him were old pals, Ganger. Over the blu-bloomin' top, and the best of luck and down wallop into the tipper. My holy blu – 'scuse my lettin' a few out! – but d'ye mind the night we went on the raid at the brickfields and you took the bay'net to help a man to God –'

'Moleskin!' entreated the Ganger.

'But didn't you, Father Nolan?' asked Moleskin.

'We'll forget all about that, Joe!' said Father Nolan.

'You, a man of God, playin' about with a bay'net like a soldier?' asked the astounded Ganger.

'God forgive me, I had to,' was the priest's admission. 'The Cross was of no avail that night.'

'But you hadn't to come, Father,' said the relentless Joe. 'And you came 'cos you had the guts. That what I like!'

The Ganger, utterly aghast, sat down and tapped the dottle from his pipe.

'The next thing you'll do is offer Father Nolan some of that mountain dew!' said the old man in tones of disgust. There was certainly no depths to which Moleskin would not sink.

'Just what I'm goin' to do,' said Joe, rushing to the sack, bringing forth a jar and uncorking it. 'It's the best we've made yet.' He poured some into a billy-tin. 'The blend, Father, the blend! It is the stuff that'll make you do things that you've never done before, love them that you hate, hate them that you love, pray instead of swear, swear instead of pray. Come, Father, put this down your thrapple and see what it does to you.'

He thrust the billy-can into the priest's hand. The priest looked at it for a moment, then placed it on a form and sat down beside it.

'I want to speak to you, Joe,' he said. 'If you'll just sit down it will be much easier.'

'I'm roostin',' said Moleskin, flopping on a form. 'Now, spit it out whatever 'tis.'

'When were you at your duties last?' Nolan inquired.

'Duties?' Moleskin inquired, a puzzled look overspreading his face.

'Your duties, Joe. Confession and Communion,' the priest explained.

'Not since the war, Father,' said Moleskin airily. 'That gadget was all right then, but now, no cop.'

'Eh!' the priest exclaimed.

'Well, you know yourself how 'twas then,' said Joe. 'Church of England parade too early, Jew parade cook-house fati-gew, R.C. parade cushy, tray bong, so I signed on as an R.C.'

'You mean to tell me that you weren't a Catholic before the war?' The priest was aghast.

'D'you mean to tell me that it was any good being anything like that before the war?' asked Moleskin. 'I lived my life in my own way and have pulled through. I've heard the parsons spout, but what they say carries no weight nowhere. One bloke I heard say: "Knock and it will be opened to you!" and when I knocked a polisman on the napper the door of the quod was opened and I went in, but when I knocked to get out it only meant a second padlock on the door. No, Father, it's without sense. Tip that tipple into your gullet and you'll know that there's a good time comin' though you may never live to see it.'

'No, Joe, you confirmed unbeliever, I'm not drinking,' said the priest with a smile. 'I'm not saying that you are a bad man, for you are not, and the only consolation I have for not asking you years ago if you were a Catholic born, is in the fact that the time you spent at Mass saved you from getting into mischief.'

'Look here, Father,' said Moleskin, springing to his feet. 'I'll make a bargain with you and call it square. I'll be a Catholic again, for two months, if you drink up what's in the billy-can.'

'Moleskin Joe!' reprimanded Father Nolan.

'Well, say three months.'

'No, Joe, we've said enough about it.' Father Nolan rose to his feet and went towards the door. 'Perhaps tomorrow, when you're sober –'

'Father Nolan, I'm not boozed!' He stood in front of the priest, and a pained note was in his voice. 'I haven't tasted one drop for the last five months, since I left the town of Carlisle.'

'You were there five months ago?' asked the priest.

'Five months ago,' said Moleskin. 'Have you ever struck Carlisle in your travel?'

'Have just come from there,' said the priest. 'A small railway job where Ganger Sorley has some eighty navvies working. Know Sorley, Mr Davis?'

'Aye!' snorted the old man. His face had the air of one fitted to pass judgment on a fellow craftsman. The judgment was held in the snort and was decidedly unfavourable.

'You were in Carlisle?' asked Moleskin tremulously.

'Yes, Joe, in Carlisle.'

'Did you see anyone there that you knew?'

'Several,' was the priest's answer.

'Anyone askin' about me?' Moleskin looked at the priest with eager questioning eyes.

'Not that I remember,' said Father Nolan. 'Is there anybody there that you know?'

'No. Yes. I mean no.' Moleskin's face went suddenly red. The Ganger noticed it.

'A woman!' chuckled the old man. 'A wench, a petticoat. That's what's troublin' Joe, the gadabout. Now, Joe, you were once speakin' about a wench to me. Who was she?' His brow wrinkled in thought, his eyes were the eyes of a year-old potato, his gnarled fingers scratched at his rusty beard.

The thought process of the Ganger was interrupted at that moment by the entrance of Carroty Sclatterguff. His wet beard, reflecting the naphtha light, had in it the lustre of sun-kissed gossamery whins.

'Your pecun'ry reward, Moleskin!' he chortled. 'One jar, is it?' As he spoke, Carroty put his hand in his pocket and rattled some money which it contained.

'One jar it is,' said Moleskin. 'The other two is: one for Macready's shack, and the other for Moran's. Enough to make every man in the job merry for twenty-four hours.'

'You don't make it all yourself, Moleskin Joe?' asked the priest.

'I've a mate,' said Moleskin. 'It's him that does all the heady work, the mixin' and the blendin'.'

'What's the man's name?' Father Nolan inquired.

'Ah, that's it,' said Moleskin winking.

'But where is it made?' the priest went on. 'Near here?'

'If everyone knew where it's made, I'm afraid the job would soon come to an end,' said Joe. 'Now, Carroty, empty this jar into something. I want it, when I'm goin' back. If I haven't the jars back with me, no whisky tomorrow night.'

At one o'clock in the morning a slight breeze made its way along the foothills and the fog cleared. It was now an easy matter for Moleskin to get back to the distillery, where he and his mate laboured. With three empty jars in his sack he started on the journey, feeling for some reason very cross with himself. He should have asked Father Nolan for news of Sheila. The girl was a Catholic, and the priest would certainly have known her. Possibly he had met her when last in Carlisle. But Joe had not the courage to put the question.

Ganger Billy would hear him ask; also Carroty Sclatterguff. And on the day following every man in Glencorrie would know that Moleskin was in love. And love – what was it? Weakness, of which no navvy worthy of the ancient traditions of navvydom should be guilty. The men went with women at times, harridans, trollops, when they had money to spare. But that was not love. Afterwards they spoke of intimate relations, their speech a medley of shameful expletives and filthy suggestions. But the women were no better than the men; their language as immodest, their attire as slatternly, their appetites as bestial.

With them Moleskin had never any truck. He dreamt of women, but of women so entirely different that he could never enter the charmed circle in which they moved. He was a navvy, a creature moving on the lowest order of the social plane, miles below the factory hand, the domestic servant, the typist.

And then came Sheila Cannon, came and stayed, and was still filling his life as much as she did years ago. He was thinking of her now as he entered a little cutting in the shadow of the hills. The passage, a short narrow fissure between two rocks rising fifty feet sheer, allowed passage for one individual only. Moleskin was almost through when his foot caught in a rope. He fell to the ground. Immediately something as weighty as the rocks which he had just passed fell upon him; a hand caught his throat, another gripped his arm, three or four fastened on his legs, a jar fell and was smashed to smithereens. His eyes gaped at figures that suddenly peopled the night; he took in the gleam of polished buttons, the brown of faces and the smell of uniforms which he knew too well.

'Easy!' he grunted. 'Easy. I'll come like a lamb!'

And from then for a little while Moleskin Joe was a guest of His Majesty the King.

CHAPTER 6

THE CAVE

Have you seen them at all,
On the green grass,
The white feet that softly pass
On the dewy sod?
And the dews of God
Hang as they hung
On the heather, the flower and the grass
Where their feet have trod.

– *From* Girls.

Had Moleskin Joe continued his journey he would have made his way into a combe, a precipice girt cul-de-sac that came to an abrupt termination at the base of a cliff, two hundred sheer slippery feet in height. Branching off at right angles from the cliff was a deep narrow defile overhung by hair-poised boulders. Here eternity was solidified – an aeon-old upheaval was made quiescent.

At the termination of the gorge a dark cave burrowed into the earth and had within it the first necessity of distillation – a sufficient stream of water falling from a height. This dropped through a fissure in the roof and fell to the floor.

Near the entrance a slow peat fire burned in a circle of stones, and round this was an assortment of barrels, jars, and pails. The whole close atmosphere was filled with the putrid stench of warm grain, disused barm, smoke, soot, and sediment.

The place was abject and filthy, the dull fire intensified the squalor of the oozing walls, filthy roof and the mucky floor. Black obscurity bundled itself into angles, recesses and unfathomable corners, as if cloaking something fell and hideous.

In this darkness a shade moved, came forward, and entered the circle of firelight. The shade took on the form of a young man of thirty or thereabout – Moleskin's partner, Tom Jones.

Throwing a block of wood on the fire, he stood for a moment looking moodily into the dying embers, then, as if overcome with some emotion, he sat down on the floor, buried his face in the cup of his hands and sank into reverie. The fire blazed up and lit the cave and all the appurtenances of the work carried on there – a still, with its worm, condenser, and spigot; barrels of fermenting malt and quiescent wort; jugs of hop juice, sacks of grain, bottles of paraffin. The water falling from the roof gurgled as it dropped into a slough on the floor, then, gleaming in the firelight as if endowed with life, it sidled like a snake into the darkness.

'Dammit!' grunted the man, raising his face from his hands and looking round. A dark flush overspread his countenance. In the light of the burning log his face was almost handsome. 'Dammit! 'twasn't altogether playing the game!'

Tom Jones, otherwise Malcolm Davis, was the son of Ganger Davis, and the only child. His father, with that respect for book-education which is so often the property of the unlearned, conceived hopes for his son and sent him to a good school where he gained a scholarship. In due course the son went to a University, but there his ways were disappointing. The youngster was dilatory in his studies, even in the study of that in which he took more than a passing interest – chemistry.

On one subject, however, he had no compeer – Chances and Recurrences as exemplified on the Turf. He had a system, sound in theory, though shaky in practice, of spotting winners. He generally backed losers. On the money the father sent the son to get books (and the books he needed!) the bookmakers fattened, and the student of Chances and Recurrences became base.

He left the University with a paltry degree, but by virtue of a knowledge of chemistry, which, though ill-arranged, had tokens of future possibilities, he obtained a minor post in a pharmaceutical laboratory. Davis worked here for some three years, putting in barely the necessary number of hours, never early in arrival in the morning nor late in leaving at night – a worker with no zeal and no ambition. His theory of Chances and Recurrences was as yet invalid in practice. The father still sent the money for the son's books. Old Ganger Davis, filled with the untutored simplicity on which live the sharks of society – sharks financial, religious and medical – paid and paid, and gloried in the paying. That the son needed so many books was sufficient guarantee of gentlemanly accomplishment.

In the early days of the war Malcolm obtained a commission in the army. His service in the field was without blemish, and without distinction. The war at an end, he came back to his post in the laboratory, but left in disgrace a few months afterwards. Cheques representing payments of debts had been dishonoured, his tailor, landlady, and tobacconist being amongst the creditors. The alias, 'Tom Jones', a facetious borrowing from the book of that title, was adopted on several occasions, and finally made permanent. Of this change of name the father knew nothing. He still addressed letters to Malcolm Davis, Esquire, Street So-and-So, thought by the father to be the boy's lodging, but was in reality a bucket shop – anyone's address on payment of a penny or two for each letter received.

'Tom Jones' had been necessary for many reasons, but principally to hide himself from his two wives. He had married twice: his first wife was a pretty golden-haired little nurse, who attended him when he came wounded to a base hospital in France. He was sent to London; the girl followed, and in the summer of 1916 the pair were married. A fortnight's honeymoon was spent in Devon, and in that fortnight they found that they had very little in common. Marjorie prided herself on her musical accomplishments and wished her talent to be appreciated; Malcolm was tone-deaf and hated the piano. He was a cynic, she a sentimentalist; he read Goethe and Heine, she Corelli and Wilcox; he was interested in horse racing, and she considered betting one of the evils of civilisation. The only bond between them was a physical one – the shortest lived.

At the end of the honeymoon they went their various ways – he to the trenches, she to her duties as a Red Cross nurse. Afterwards he heard that Marjorie was carrying on a mild flirtation with a medical officer named Taylor, who worked in her hospital. Time enough to see about that when the war was at an end, he thought. Anyhow – it did not matter a damn, was his ready reasoning. He would act in the same way.

Towards the end of 1917 he came to England on leave, and in the mad, feverish moments of ecstasy which were those of young men reprieved for a moment from the gouged alleys of death and destruction, Malcolm met a girl and fell head over heels in love with her.

She was a Catholic working girl, intellectually far beneath him, morally far surpassing him. But her faith and innate purity kept her inviolable in the emotional epidemic of the period; her honour was proof against the blandishments of an officer's uniform. Davis, knowing much of the world, was prone to love and ride away. But this girl was different from any he had previously known. The intimate dalliance which he desired was denied him as a lover. He married the girl.

As with the first, he regretted the second marriage contract almost as soon as it was made, although the first few days and the few others which made up his leave from the battlefield had a certain piquancy of their own. Simple and unlettered, the girl nevertheless managed to be interesting for a time, but when the war came to an end Malcolm realised that from then on she would always be his – his company noon and night, waking and sleeping. He had to take her with him wherever he went, his house hers, his table hers, his bed hers. Then would come children – and these he hated. Squalling ragamuffins! He had been caught in a snare.

Free from khaki, he lived with her for a fortnight in the town of Carlisle. At the end of that time he spoke to her:

'I'm going to Edinburgh,' he said. 'I've work to do there.'

'A job, Malcolm?' she queried.

'I would not exactly term it a job,' he said coldly. 'It is a continuation of my studies in chemistry.'

She felt that he was talking down to her. Studies in chemistry were far beyond her province. Apart from her book of prayers, she had not read a book in her life.

'And when will we be going?' she asked him.

'I am going alone,' was his answer.

'Without me?'

'Well, what can you do?' he asked. 'I must get rooms. You'll have to pull along by yourself for a while. I'll send you money.'

'But when can I be with you, Malcolm?' she entreated. 'I must be with you when, when –' she stammered, blushed, and was silent. The man cast a covert glance at her figure and noticed that the lines of the girlish body had lost a little of their maiden symmetry.

'Well, you cannot come with me now,' said the man. 'In a week or a fortnight; as soon as I can get a place ready.'

He went away. For a while he sent money; not very much, but the young wife was able to pull along somehow. Then when his job came to a sudden termination, when he was flung out on the houseless world without prospect of reinstatement, he ceased writing to her.

Thrown in the cul-de-sac of incompetence, the future held no prospects for Malcolm Davis. All objectives were blotted out; there was nothing for him unless he worked with his hands. Even this labour was difficult to obtain, and there was no out-of-work dole – there was nothing.

The little spark of manhood which was his forbade him calling upon his father in the difficulty. When he worked there was always the possibility of repaying the old man one day. But stronger than compunction was his conceit, that conceit which debarred the young man from introducing his illiterate father to his stylish mates in the old days. Perhaps that prevented him from soliciting the old man in his present predicament.

His father, however, helped him in an indirect way. When very young, Malcolm came into touch with the navvies and got to know their ways and their needs. Going out as they did into the wildest heel-ends of the country, building bridges, railways and waterworks in places miles removed from public houses, they thirsted for strong waters. Why not bring the public house to their doors? Malcolm argued. This was the idea in his mind when he encountered Moleskin Joe. Testing Moleskin as he did, and finding him a man fit for any emergency, he joined with him, and the two brought the pub (unlicensed) to Glencorrie waterworks.

For five months they had worked together, each in his own particular way. Davis was treasurer and distiller and remained in the confines of the cave. None of the navvies, as far as he knew, had ever set eyes on him. Moleskin was the man-of-all-works, especially the works that were dirty and difficult; it was he who scrounged the moorland for peat and kindling, the navvy habitation for pails and barrels; it was he who did the weekly journey to Dunrobin, purchased barley grain, oatmeal, meal seed, and induced carters to cart it to Glencorrie. Where the roads panned out and man was necessary as a beast of burden, Joe became the beast of burden and delivered the goods to the mountain distillery. Afterwards he traded with his mates, supplied them with the liquor they loved, and received payment. This money was kept in trust by Davis. At the end of the season, when the job would come to an end, profits would be divided between the two.

The police had got wind of the business at a very early date. Two Dunrobin officials, strong Highlanders, came and made inquiries. Of course no navvy had ever drunk mountain dew; they had heard of people making it, not in Glencorrie, of course, but in Wales. They remembered years ago when building the waterworks in Tonypandy. But to drink it? No! It never sat on their stomachs! . . . And even when listening to the story, the police smelt breath that was flavoured with illicit tipple distilled less than twenty-four hours previously.

The police withdrew, and returned a few nights afterwards.

It was then that Moleskin Joe ran across them. What occurred on that momentous occasion was never known, but Dunrobin gossip has it that one man returned to the station without his tunic and the other without his trousers.

For a while afterwards the distillers lived in comparative security, but eventually the law appeared in stronger force, less obtrusive, but more deadly. New workers came into Glencorrie, men attired in the ancient appointments of the time-bitten pioneers, and obtained work. Moleskin Joe, when going back with his jars at midnight, found himself followed by two of these men. He had never trusted them, for though their clothes were fitting, their manner of handling a crowbar and shovel was not above reproach. Plying them with questions, Joe found that they knew little of the traditions of the trade – that they were, in fact, C.I.D. merchants. Moleskin handed them over to Sid the Slogger, Tom the Moocher, and others, and on the following morning they left for the nearest hospital and never returned again.

The State was not done yet, however. At the end of four months it sent its paid servitors to scour the glens and hills of the district. Policemen were suddenly found springing up from the most unexpected quarters. A navvy would go out in the evening for a pail of water. Just to boil up for a billy of tea, or bathe an aching foot. On his way back a hand would suddenly spring out of the darkness, fasten on his collar. The pail would be taken from him, its contents smelt and tasted by men in uniform.

Getting back to his shack, the yarn told by the navvy would lose nothing in its telling. Immediately his mates would go out, armed with picks and shovels, and spend hours in fruitless search. Coming back they would beat the man who sent them out on such a wild-goose chase.

Malcolm Davis heard of the happenings and was much troubled. He could carry on for six months more, to the finish of the job, if the police did not disturb him. By that time he would have some six thousand pounds in his possession. Half that would go to Tom Jones, half to himself. But he did not intend to give any to the trustful Moleskin.

Something had to be given to the uniformed hounds however. A bone, and what better than throwing Moleskin to them? Give Moleskin up, lie low for a fortnight, until all suspicion was over, and then start again. This was the plan of Malcolm Davis.

The first move was successful. Moleskin was already on his way to prison. Tomorrow Malcolm would leave the district, put most of his money in the bank, have a jolly good time and return to the still at the end of a fortnight. Then a few months' hard work, and by the time the police troubled again about the place the job would be near its end and Malcolm Davis in possession of a snug little fortune.

These were his dreams as he sat in the distillery, smoking endless cigarettes and now and again throwing wooden blocks into the fire. He was happy. The future stretched before him, rosy, resplendent; the past had no regrets.

He sat there entirely unashamed of any action committed. The women he loved and who loved him were past history. He thought of Marjorie, the golden-haired nurse, of Sheila, the little workgirl. They no longer existed for the man.

The father who adored him was flouted, the mate who trusted him betrayed, and Malcolm Davis, smoking his cigarettes, was at that moment wondering which would afford him most enjoyment, a week in Paris or a fortnight in London.

'That is the only thing to be done,' he told himself. 'I've got to leave here for a while, and I think it has to be Paris. But I'm going to be careful –'

Where and when he had to be careful was never disclosed at that moment. He was looking towards the door, his eyes taking in vaguely the glint of wet stones reflecting in a sombre way the glow of the still-room fire. Nothing was to be heard save the sough of the wind on the hills, and the lower croon with which it felt its way along the nearer boulders. Something which might have been taken for a white stone, socketed in a dark niche of the defile immediately opposite, altered its location in space. It moved. Davis breathed hard for a moment, his eyes dilated and one hand slid quietly towards his pocket.

'It's nothing!' he told himself. 'A splosh of light, a sheep, a bird!' His eyes were still on it, whatever it happened to be. It stood quite still now, like a rather bedraggled mask glued on to a wall of dark muslin.

'It's all damned nerves!' he grunted angrily, pulling a cigarette box from his pocket.

At that moment the face moved, and came towards him. Davis gasped, and sprang to his feet, mesmerised. The eyes which he fixed on the face were dreadfully vacant. As in a dream he saw the face settling itself down upon the shoulders and body of a human being dressed in a waterproof coat.

'Well, Mr Davis, is this where I find you again?' was the newcomer's question.

'Yes!' Davis stammered, still in a trance. 'Who are you?'

'You don't remember me?' asked the stranger. 'I'm told that I look very young for my years. But you, Mr. Davis, have aged a little since I saw you last.' The speaker unbuttoned his waterproof and disclosed a cleric's uniform. 'Know me now, Mr Davis?' he inquired.

'I'm afraid I do not,' was the distiller's answer. But he had in reality recognised the clergyman as Father Nolan, whom he came across at one period of his life. 'Have you got lost, sir?' he asked.

'No, I haven't got lost,' the priest made answer. 'But I am looking for one who has; for you, Malcolm Davis. Now, you know me, Father Nolan, the old priest who married you to Sheila Cannon four years ago.'

'Married me?' asked Davis, feigning mystification. 'Please sit down, and we'll discuss this matter.' He shoved a block of wood towards the priest. 'I'm sorry that I cannot offer you a better seat, but as you see, I'm labouring under certain disabilities here. You'll have a cigarette?' he suggested as the priest sat down.

'No, thank you,' said Father Nolan, whose eyes were fixed on the younger man. 'I seldom smoke –'

'Or drink?'

'Or drink.'

'You're a wise man,' said Davis, toying with a cigarette. He felt quite at ease with himself now. A parson! Well, what was a parson anyway? No great shakes! Simple souls, most of them! Anyway, he was glad Nolan had come. It would pass a few hours. Davis sat down, lit his cigarette, and stretched his legs out to the fire.

'I'll make a pot of tea,' he said. 'You would like that, wouldn't you, Father Nolan?'

'No, thank you,' said the priest. 'If we come to an agreement on the matter which has brought me here, I wouldn't mind having a cup of tea.'

'Of course you wouldn't,' Davis acquiesced. 'Now, begin at the beginning and tell me how you got these ideas into your head and how you found your way here.'

'I'll tell you all,' said the priest readily. 'In the first place I, in the year 1917, in the town of Carlisle, performed a religious ceremony, the sacrament of matrimony, over two individuals, one an officer in His Majesty's army, known as Malcolm Davis, the other a girl, known as Sheila Cannon. The first was the son of William Davis, a foreman ganger, the other the daughter of Michael Cannon, then deceased. Do I make myself plain?'

'Yes, you do, Father Nolan,' Davis admitted.

'A year ago, four years after the marriage ceremony, I went to Carlisle again and there I met Sheila Davis,' the priest went on in a quiet voice. 'She was very unhappy, her husband had left her, and she had a little boy. She was out of work, a little hungry and a little ragged. Where her husband was she did not know.'

'Why didn't she write to her husband's father?' Davis inquired. This was a feeler. Davis did not want his father to know.

'The navvy, like the bird of the air, has no address,' said the priest. 'The woman asked me to find out where her husband was and in my humble way I made inquiries. I got into touch with a pharmaceutical laboratory, a boarding house, a common lodging house, a navvy who knew this young Davis and saw him quite recently –'

'Ganger Davis?' asked the young man. His voice was calm, but for some unaccountable reason his cigarette dropped to the ground. The priest noticed this and pulled a cigar case from his pocket.

'Try one of these,' he said. 'I don't smoke myself, but some person has given me these. I gave Ganger Davis one a short time ago. He doesn't smoke them, but he kept it – for his son.'

'His son?' asked Davis in a whisper. He had a sudden weak moment. He almost threw himself on the visitor's mercy to confess, make a clean breast of the whole business, let Father Nolan know. That is, if Nolan did not know already. He did know! The thought sobered Davis, and he straightened his back. 'No, thank you,' he laughed. 'I don't care for cigars.'

For a moment there was a strained silence.

'And does the father know where the son is?' he inquired.

'He doesn't know, and there is only one way in which he never will know and that rests in the hands of the son. If the son goes back to his wife, stays with her and be all that a good husband should be, give up the evil course which he has taken –'

'Easy a moment, Father Nolan,' said Davis. 'This is a very interesting case. There is a lot to be said in favour of the wife, in favour of the father, but perhaps we may find excuses for the husband and the son.'

'I am ready to listen to any excuses,' said the priest.

'At the start, Father Nolan, you'll grant that war changes the outlook of most people?' asked Davis.

'Yes, God forgive us.' Possibly at that moment the priest recollected his own misdemeanour with a bayonet.

'Now suppose an officer came back on leave from the trenches, that this officer had no home, that he was an educated man, that he had a feeling that it was ten to one against his living through the next six months of flying scrap-iron, that he had all the joy and urge of life, that he met a young maiden, simple as Hardy's Tess, beautiful as Romney's Lady Hamilton, and fell madly, head over heels in love with her, that he would have gone to hell for her at that moment, that love to her meant marriage, what should he have done?'

'Get married to the girl if she returned his love.'

'He did,' said Davis, 'and regretted it ever afterwards.'

'But he should have considered this beforehand,' said the priest.

'They never considered; not, anyway, at that period of the world's history.' The face of Davis had not changed. 'The life then, Father! Careless, unmoral, gallant, French. The sinful young men were the fashion then. Nothing was too good for them. Promiscuity, adultery, was exuberant life force seeking an outlet. Funk saw sin with kindly eyes. Young men were going to die. Young girls gave them their bodies; old women gave them their blessing. Medals for the war-babies! Free medical treatment for the prostitutes!'

'This young man?' the priest inquired.

'He came back,' said Davis. 'If the gods did not want to

laugh at him they would not have allowed him back. He found that a woman's piquant lack of polish, artificial allurements, and grammar, though a dainty relish for a month of love, is poor substance for a steady diet.'

'And then?'

'For some people attainment spells the end of desire and this young man was one,' said Davis in a cold dispirited tone as if the matter had no further interest for him.

'And if this man knew that the girl loved him very much, that she wept long and sorely for him, that in agony she bore a child which is his, that her heart sorrows for him still, would he not in pity, if not in love, go back to her again and make her happy?' asked the priest.

'But how can he go back?' cried Davis angrily. 'He left her, his purse as empty as hers. For a while he was able to make a little and he sent her part of this. Then came poverty and ever since 'tis poverty, poverty all the time –'

'But he is making money now,' said the priest; 'making it in an evil way, God forgive him, and why doesn't he send her some? Why doesn't he?'

Having spoken, Father Nolan's hand shot out suddenly and rested on the arm of Davis, rested and gripped. The one held, gazed open-mouthed at the clergyman.'

'What do you mean, sir!' he stammered.

'Mean!' Father Nolan got to his feet and looked at Davis. 'Mean, you dirty little shrimp! I mean, God forgive me for it, to give you the best hiding you've ever got in your life. I'll have that hand, too!' he grunted, catching the one that was sliding towards the hip-pocket. 'Didn't know me, eh? You'll know me before I'm finished with you. If it wasn't that I respect your poor father so much, I'd have taken the police here; if it wasn't that I respect your wife so much, I'd take you to the police. Trying to get away, you squirming rat!' Father Nolan twisted him round a few times. Davis was as nothing in the priest's powerful arms. 'Sit down there!' He shoved him on the seat, still keeping grip of his hands. 'For her own safety and her own happiness you had better stay where you are, but every penny you possess is handed over to me now, and the money goes to your wife in Carlisle tomorrow morning!'

On the following morning a letter, accompanied by a postal order for twenty pounds, was sent to Sheila Davis. Father Nolan was the sender.

CHAPTER 7

THE RETURN

When a nail in the sole of your bluchers is poking your foot like a pin,
With every step of the journey driving it further in –
Stomach as empty as pity, homeless and down at heels,
With a nor'-easter biting your nose off, then you would know how it feels
To tramp on the great long roadway. You find when you go abroad
That the nearer you come to Nature, the further you go from God.

– *From* Padding It.

In the fact that on that evening Sid the Slogger transferred a noggin of spirits, raw and illicit, from mouth to stomach without moving his Adam's apple, that Pig-iron Burke swore for five consecutive minutes and never used the same swear word twice, that ten gamblers, sitting to their game of cards, had ten pick-shafts in readiness for a row, that each player had at least one card up his sleeve, that Digger Marley concealed a pack and mixed it with the other cards to his own advantage, there was nothing unusual. These facts, taken as a whole, were the ordinary of an evening in Windy Corner, Ganger Billy's shack in the Glencorrie Waterworks.

'Sclatterguff, what the devil's keepin' you?'

This was Pig-iron Burke's question shouted from the gambling table and directed to the crook-backed man, who was going round the apartment, a two-gallon jar under his arm, a pannikin in his hand, serving spirits to the drouthy ones.

'I'm trudgin' laboriously towards you,' Sclatterguff grunted. Now, as always, he loved long words and generally pronounced them incorrectly.

'Dish out more!' growled Tom the Moocher, gulping his portion and wiping a cavernous mouth with the back of his fist. 'I'vn't my full share nohow!'

'*Your* full share!' grumbled Marley. 'You'd only have that with your ugly mouth to a 'stillery pipe!' Giving utterance to this time-bitten pleasantry, he emitted a laugh from which the property of humour had long since vanished.

'Dunno how old Moleskin's gettin' on tonight!' said Pig-iron Burke, smacking his lips in anticipation of the drink that was coming.

'Dunno,' said the Moocher, licking his lips in remembrance of that which had already passed. For some inexplicable reason the woes of a fellow creature gave relish to their particular moods.

''Twas dirty, lettin' Moleskin be run in,' Sclatterguff remarked. ''Twas all a made-up thing, that's what I say.'

'What do you know about it?' asked Ganger Billy. 'You're full up!'

'Full, I may be, but firm,' said the man. 'Joe's a scrapegoat; that's what he is, a prawn in the game!' He refilled the billy-can.

'Then more a fool him to let the polis nab him,' the Moocher remarked.

'Ah!' Sclatterguff's grunt was one of mystery. 'He was caught in a net. 'Twas the sword of Dam-o-cockles!'

'As long as we get this duty-free what else matters?' Sid the Slogger addressed the shack.

'Nothin' else matters, if we get enough,' was the answer, given with full-throated feeling.

'It's wrong!' shouted Sclatterguff, putting the jar on the floor and sitting on it. 'I'm an old man, but I hate dirty work, and I don't like to think of my ole pal, Moleskin Joe, in the lock-up.'

'Turn on the sluices!' growled the Moocher. 'It's only when you're half-boozed up that you care a rap where anybody is.'

'Sentimental!' laughed Ganger Billy. High in the soot, stench and smoke rose his head, a guttering 'clay' resting on a beard the colour of rusty iron.

'What is Moleskin?' asked Sclatterguff with feeling. 'A big child, and nothin' more. Who'll say no to that?' He was suddenly aggressive. Under the naphtha flare his face had the hue of dry time-worn leather. 'I know more about Moleskin than most of you know. He was gone on a wench!'

'Eh?'

The eyes of the gamblers, sunk forward to within an inch of their favoured cards, as if trying to read the secret which their turn-up would reveal, swerved round and rested on Sclatterguff. In the man's admission there was something of astonishing import. Moleskin Joe in love.

'Who's the wench?' asked Ganger Billy.

'A girl named Sheila Cannon,' said Sclatterguff.

'The one that was almost drownded when the Hermiston Waterworks broke seven years ago, her that Moleskin saved! Is that the wench?' asked Tom the Moocher.

'That's her.'

'Handsome piece of goods!' was Ganger Billy's dry comment. 'I've never seen her since then.'

'Moleskin lost sight of her when you did, and didn't see her either up to six months ago,' said Sclatterguff. 'Then he saw her in Carlisle goin' by on a tram-car, so he came up here!'

'Up here!' exclaimed Ganger Billy. 'What the hell did he come up here for? That's always the way a wench gets what she wants, runnin' away from it. But a man's way is different.' He tapped the bowl of his pipe on the stove, and looked at Sclatterguff.

'Oh! every trick the lassie knows, she plays from dusk to dawn;
The more she puts a fellow off, the more she leads him on!'

sang Sid the Slogger, in a deep baritone.

'Moleskin hadn't a penny at the time! said Sclatterguff.' He was broke, and once he had two hundred and fifty pounds. He made it all in the war, and he wanted to marry the wench when he got out o' the army. He didn't know where she was, so he set out to look for her.'

'A needle in a hay-stack!' said the Ganger.

'And one night, when he was in Sam Lighter's lodgin' house in Newcastle, somebody pinched his money, and what took place then was a terrible collusion.' Carroty spat into the stove. 'He put his back to the door and searched everybody. And there were tough cusses there, but none as tough as Moleskin himself. He didn't get the money. He got six months for kickin' up a dust. But when he saw the lass in Carlisle he came here to make a fortune by the mountain dew. He was goin' back to marry her. But see where he is now! Doin' three months' hard because he trusted his pal, that red-haired limb of the devil, Tom Jones.'

'What had Tom Jones to do with it?' asked the Moocher.

'The polis were about here at the time, and Tom Jones knew that if one man was caught, the polis would be satisfied for a time, anyway, and he was right. They haven't come back here since then, and Jones is making the booze as prior.'

'But they're on the look-out again,' Tom the Moocher remarked. 'The county police offer a reward for anyone that will give the booze merchant up!'

'Fifty pounds it is again,' said the Ganger thoughtfully.

'Fifty pounds, and all that's to do is to tip the police the wink,' somebody remarked.

'Big money for a wink!' Marley grunted.

'But bigger risk, Poultice Face!' Sid the Slogger spoke and got to his feet, his eyes afire. The whisky was already in his head. He was a low-set, bearded man of enormous width and strength, for whom the nickname Slogger was a fitting appellative. 'We're a score of miles from a boozer; we want our drop of tipple, and God keep the man that goes between us and it. If anyone does, I'll brain him, catch him by the thrapple, twist him round, down him and gouge his eyes out.'

He hit the table with a calloused fist; the money danced, the cards rose in the air and fluttered to the ground. 'That's what I'll do!'

'That's what you won't do, Slogger!'

At the sound of the loud strident voice the gamblers sprang to their feet. Sclatterguff rose so hurriedly that he overturned the jar but was not conscious of the calamity. All looked at the speaker, a man of some thirty odd years, who had just entered. The newcomer was six feet or more in height, clean-shaven, magnificently built and not unhandsome. He wore an overcoat, and one of his hands was fastened on the collar of Sid the Slogger.

'Holy hell! it's Moleskin Joe!' The Slogger looked up at the man, then round at the others, as if calling evidence to verify what his eyes were seeing. 'Where – where,' he stammered in great trepidation, 'where have you sprung out o'?'

Eyes glared out of the smoke laden atmosphere, one or two men stepped timidly towards the new arrival. Sclatterguff caught Moleskin's hand and felt it.

''Tis Moleskin!' he shouted. 'I wouldn't go by his face, it's too clean. But I'd know him by his fist. Never saw anything more like a sledge-hammer in my life. My soul to the devil, but I'm glad to see you back, Moleskin Joe!' he laughed, hitting Moleskin on the back.

'But – but you're supposed to be doin' three months' hard!' The look which the Slogger fixed on Moleskin was vacant and helpless.

'Three months,' was the newcomer's grim admission.

'But you were only in a month!' gasped Marley. 'How did you get out?'

'Got your ticket?' the Ganger inquired.

'Got it,' said Moleskin loosing his grip on the Slogger's shoulder. 'But it took coaxing! I coaxed the warder to give me his coat and hat. My thumb was on his thrapple at the time –'

'Ah, well!' exclaimed Marley, who saw the solution of the problem before the others recovered from their surprise.

'Then the bloke at the gate asked me to show my pass as I was goin' out. I showed it to him,' said Moleskin, making play with his fist.

'Some pass, that!' said the Moocher.

'When well used,' was Moleskin's admission. 'Then I took to my heels with all the polis in Glasgow after me. The ones that chased me were unlucky, but not as unlucky as them that tried to stop me. And here I am now – and for the love o' Mike give me a pipe!'

Three pipes, loaded and lighted, were handed to the newcomer.

'But that's not the overcoat you left quod in?' asked Sclatterguff, fingering Moleskin's appointments.

'A little bit o' Heaven!' Moleskin remarked, sitting down and puffing mightily. 'I had a change in Paisley, changed with a rag-picker in a doss-house, and left while the rag-picker was explainin' to the polis how he had got the coat. 'Twas a close shave that time!'

'Moleskin!'

Ganger Davis spoke.

'Well, old cock?' asked Moleskin.

'If I may tip you the wink, clear out't,' said the Ganger. 'There are too many polis about, too many.' He fixed a startled look on the window. 'It's not safe.'

'There's not much in life, if it's always safe,' was Moleskin's admission. He was almost hidden in the wreaths of his own smoking. 'How many polis round here?'

'Thirty, if a man,' said the Ganger.

'How many navvies?'

'Four hundred.'

'Well, it's a mangy gatherin' of toe-rags,' said Moleskin with the dispassionate air of one who looked on matters from a distance. 'In the old days one buck-navvy sober was as good as three polis and drunk as good as a score.'

'That's the game!' chortled the Slogger. 'But what did you mean, Moleskin, when I said that I'd do anyone in that would give our tipple merchant up, and you said what you said? You're not goin' to help the polis, are you?'

'Me!' There was rebuke in the syllable, the chilling rebuke of a man whose first law was the impeding of police in the execution of their duty.

'Well, what's the game?' asked the Moocher.

'This is the game!' Moleskin got to his feet, took off his coat and disclosed a convict garb worn beneath. He pointed his finger at a pannikin which stood on the table. 'I want to settle up with the bloke who makes this, the bloke that got me into this uniform. That's all!'

'Aye,' was the remark of the shack. 'And what are you goin' to do?'

'When the polis were takin' me off that night, I found that one of them was an old butty o' my own in France in the old days,' said Moleskin in a slow quiet voice. 'He was a good fellow, and a great pity that he wasted himself on a job like a polisman. But anyway, he tipped me the wink that it was Jones, my mate, that gave me up. Course, the polisman didn't know that he was my butty –'

'And what now?' asked Sid the Slogger. 'You're here and he's still on the doin's, sellin' it by the gallon. He got you out of the road, and the polis thought it would stop when they had you, and now your old mate has the free hand.'

'Aye, and what are you goin' to do?' queried Tom the Moocher. What had happened was losing radiance, what was to come held the navvies under a spell.

'What would you fellows do with him?' asked Moleskin. 'That is if you were in my place?'

A few tried to look as if the point-blank question was no concern of theirs.

'Now, Ganger Billy, what would you do with that man if you were me?' Moleskin looked straight into the old man's eyes, and the old man returned a glance as straight as the interlocutor's.

'I'm not in your skin to know that,' was the Ganger's answer.

'Now, if I'd do him in?' Moleskin propounded.

'You'll swing for it!' The Ganger's voice was grim.

'Well, I, for one, would as soon spend a minute on a rope as spend years on a plank.' Moleskin spoke very slowly as if taking pleasure in his words. 'And, anyway, there's a good time comin' though we may never live to see it!'

'Then put this into you!' said the Moocher, handing Moleskin a full pannikin. 'If you're wantin' to do a man in, I don't see why the devil I should spoil your game. I'm not the one to have a grudge again' you when you're takin' a thing so much to heart.'

Moleskin drank deeply, rolling the liquid round his mouth to get the full flavour of the liquid. Appreciation showed in his eyes. It was good stuff, surely.

'Not much to write home about,' he remarked casually when he handed back the pannikin. His eyes made a studied survey of the apartment.

'Could be worse,' said the Moocher philosophically.

'Not much,' Marley grumbled and turned a card idly. His voice, coming from a great depth, rose sluggishly; under a tweed cap his brow was steeped in darkness as if the night had settled there.

'Still up above in the cave, is he?' Moleskin inquired, bending his thumb towards the hills.

'Aye; still roostin' there,' said Sclatterscuff. 'Why're you askin'?'

'Was only just puttin' the question,' replied Moleskin and relapsed into silence.

For a moment there was quiet, and outside could be heard the wind whistling on the hills like a lost thing that knew neither peace nor sanctuary; then came a sound as if somebody were knocking at the door. But none except Moleskin was conscious of this. Under the exceptional circumstances he was alert to every noise.

Tom the Moocher was on his feet, drowning the memory of gambling losses in song. As he sang the men disported themselves, some dancing to the measure, kicking at all inanimate objects within leg reach; two engaged in mock fisticuffs, but accidentally or purposely drawing blood, set to battle in grim earnest, that earnest of navvy fighting, which has neither limitation of means nor discipline of method. All measures are therefore legitimate, the stamp of heel on tendon, the blow of toe-plate on shin, the knee-shove to abdomen. Apart from the two disputants nobody was particularly interested in the fight. Such happenings occurred hourly, futile squabblings which were an active expression of the meaninglessness of their lives.

'Somebody's knockin'!' said the Moocher, coming to the end of his song. 'Some potwalloper from Glasgow out o' a job!'

'The polis, maybe,' said Moleskin, his lips tightening as he rose to his feet. Lifting a pick-handle he went to the door, stood to one side and pulled it open.

'Come in!' he called. 'But if you're up to bleedin' mischief you'd better stay out!'

With hand taut on his weapon, he waited.

CHAPTER 8

CUNNING ISAACS

Not for him is the Christmas and all the sweets it brings,
Nor does he share the New Year's hope of bright and beautiful
things –
And never for him is the festal board with Nature's bounties
piled.
The wan-eyed bootless bairn – the poor, uncared-for child.

– *From* Songs of the Dead End.

He who had been knocking came in, took two steps forward, one back, and with finger in mouth looked at the assembly. The assembly's eyes turned to the door and focused themselves on the visitor. For a moment there was a great silence and the cumulative glances had in them one expression – wonderment coupled with awe. The one who stood at the door was a little boy.

His age might have been four, his hair, brown and curling, hung down in ringlets over a charming little face, pitifully pinched and drawn. Poorly dressed, his clothing was a mere gathering of patches insecurely held. He was bootless, but as if to make up for this deficiency he wore two socks on each foot, each sock differing in texture and colour from its neighbours. These, having nothing to hold them up, curled down over the boy's ankles, and as the trousers, enormous in width, came no lower than the knees, the youngster's shins, white where the skin was taut on the bone, and blue where the flesh had more body, were a sad testimony to the cold night outside.

'Gawr!' exclaimed the startled Moleskin, withdrawing a pace and dropping his weapon to the ground. 'A nipper! Where have you come from?'

The youngster gazed at Moleskin for a moment, then looked to the floor again.

'Here, what do they call you?' The convict came a step nearer and put his hand on the boy's shoulder.

The youngster shook his head, without looking up.

'Now, nipper,' said Moleskin coaxingly, 'what does your daddy call you?' Again the boy shook his head.

'Well, your mummy, now?'

'Cunnin' Ithaac,' was the astonishing answer.

'Hear that, boys!' roared Joe. 'Cunnin' Isaacs! Ha! ha! And are you a cunnin' nipper?'

Isaacs nodded vigorously. There was no doubt about it.

'You're startin' early,' said the Slogger, who was now so interested in the newcomer that he left his cards on the table, as well as a few shillings which he had made. That Marley pocketed the money was a fact not noted at the time. The boy nodded in answer to the Slogger's query, but shrank in terror when the questioner approached him, and when the Slogger stretched a miry hand towards him, the youngster rushed to Moleskin, gripped the convict's trousers and hid behind the man.

'Now, don't be feeard o' him, but tell us where your mummy is?' Moleskin patted the boy's head as he put the question.

'Mummy dorn away.'

'Away? Where?'

'Dorn away,' was the vague answer. 'Wanted Mummy. Then I wunned away. Was fwightened, vevy fwightened! Where Mummy?' he sobbed, clinging to the convict's leg.

'Well, ask me another!' said the mystified Moleskin. 'It's more than I know. But it's all right. She'll be back, if you just sit down here and warm yourself.'

He caught the boy, carried him to the stove and placed him on a form before the fire. Tom the Moocher brought a pillow from the bunk, and held it out to Moleskin.

'Put that under the poor wee devil!' said the Moocher. 'What age are you?' he asked the boy, whom Moleskin duly installed on the pillow. 'Are you very old?'

'I'se vewy old,' was Isaacs' reply. 'And mummy's goin' to get me a hoss, a big white hoss!' he went on, with childish irrelevance.

'A big white hoss!' said the Moocher. 'And your mummy will get it for you?'

'But she dorn away.' The boy looked round the room.

'Now, settle down, and warm yourself!' said Moleskin hurriedly. 'And I'll bet that you're very hungry.'

'I'se vewy hungwy.' The boy spoke with emphasis. 'And mummy vewy hungwy, too.' He rubbed his eyes as if on the point of crying.

'Now you're not to cry,' said Sclatterguff. In his maudlin voice there was sympathy. 'A man that's goin' to be a buck-navvy never cries. He doesn't care a hang what he meets. And don't you want to be what God didn't start and the devil finished – a buck-navvy?'

'I want to be buck-navvy,' said Isaacs, with a choke in his voice.

The other members of the squad were now engaged rummaging amidst their appointments, dragging forth articles of food from the secret recesses of clooty confinement. Digger Marley produced a silver-plated teapot and brought it to Moleskin. The convict had just placed a billy-can of water on the stove.

'Make the tea in this,' ordered Marley. 'It's better'n the 'billy.'

'Silver! Where did you pick this up?' Moleskin exclaimed, catching the teapot and scrutinizing it. 'And what's this writin' on it? "Station Hotel, Wigan." H'm!'

'And here's a mug for the nipper!' said Pig-iron Burke, placing a delft mug on the form beside the boy. 'Y.M.C.A.,' he explained.

'Now, put that into your wee tummy-wummy!' Tom the Moocher ordered, handing the boy a sandwich, and at the same time tickling the youngster's ribs. 'Tummy-wummy-wummy!'

'Here, sit on my knee and I'll give you a nice ride!' Sclatterguff, not to be outdone, caught the child and lifted him on his knee.

'What are you stickin' yerself in for, Sclatterguff?' grumbled the Moocher. 'Always comin' where you're not wanted! What d'ye know about kids?'

'Have kids as big as you if I knew where they were,' said Sclatterguff, settling himself on the form, Cunning Isaacs on his knee. 'Now, my wee laddie, you eat up and I'll sing a song to you.' And without another word, Sclatterguff, who had a bit of a voice, even in drunkenness, let himself rip, to use his own words:

Hee-up, my little hoss,
Hee-up again, sir!
How many miles to London town?

Three score and ten, sir!
Hee-up, my little hoss!
Hee-up again, sir!
Can I get there by candle light?
Yes and back again, sir!

'Gawr! It's a long while since I've sung that,' said the singer thoughtfully, and there was a note of sadness in his voice. 'And you' – he looked at the boy whom he was dandling on his knee – 'that's the song for you! There's the hoss, a white one, and you'll go to the town –'

'Polis in town,' said the youngster. 'Mummy not like polis. They tell her "move on!" '

'There'll be no polis in the town when you go, my boy,' Moleskin remarked, handing a mess-tin of tea to Isaacs. 'We'll go with you, and we'll put the polis into the river and sit on them!'

'Sit on them!' laughed the boy, taking the mess-tin. He took a sip of tea, burying his little white face in the utensil. 'Nice,' was his syllable of approval, after a series of gurgles.

'That's the style, Isaacs!' The delighted Moleskin handed him another sandwich. The child had three already, three of navvy pattern – a loaf in two slices with a chop between. 'We'll make a man of you, a buck-navvy.'

'Well, I suppose we'll have to give him up tomorrow to the polis,' said the Moocher. 'There'll be inquiries made and we've got to hand him over. I suppose the polis will be here in the mornin'.'

'The polis may come, but they'll be damned lucky if they get back,' roared Moleskin. 'If his mummy doesn't come he stays here!'

'What's up your neck now?' asked Sclatterguff, looking at the escaped convict.

'Nothin' much, Carroty. But I don't want a nipper like that to go into the poorhouse. It's another shuffle when a man goes in. He can go in for the night, and come out in the mornin'. But put a boy in, he stays – he sticks! It takes the guts out o' him. I was a poorhouse brat and I haven't got over it yet. And, anyway, Carroty, you've sat there long enough! Heave out't!'

With these words, Moleskin caught the youngster in his arms, heaved Sclatterguff aside, and sat down with Isaacs on his knee.

'But what can we do with him here?' asked the Moocher.

'Start a baby crutch, eh?' Sclatterguff inquired. The old man was sarcastic.

'Well, I don't see anything wrong with us housin' him here,' said Moleskin. 'A bit o' a bunk and a bit o' grub, and that's all he'll want. Our sooveneer, Cunnin' Isaacs!'

'Aye, and you'll be Daddy Joe,' said the Moocher with gentle sarcasm. 'But, Daddy Joe, what will you do when the polis get hold of you? What'll you do when it comes to paddin' the hoof, on the dead-end with hundreds like you, not knowin' where to turn for bite or sup. Eh, Daddy Joe?'

'There's only one way of eatin', but there's more than one way of gettin' grub.' Moleskin assumed an air of wisdom. 'And, anyway, I've often fed myself for weeks, by walkin' in the dark and trippin' against chickens!'

'So, you're goin' to take him with you?'

'I might do worse than that.'

'And what about the man you're goin' to kill?' asked the Moocher.

'That won't take long,' said Moleskin blandly. 'But whatever else turns up, I'm not goin' to let Cunnin' Isaacs into the workhouse. Isn't that the ticket, Cunnin' Isaacs?' he inquired, looking at the boy.

'Ticket, Daddy Joe,' was Isaacs' startling reply.

'Oh, Lawr!' exclaimed Moleskin, fixing a shamefaced look on the inmates of the shack. 'Now, is your wee tummy filled?' he asked the child, who nodded emphatically. 'And aren't you tired?'

'Vewy tired,' said the youngster. 'But must say pwayers. Mummy cwy me not say pwayers!'

'Well, I'm damned!' Moleskin exclaimed. For a moment he felt nonplussed.

Sclatterguff, utterly aghast, made some remark regarding prayers never having been said in the place before.

'Well, I'm blest!' Moleskin muttered. He had never confessed to this state of being before, but in some subconscious way he felt that the occasion demanded this avowal. 'Yes, sonny, say your prayers,' he urged. 'Spit them out . . . I mean, set about them!'

Isaacs slipped off Moleskin's knees, ran to a bunk and knelt there. Like all boys' prayers, it did not occupy much time of his waking day. He finished, blessed himself and got to his feet.

'Now, come on, old son.' Moleskin caught the little one in his arms. 'There's only one thing to be done with nippers when they're tired. Come on, Ikey Mo!' He threw the child on a bunk, and tickled his ribs till the youngster crowed with delight.

'Ho, Dempsey, wot've ye got to say now? Nothin'? Well, close your eyes and get to sleep!' and with this injunction Moleskin wrapped the tiny body in a blanket, on which stood out prominently the rough scrawl that testified to the Ganger's ownership: 'Stolen from Ganger Billy.'

'He's a nice wee nipper,' said Sclatterguff, coming to the bunk and looking at the youngster. 'Gawr! was I ever like him!'

'No, you were born with whiskers,' the Moocher remarked.

'Now, cuddle up and ye'll be as snug as a bug in a rug,' said Moleskin to the child.

'Who was it that was goin' to kill a man?' asked the Moocher in scorn. The man was jealous.

'Daddy Joe!' roared the shack in unison. The feeling of envy was not the Moocher's alone.

'And who was it that wanted elbow room?'

'Daddy Joe!' came the instant reply, bellowed in a chorus.

'Lookin' for trouble, some o' ye, ain't ye?' Moleskin inquired, glowering at the assembly.

'Go on! Can't you take a joke?' asked the Slogger.

'We're fond o' the kid as you are, Moleskin,' Tom the Moocher grumbled. 'Guess I'll take a share in him.'

'So will I,' said Pig-iron Burke. 'Gawr! it's years enough since one o' 'em came my way. Come to think of it, I've taken a fancy to the nipper myself!'

'And what about me, eh?' asked Digger Marley.

'I heard him knock first,' said the Moocher.

'And who sung to him?' asked Sclatterguff.

'Aye, but who did he come to first of all?' Moleskin rose to his full six feet two, as he put the question. 'Whose leg did he grip hold of' – he slapped his trousers as he spoke – when he ran away from that hairy-faced lodgin' house smelt!' He pointed a withering finger at Sid the Slogger.

'Me love Daddy Joe!' came the little voice from the bunk and Isaacs peeped across his blankets at Moleskin.

'There!' said the big man, proud of the recommendation. 'There, is that not enough for all of you?'

'And love me, too, Isaacs?' asked the Moocher, coming to the bunk.

'And me?' inquired Pig-iron Burke.

Isaacs favoured both his admirers with a bright nod, but shook his head when the Slogger asked a similar question.

'Don't like me! What's wrong with me?' asked the crest-fallen Slogger.

'Whiskers!'

'Whiskers. Oh Gawr!'

'Whiskers every day?' inquired the youngster.

'Aye, every day until he's able to pinch somebody's soap!' the Moocher explained.

The child, with that swift play of thought which runs to subjects that have no palpable connection with anything that has gone before, lay back in his bunk, and looking up at 'Daddy Joe', informed him that there was a big blister on his heel.

'A big blister, sonny?' Moleskin was all concern. 'But don't trouble. It will be away tomorrow!'

'Not want it go 'way,' said the rascal. 'Mummy very good to me when I have blisters! Gives me picky-backs!'

'Of course! You'll have two in the mornin'. Now, just stretch yourself out and have a doss,' said Moleskin coaxingly. He had no idea what 'picky-backs' might be, but guessed them to be something to eat.

'When will mummy come?' asked the boy, stretching himself out as Moleskin suggested.

'Tomorrow morning as soon as you wake up, she'll be here. Now get to doss. And you' – Moleskin looked fiercely at the inmates of the shack – 'keep quiet!'

Talk was hushed. The men, when they spoke, did so in whispers, and when they moved, changed their location in space on tiptoes. At the slightest movement, Moleskin, who sat on the corner of the bunk, made violent gestures of disapproval. The boy's eyes were closed.

'And the big white hoss?' he suddenly asked, sitting up.

'Your mummy will bring you the big white hoss, sonny,' said Moleskin.

'Many miles to London town?'

'Two! Now go to sleep. I'll sing a song to you. Have you any other song?' Moleskin inquired in a whisper, as he looked at Sclatterguff. 'Not about hosses.'

'Try the "Bold Navvy Man",' advised the Moocher.

'Not a good song, that,' said Sclatterguff. 'It's smutty.'

'"Put your duds, dirty dog, up the spout", is a better one!' Digger Marley suggested.

'None o' them's any good for a wee nipper,' said Moleskin. 'But I have it! Turn down the light, Carroty.'

Carroty did as directed, and the shack was plunged into darkness. All sounds, all motion suddenly ceased, but here and there could be seen, when the eye became accustomed to the obscurity, the blurred outlines of seated figures and the dull glow of drawn pipes. The smell of the place, of damp wood, wet earth, rotten meat, decaying vegetable matter and rank tobacco, was heavy in the nostrils. From without came the wail of the wind playing on the caves, and within a queer rasping sound, as if emery paper were being drawn along a rusty file. Sid the Slogger was shaving in the darkness.

And in the midst of all this sound could be heard the voice of the convict. He was crooning the child's lullaby.

Two lovely black eyes!
Oh, what a surprise!
Got 'em for tellin' a man he was drunk –
Two lovely black eyes!

'Dossin', Cunnin' Isaacs?' he inquired in a whisper.

'Dossin', Daddy Joe,' said the youngster sleepily.

The song was continued softly:

Two lovely black eyes!
Oh, what a surprise!
Oh, what a surprise!

'Dossin', Isaacs?'

There was no answer. Moleskin rose to his feet.

'Well,' he remarked. ' We've got him now, and what the hell are we goin' to do with him? And where has he left his mummy?'

CHAPTER 9

THE OLD GRIND

Have you sweltered through the Summer, till the salt sweat seared your eyes?
Have you dragged through plumb-dead levels in the slush that reached your thighs?
Have you worked the weighty hammer swinging heavy from the hips,
While the ganger timed the striking with a curse upon his lips?
Have you seen the clotted point-rods and the reddened reeking cars
When they've drawn your trusted matey through the twisted signal-bars?
Or seen the hooded signal as it swung above you clear
And the deadly engine rushing on the pal who didn't hear?
When working your salvation in the way the navvies do
These are the little trifles that are daily up to you!

– *From* Daily Bread.

Early the next morning the Glen showed itself to Moleskin's eyes. Westward the stars were bright over the hills, though the east had the first colours of the day. The air was fresh, and from afar came the sound of the gathering sea.

Round Glencorrie tarn, amidst the puddle piles, were the various implements of labour, cranes fixed and portable, carrying empty clay-crusted drums, a rake of muck wagons on the light railway, a feather of smoke already rising from the engine in front; claw-bars, crow-bars, huddles of iron, steel, wire and wood.

It must be confessed that the sight of the place in the early morning did not present a cheerful spectacle, though on the previous night there was a certain element of romance in the scene when Moleskin arrived there and looked upon the lighted shacks, the workers labouring in the halo of the naphtha lamps, and heard the broad jokes and loud laughter of the workers.

Now the whole had a particularly bald, depressing effect. The shacks, tarred and canvassed, stood in miserable disarray, the rain was still dripping from the roofs. Every front door was a muck-wallow, the windows had three panes of their customary four boarded, and to add to the drab picture, two revellers, who had steeped themselves unwisely in liquor overnight, were still steeped in the mud into which they had fallen when their revels were at an end.

The second largest shack belonged to the ganger Macready, and it was to this shack that Moleskin directed his footsteps when the day cleared. Opening the door his nose was met with the exhalations begotten of night in a close sleeping place. There was nobody astir; all were still asleep, some in bunks, their territorial rights by virtue of the sum of fourpence paid to Macready. Others slept on the mucky floor.

Moleskin stepped across the shack to a bunk which one man had to himself. The other bunks contained three souls apiece, but Macready, for some unexplainable reason, was upholder of the one-man-one-bed principle and lost eightpence nightly on the whim.

'Macready!' Moleskin called, pulling down the sleeper's blanket.

'Wha-r-r-r!' grumbled the sleeper.

'Show a leg!' Moleskin commanded, pulling the blanket down a little further.

'What the devil are you pullin' at!' growled Macready, sitting up and fixing baleful eyes on the one who disturbed his slumber. 'Canned every night the whole – Moleskin Joe!'

He put out his hand and gripped that of his visitor. Handshakes are uncommon amongst navvies. But the occasion demanded something superfluous.

'Carroty told me the story of your comin' last night,' said Macready, his eyes still fixed on the visitor. 'And he let split about a nipper that said his prayers, and your hymn singin', and "Liar!" says I to Carroty, and "Liar you!" says he, the gin-gutted whelp, so I heaved him out. 'Twas at twelve o'clock, too ... And it is you?' he asked.

'To the nail of my big toe!' Moleskin admitted.

'Heave out't, you smelts,' Macready roared, springing to

his feet, and running along the line of bunks cleared them of their blankets. The sleepers, mother-naked, in shirts, or full working habit, grumbled into wakefulness. 'Aye! what about it?' he asked, coming back to Moleskin.

'A job,' said the ex-convict.

'Time?' inquired Macready.

'Never worked on time all my natural,' said Moleskin. 'Any piece work goin'?'

'Aye, Moleskin,' said Macready thoughtfully. 'There's a job goin'. There's an eighty-yard trench to be dug, for the pipin'.'

'Ten yards off from the front of breastwork?' asked Moleskin.

'That's it.'

'Depth?'

'Eight foot – but most of it mud!' said Macready.

'Aye! mud,' laughed Moleskin. 'We'll need more dynamite than shovel. One hundred and twenty pounds and I'll start. Somethin' in advance and new clothes.'

'It'll have to be done in a week, and the price is fifty,' said Macready.

'It'll be done in a week and the money is as I've said.' Moleskin drew himself to his full height. 'It's worth two hundred, that job. I'll go and ask the engineer what he's offerin'.'

Moleskin of old had bested Macready on matters of finance, and the man feared him. Macready had really been offered two hundred guineas for the job, but wanted it done as cheaply as possible so that he could make a little on the transaction.

'A hundred and ten,' he suggested.

'Twenty,' said Moleskin.

'All right, and to the devil with you,' was Macready's gentle acquiescence. 'But you'll need a score of men.'

'I'll do it with five!'

'Then you'll sweat!'

'We'll lather,' said Moleskin. 'Now, duds,' he suggested.

'On the nod, of course?' Macready remarked.

'Put it down against my screw,' said Moleskin. 'I want a jacket, double-breasted, a waistcoat, moleskin and ivory, a sweater, cap and bluchers.'

'Well, I'll see what I can do to oblige a pal,' Macready muttered, taking a mighty key from his pocket as he spoke. His working garb was also his suit of pyjamas, which meant that he never changed clothes even to sleep.

Going to a large chest which stood in the corner he unlocked it, threw the lid back, and pulled out a varied assortment of apparel, jackets and trousers, army and civilian, sweaters, waistcoats, singlets, pants, 'grey-backs', caps, socks and boots.

A certain amount of trading is carried on amongst the navvy fraternity. Those older in the craft, who are gifted with a business acumen, and can govern their thirst, lay in stores of food and clothing which they issue to the men on credit. The heel end of payday generally sees the men without a penny, and from a drunken sleep they often awaken skin-naked. Then the petty trader comes in and feeds, clothes at exorbitant prices. The trader is generally a ganger, who, in due course, will pay out the wages, and is never a loser on his transactions.

Moleskin was now busy trying on a sweater. The broad-arrowed tunic lay on the floor at his feet.

'That sweater becomes you, Moleskin,' said Macready drily. 'The right colour.'

'A jacket now.' Moleskin spoke with business promptitude.

Macready handed him one. The buyer held it out at arm's length and surveyed it. It was decidedly sparse. He shook his head.

'Try this'n,' said Macready, handing him another.

Moleskin tried the second one, buttoned it, pulled down the sleeves and squared his shoulders.

'Made for you, Moleskin, my boy!' There was approval in Macready's voice. 'Your second skin! Born in it ye were!'

'Bluchers,' Moleskin remarked.

'But there's nothin' wrong with them you're wearin,' said Macready.

'Nothin',' Moleskin agreed, 'but they're what I came out in.'

He shed the slough of his servitude, the penal appointments, and went out from Macready's shack in moleskin and ivory, knee-straps and bluchers, the traditional garb of the hard-homed navvy. Attired thus, he bore down upon Windy Corner.

Though verging on ten o'clock the child was still asleep and the navvies were only getting out of their bunks. Many of them had been out until three of that morning, searching for the mother, who, according to the child's confused statements of the previous evening, had come to Glencorrie. But who she was, what she was and why she had come to such a locality, was a matter of very vague conjecture. Women never came to such a place. The search in the darkness had been fruitless.

'There are fellows here as have run away from their old women,' Pig-iron Burke remarked, resting his head on his hand. 'I know dozens as have.'

'You'll save time if you tell us the ones as haven't,' said Tom the Moocher. 'Lawr! my poor head!'

'She ain't much o' a woman, whoever she is, gallivantin' about the country, throwin' her kid on anybody as is fool enough to take care o't!' said Digger Marley, looking at the sleeping cherub.

Moleskin came across the floor and seated himself on the child's bunk.

'A reg'lar wash-out she is!' grunted the Moocher.

Moleskin looked up sharply.

'Who're ye speakin' about?' he demanded.

'Her that ran away and left the nipper here on our hands,' said the Moocher.

Moleskin sprang to his feet, crossed the floor and looked down at the man.

'D'ye want to go out and do your work today?' he asked. 'Or do you not want to go?'

'I should smile,' said the Moocher, who looked a trifle uneasy.

'You'll smile on the other side of your mouth if you say another word against the nipper's mother,' said Moleskin. 'The same to you, Marley. If any of the two of you or anybody else says a word against her you'll not be able to do any work today, tomorrow – or for a fortnight. You know nothin' about the woman. You don't know who she is, what she's gone through – and kickin' a dog that's down is damned dirty work!'

'Hold yourself, Moleskin, hold yourself in,' said Sclatter-guff, who had already taken the precaution to move towards the door in case his advice was not followed.

The boy sat up in his bunk at that moment, looked round with unseeing eyes, and burst into tears.

'What's wrong, Ikey Mo, what's wrong?' asked Moleskin, running to him.

'Mummy,' sobbed the youngster. 'Want Mummy!' He closed his eyes, lay back, and was presently asleep again.

''Twas you that wakened him!' Moleskin hissed at Marley.

The youngster sat up in bed again and fixed questioning eyes on the assembly. He was now really awake. Half a dozen tins of tea were held out towards him, and Sid the Slogger, pressing a finger on his own chin, muttered, 'No whiskers', and blushed red as a schoolgirl when the admission left his lips.

'W'ere Mummy?' asked the youngster, looking at Moleskin.

The ex-convict fed the child and cross-examined him. This required very skilful handling. Fifteen minutes elapsed and the sum total of the findings was: Mummy came to get him a white horse, he had a blister, Mummy made him say prayers, he was on a tram-car and Mummy paid twopence, and he had a banana.

'Why did Mummy come to here?' asked Joe at the end of twenty minutes.

'Get me a white hoss.'

'A white hoss – and – and –'

'A daddy!'

Moleskin whistled, and looked at Ganger Billy.

'That's it!' he exclaimed. 'His daddy's here. How many married men on the job?'

'Scores!' was the Ganger's ready response.

'Do you think any of them is –'

'How the devil am I to know?' was the Ganger's answer. 'I don't carry their marriage lines about with me.'

One fact was now more or less clear. The child's mother had come to Glencorrie, and the father of the child was, or had been, in the locality. The only thing to be done now was to continue the search, find out what had happened to the mother and keep Cunning Isaacs until she was discovered.

'He's ours and it would be playin' it dirty on the nipper if we don't do all that we can do to make him as easy on it as we know how,' said the ex-convict.

'We ain't goin' to gobble 'im up,' protested the Moocher.

'And you'd better not,' advised Moleskin.

'We're not bloody savages,' the Slogger remarked.

'Ye've got to draw in on your language, Sid,' muttered Moleskin. 'Talk with words like them ain't for the ears of Cunnin' Isaacs!'

'Cunnin' Isaacs!' Sclatterguff pronounced the words slowly and finished with a snort of disgust. 'That ain't a name to give the child! Low, common is what I calls it. Percival! That's the name for him.'

'Too nobby,' commented Moleskin after a moment's hesitation.

'If he was my offspring I wouldn't give'm the gastrinomic of

Cunnin' Isaacs.' Sclatterguff's voice was charged with pedantic censure. 'Entirely agnostic to't, I'd be!'

'He blew into us as Cunnin' Isaacs,' said Moleskin. 'And that's his name till he blows out again. And now,' he added, his voice rising, 'there's a job on for anyone as wants to work as the Almighty never asked a man to work in all his natural!'

'What is the nature of the operations?' asked Sclatterguff.

'Have you got rid o' them pains in your lummar regions?'

'They've utterly forsook me,' said Sclatterguff.

'This job will give you them again,' said Moleskin grimly.

'I'll risk it,' was the reply of the valiant Sclatterguff.

'Pig-iron, Slogger, Marley, Moocher and Sclatterguff. That is five. Then I'm in, making seven!' Moleskin spoke thoughtfully and there was no trace of conceit in his voice. The men named gathered round him.

'What's the job?' asked the Moocher.

'Cock up yer ears, till I spit somethin' into them. I've struck up a bargain with Macready about the pipin' –'

'Con-dew-it,' mumbled Carroty.

'Hold your cack!' Moleskin shouted. 'Eighty-yard trench in front of the breastwork, eight foot deep, hammer and jumper graft. A week for the doin's. A hundred and twenty quid for the gadget. Chancin' yer arms?'

'Six men for the job!' exclaimed Burke, and whistled.

'Felladeezy, meanin' suicide, when you should have known better,' said Carroty.

'Pig-iron and Sclatterguff are out o't,' said Moleskin. 'They love work so much that they could lie beside it all day and look at it. I must get two others.'

'I'm on it,' said Burke.

'So'm I,' said Carroty. 'My remarks were irrelevant.'

'That's settled then,' said Moleskin. 'Fair sharin' of the dough when it's over. I'm boss of the show. I give orders and I'm obeyed sharp. You've to run to it! If you fall don't take time to rise. No man to be three sheets in the wind, awash! If that happens all his dough is shared out equal with his shipmates. Doss as if you don't hold with it. Grub as if it's a waste of time. Now to it, under weigh! Carroty, picks and shovels! Slogger, hammers and jumpers! Marley, dynamite! Double, the whole damn lot of you and get the tools!'

And so the work started. The men, usually careless and indifferent, seemed to undergo a transformation. A frenzy seized them and increased from moment to moment. They panted from their exertions, and though the day was sharp and bracing their faces were never dry.

'It's four o'clock,' said Carroty on one occasion when they lay in the shelter of an atoll waiting for the dynamite to explode.

'Get a naphtha lamp, Slogger!' Moleskin ordered. 'It'll soon be dark.'

Under the torchlight they worked till nine.

'Carry on!' Moleskin commanded. 'I'm goin' into Windy Corner.'

'Grub?' inquired Marley.

'To put Isaacs to bed,' was Moleskin's explanation.

They fed mightily at midnight, and set to work as soon as the last bite had crossed their lips. Moleskin, gifted with an enormous stock of energy, was indefatigable, and could speak, command while he worked. The others were silent, their muscles called on every atom of power that their bodies contained. All smokers, they had no recourse to pipes. Lighting was a waste of time; they chewed.

Their work saw the dawn in, the sun at meridian and setting. The stars came out again and sorted themselves in their eternal order. A naphtha lamp flared over the heads of the six workers, whose crowns were flush with the lip of the dug trench. The shack inmates were out watching the operations.

'Thirty-six and a half hours,' said someone from the crowd. 'Horse Roche did thirty-six and three-quarters.'

Horse Roche, the noted figure of ancient history, was he who had handed in his check on the Somme battlefield.

'We'll go a quarter better,' said Moleskin, and they did. Thirty-seven was their tally of hours.

That night, as on the previous night, they drank nothing. There was no drink to be obtained. Report had it that Tom Jones had packed up and gone for good.

'I must see into this bisness,' was the comment of Moleskin Joe, and accompanied by Ganger Macready and a dozen others who wanted to see vengeance fulfilled, he went to the cave where the bootlegger carried on operations. The place was deserted. Tom Jones had gone.

'Must have heard of your gettin' out!' was the comment of Macready.

'Must have,' said Moleskin in a despondent voice. 'That's what comes of workin' too hard.'

'Might as well have stayed in the lock-up, eh?' muttered Ganger Billy, who was one of the party.

'Ah! but there's Isaacs, ain't there?' asked Moleskin.

'Tom Jones hasn't broke the worm, burned the vat or done away with the still, so I think I'll try my hand at makin' the tipple myself,' said Macready. 'Never tried my hand at anything that I wasn't able to make a fist o'.'

'But the blend, that's the thing,' said the Slogger. 'The knowin' how far to go and the knowin' when to stop!'

'I'll do it as good as any o' 'em!' Macready squared his shoulders and assumed the air of one who was fit for any project.

'But it ain't to be drunk at Windy Corner!' Moleskin, as if in answer to a challenge, squared his shoulders. Standing thus in the opening of the cave, his attitude gave one the impression of irresistible strength and power, and an inborn natural ferocity which he was keeping well in hand. 'Not when the nipper and me's there!'

The next day the men were at work early and again the next. On the fourth day a tragedy happened. Pig-iron Burke was damping a charged bore-hole when a premature explosion took place. A flying rock hit his forehead and killed him.

'Poor Pig-iron!' said Marley, with some show of feeling. 'Never saw one like him for slippin' an extra ace up his sleeve!'

'Had clever paws,' said Moleskin. 'Now, Carroty, you slap up a whack o' grub. There's the nipper comin' across to us. It's not a sight for him. Take him back to the shack, Slogger. Me and the Moocher will get a barrow. Marley, you dig the tippin'-hole.'

Returning with the barrow, which they had cleaned for the occasion, the two men found their dead mate barefooted. Someone had stolen his boots.

'Pinchin' the boots off a stiff!' grunted the Moocher. 'It's not above board!'

'No, it's not,' was Moleskin's philosophic admission. 'We ought to have took them off afore we went away.'

Five-handed the work was continued; at noon on the sixth day the job was completed, and the workers were paid their wages.

Things were fairly quiet in Glencorrie, particularly in Windy Corner, where no whisky was drunk despite the fact that Ganger Macready was distilling with a certain amount of success. Tom Jones had disappeared and his whereabouts were unknown. The police visited the place no more.

CHAPTER 10

NEW DUDS

Keep your own counsel. A secret will be
Roared to the world if whispered to three!

– *From* Wayside Proverbs.

From the start the stray child was everything to the ex-convict, and his coming had a great influence on Moleskin. The rugged man had changed, had become transformed in one night. He shed his old life, his manner of living, as one, becoming healthy after illness, sheds the trappings of the invalid state. All that was life to Moleskin of old had become insipid and tasteless. Drink and cards were thrown aside, and the big man settled down to good honest grind. As soon as the first job came to an end he got a second, which, like the first, was paid for the work done, not for the hours laboured.

He was nurse to Isaacs, schoolmaster and guardian, and as guardian he strove to make Windy Corner fit for the little occupant. A shack containing Moleskin in the old days was generally one of the noisiest, but now Windy Corner was as quiet as a mission hall. Swearing was taboo, cards had to be played in a spirit of decorum, no fighting or drinking was allowed. The nipper had a bunk to himself; he retired to rest at nine-thirty; lights were out at eleven.

But it must be admitted that this curtailment of liberty was not favourable in all eyes. The wilder spirits of the assembly, those who loved late hours and excesses, faded away into shacks where discipline was not so strict and where various individuals traded in spirits crude and raw. Equipoise in lodgement was maintained, however, by the more peaceable workers taking up their abode in Windy Corner.

Ganger Billy, who never gave unmerited praise, and was

even loath to give it where deserved, saw reason to bless Cunning Isaacs. His furniture suffered no more from the rough usage of drunken men. The child served as a chucker-out, and fulfilled this duty without payment.

For the first few nights Isaacs cried for his mummy before falling asleep, and often called for her in his slumber, but after a very little while he seemed to have reconciled himself to his new surroundings. In fact, this new life was much more interesting than the old. The world was filled with wonders.

He soon knew the waterworks from end to end, and made one of his own construction, thirty-six inches by eighteen. He had no great liking for his own shack, because it was an abode of peace under Moleskin's jurisdiction, but loved other domiciles where so many quarrels were settled with the fists. Bloodshed delighted him.

From the beginning he was the pet and plaything of all. A whole job would come to an end when he appeared, pennies were given him, he obtained a heavy-hafted clasp knife from the Slogger, the Moocher would pull out his teeth for the boy to handle, then put them back in his mouth again. This raised the Moocher in the youngster's imagination. 'De man with the pull-out teeds!' he called him. No one else had such a faculty, not even Daddy Joe. The Moocher did it every time Isaacs ordered, for in the empire of Isaacs, which had an ocean (the reservoir), a country (the puddle heaps, slades and knolls), a light railway with traffic thereon and a fleet of ships (fashioned by the navvies in their spare time), no one dared disobey the capricious Emperor.

None except Moleskin Joe questioned the authority of the tyrant, and this questioning occurred on two momentous occasions. The first was when Isaacs saw a dead crow lying in the reservoir and walked out to bring it in. He was discovered when his head and shoulders were only visible and the dead crow still some ten yards away from his reach. Moleskin brought the youngster out.

'What the hell have you been muckin' in here for?' The bit of propriety had fallen from Moleskin for a moment.

'Birrrd, tippin' hole!' was the explanation of the drenched monarch.

'Wanted to bury it, did you?' asked the ex-convict. 'Lucky thing we hadn't to bury you.'

He brought the boy to his shack, stripped him and wrapped

him in the blankets while his clothes were left to dry by the stove.

'Never do it again!' Moleskin ordered. 'If you get wet you'll get cold and kick the bucket.'

Isaacs, realising that there was something very serious in the escapade, promised Daddy Joe that he would never go into the water again. Seeing that Moleskin was somewhat mollified by the promise, the rascal turned it to account and asked Daddy Joe to make him tea in the 'silva teapot', and then fell asleep. When he awoke the tea was ready and the dead crow was lying on the bunk.

The second occasion on which Moleskin Joe exercised his authority was one more dire in its consequences. The youngster was discovered climbing the jib of a crane. Moleskin took him down, took him down quietly, so quietly that the youngster was frightened. What was going to happen? Isaacs had certainly fallen from grace. But what did happen was nothing really awful and it gave the young savage intense joy. Moleskin went to the crane-man and inquired: 'Was it you, you doss-house flea, that let the nipper go up there?'

'Wharr ye ridin' the 'igh 'oss for?' asked the man.

'Take that for doin' it!' said Moleskin, drawing a heavy left on the crane-man's ear. 'And that for lettin' *him* do it, and that to keep ye from doin' it again!' The second blow differed from the first in that it was heavier, and the third had the force of the first and second put together.

'Do it again, Daddy Joe,' ordered the nipper when Moleskin stayed his hand.

It must be recorded that an event like this was sauce for the boy. He liked to see blows given and received, though the cause and outcome of a fight was of little consequence to him. The struggle was the thing. Moleskin was the best man in Glencorrie he knew, but for some reason or another he wished that Daddy Joe would fight more.

Moleskin laughed these childish wishes away. He was filled with a great gladness, gladness for everyone, for his mates, for the child, for himself. He was ridiculously happy and happiness is no illusion. Therefore, he did not want to fight.

Sometimes the ex-convict would sit for hours with the boy on his knee, telling him stories, stories of heroic deeds on sea and land, of strange places visited, southern seas and islands, northern capes and frozen waters. Joe had been a sailor and a soldier and saw many queer things, underwent various hardships and risks in far seaports where the knife-thrust was common answer to the chiding word, and where the thoughtless impulse led to ready action. The boy loved these stories and the bloodier the tale, the greater the interest.

One evening he asked the boy his mother's name.

'Mummy,' was the answer.

'Would everybody call her Mummy?' Moleskin inquired.

'No,' said the boy. 'They call her Seela.'

'Sheila?'

The boy nodded.

'Sheila is her name?' Joe queried.

'Not Seela. Mummy,' was the answer. 'Me now peepy. Want doss.'

Moleskin placed the youngster in the bunk and wrapped him up. Then seating himself in a corner, lighted by the naphtha lamp, he took up scissors and needle and continued a tailoring job where he had left off on the previous evening. A khaki uniform had been procured on credit some time before, and immediately afterwards followed a mysterious rite in which Isaacs played a prominent part.

The boy was measured to see if he were growing up. Marley did the measurement in tape and Moleskin tabulated the findings in figures. Afterwards a foot of selvedge was shorn from the tunic, the back panel removed and what remained was sewn together. The sleeves were docked and half the trousers' legs cut away. It was a period of hush, secret nods, meaning looks while the work progressed, and everybody with the exception of Isaacs knew of the job, which was now nearly completed.

What a strange thing that the name of the boy's mother should have been Sheila, Moleskin thought, as he busied himself with the scissors. He knew a Sheila, the girl who happened to be the only woman he had ever loved.

He recollected the time, years ago, when he had met her. Then came to him, for the first time, that desire for a woman, the need for her sympathy, her caresses. He recalled it all, how he was affected with the fever and fret of love-sickness, how he carried on in much the same manner as any other bashful swain. The days on which he saw her were days of brilliant colours, the shack in which she lived borrowed magnificence from the figure which it sheltered, the oil-lamp which stood on her table had the roseate hues of some romantic dawn. Moleskin saw the lamp from outside; he never had the courage to enter the sanctuary which it lighted.

On the night when the impounding reservoir of Hermiston broke its breastworks, when he saved the girl from drowning and almost got drowned himself, he remembered how, coming to, he found the girl kneeling by his side, kissing him, speaking sweet things, telling him that he was the best and bravest man in the world. Probably all was due to that hysteria which is fellow to danger and death. He did not know and never strove to analyse it. The emotional complexities of womanhood were beyond him, but that evening was something to remember, the kisses he received and did not return, because he was a rough rung of a man.

'No,' he said, putting the needle in the lapel of his jacket and rising to his feet; 'I ain't a hand with the wenches!'

On the following evening the work was completed. Windy Corner was crowded for the occasion; and many who had never entered the shack were there that evening.

Moleskin, wearing on his face the solemnity due to the event, drew a bundle wrapped in a red muffler from his bunk, and went to the form by the stove. Isaacs was seated there.

'Somethin' for you, Isaacs, you wee devil, you!' said Moleskin, placing the bundle on the floor. The concluding epithet was a term of endearment. 'Guess what it is. Three guesses!'

'My new suit,' said Isaacs.

There was a dead silence. Sclatterguff, for some reason, took a step towards the door, but Moleskin's arm, with a great stretch, shot out and the retiring man was held.

''Twas you, you doss-house smelt.' The scruff of the neck is a good hold for the one who forces another to do a pirouette. If Sclatterguff had been toothed like the Moocher his teeth would have lost grip during his forced revolutions.

''Tw – 'tw – 'twasn't me!' hiccoughed the unhappy man.

'Then who was it that blew the gaff?' thundered Moleskin and forebore to stay his hand.

'Dunno!' mumbled Sclatterguff.

'If you don't know who 'twas, then 'twas you!' Moleskin's ready logic was as pitiless as his arm.

''Twas Pig-iron Burke,' said Sclatterguff, wallowing with that admission into unbroken shame.

'Hidin' behind a stiff!' snorted Moleskin, releasing Sclatterguff and turning to Isaacs.

'It is a suit, nipper,' he said, unloosening the bundle and bringing it out. 'Now try it on, my lad.'

The trousers were donned, and had a certain relation to that for which they were intended, even though the upper rim of the waist rose to the boy's neck.

Ganger Billy made some humorous remark regarding them. They were the first pair he had ever seen forming that for which God had intended them and a waistcoat and muffler into the bargain.

The jacket was put on, and the tailor eyed the infant Beau Brummel with a proprietary air.

'Isaacs, it fits you all right, as far as I can see.' Moleskin trimmed a few stray tails with his scissors. 'Stand off a bit till I get a proper view o' you!'

The boy stood off a bit and squared his shoulders.

'Aye, aye, man, it's all right.' The tailor was filled with admiration of his own handiwork. 'Fits like a blister! Turn round till I see you behind.'

For a few moments Isaacs performed many movements under Moleskin's directions, leant forward, and bent backward, to show if the stitching would bear strain, took three sharp paces forward to show the garb in movement, and stood at attention to show the suit in repose.

'Not so bad, nipper, not so bad!' said Moleskin, his eyes filled with the joy of an artist who looks at his completed work.

'Aye, it fits the nipper, fits where it touches,' was the dry remark of the Moocher. 'You're at the wrong trade with a shovel, Moleskin. A man that's able to do that with cast-offs, would be able to make a lady's costume from a cement bag.'

'Daddy Joe, tailor,' said the youngster with determination, 'and Cunnin' Ithaacs vewy peepy!'

'Then it's bunk, Ikey Mo!' Moleskin lifted the child in his arms, and carried him to his sleeping-place. 'You squat down here and doss!'

'Cookies, Daddy Joe?' asked the youngster, as he was being tucked up. 'I'se hungwy!'

Moleskin felt in his pocket and brought out a portion of sandwich.

'Put this inside of you,' said the man. 'It's very good.'

'Don't like it,' was the youngster's firm avowal. He was already spoilt. 'Not good! Cookies!'

'Cookies! What's cookies?'

'Cookies last night!'

'What had you last night?'

'Cookies! Moocher me cookies, when you workin', Daddy Joe.'

Moleskin turned a blazing eye on the Moocher.

'What game were you up to?' he thundered. 'What is he to you, eh? Eh! Fillin' him with muck when I'm not about. What's cookies anyway?'

The Moocher had retreated discreetly, and now looked at Moleskin from the vantage point of the open door.

'They're a sort of scones with currants on them,' the Moocher explained.

'And where did you get them?' asked Moleskin.

'At Dunsore Farm –'

'Bought them?'

'Pinched them.'

'Now, Isaacs, you go to doss,' said Moleskin. 'I'll have cookies for you when you wake up.'

He again tucked the blankets round the boy.

'Four cookies, Daddy Joe?'

'Four, Isaacs.'

'Two dozen, Daddy Joe?'

'Two score, you wee devil, you!' said the big man. 'Now, go to sleep, or you'll get none at all.'

'Moocher get some for me,' said the little diplomat.

Long legs could have done the stretch between bunk and door in five paces; Moleskin did it in three and his hand fell heavily on the Moocher's shoulder, fell and gripped.

'Out!' Moleskin yelled. 'Out and don't come in till he's sleepin'.'

'What's wrong with you now?' spluttered the Moocher.

'Nothin', but get out!' and with these words, Moleskin thrust the man through the door. 'What the devil does he know about nippers, him and his dirty teeth,' he grumbled, coming back to the bunk.

'Isaacs!' He sat down by the bunk and caught the youngster's hand. 'Do you like that toad-skin, Tom the Moocher?'

'I do, Daddy Joe.'

'Do you like me, Isaacs?'

'I do, Daddy Joe.'

'Now, tell me this. Why do you like Tom the Moocher?'

'Cookies.'

'You shouldn't eat them. He's a bad man!' said Moleskin.

'Bad man, nice cookies,' the youngster mumbled.

'If you close your eyes and go to sleep, I'll get you cookies,' said Moleskin. 'Now sleep.'

'I'se sleepin'.' The youngster shut his eyes. After a moment he opened them, looked slyly at Moleskin and closed his eyes again. For a while he breathed heavily, then opened one eye, so slightly that only a slit and glint told of the manoeuvre. Presently the glint of the pupil was clouded by the falling lash, one little arm was thrust over the coverlet and fell slackly on the blanket; Cunning Isaacs turned on his side and was asleep. Good night!

CHAPTER II

THE RIDER

The Wise Man spoke:
'Twas me to discover
That we twist the same rope over and over
And all is the same for us, man and men,
On the lift of the hill, in the lap of the glen –
We come and we go, but the end is sure;
Kind word, act, purpose, these three endure.
Though the seven threads of deadly sin
Are set in the line that all men spin,
Faith and Charity, Love and Hope,
Show in the strands of the meanest rope.

– *From* Wayside Proverbs.

Moleskin, having set his mind on procuring cookies for his little friend, lost no time in putting a hastily formed plan into action. The thought of the Moocher's ability to please galled the ex-convict. Isaacs had to be humoured, of course, but only up to a point. There was such a thing as overstepping the limit, and it had been overstepped on the cookie question. At the start Moleskin had the supreme place in the youngster's estimation, and the man looked with a tolerant eye on the Moocher's teeth. Now, however, the vantage ground was slipping under Moleskin's feet. Something had to be done, and in his own parlance, he had 'to see about it'.

Dunsore Farm was some five leagues away. To walk that distance was, of course, out of the question. The only thing to do was to ride it. The night was a good one, frosty and hard underfoot, with a moon, wasting a little, standing high over the hills, and peeping down at Glencorrie. At that moment the moon, in Moleskin's opinion, resembled the plate on which the Moocher's bottom teeth were set.

The equine stock of Glencorrie was an assortment of skin and bones, and more bones than skin. The sight of the rafter-ribbed hacks would make a veterinarian swear, turn a hack-driver green, and induce a knacker to join the Society for Prevention of Cruelty to Animals. All the hacks were patterns of superannuated weariness, long-developed guile and natural viciousness.

Moleskin went to the stable and brought one out, possibly the worst steed of the collection. Its mane showed only in places, like grass on a neglected pavement, its back was so sharply edged that Moleskin, mounted, without a saddle, had some very confused thoughts of a blunt-edged razor.

Seated, he had a look round the glen. Somewhere a jew's-harp was giving voice to 'Annie Laurie'; in the near distance a gang of men were discussing an ancient fight, discussing it with such vehemence that it was natural to expect it to end only in blows; from Moleskin's position the reservoir was quite visible, the half under the hills sunk in darkness, the other half reflecting the moonshine in little broken waves of light.

'Seein' that there ain't no saddle, we'll go easy,' was his thought. 'So, whoa, bonnie lassie!'

Nothing beats courtesy. It might serve instead of a saddle and previous experience. That there was a little doubt in his mind on this matter, must be admitted. But it was the only way. His fingers tightened on the reins which he had taken from the stable.

'Gee up, jenny!' he ordered, looking towards the cart-track which lay in the hollow below him. The animal took his order literally, geed up to the stable that stood on higher ground, and passing in, left the rider hanging by the cross-beam of the door, his eyebrow cut a little because it came in contact with that obstruction.

Moleskin let himself to the ground, procured a paling stake, and brought the animal out again.

'Now, Razor Bones, you effigy!' he apostrophised the animal as he elbowed it into the dyke. 'It's got to be settled once for all whether you'r me's to be boss!' He mounted Razor Back and Razor Back made for the door.

'Not that way!' roared Moleskin, laying tongue to a few extra epithets. 'Turn round!'

Under the urge of the stick and manipulation of the reins the horse turned round, but, like a crab, made its way backwards towards the door.

'Ye're up against it, Razor,' Moleskin grunted. 'At least, that part of you that's near the stable!' With this sound advice, he raised the stick in the air, leant sideways for elbow room and lashed at the horse's buttocks. Up till that moment it had been quiet, but now it raised itself in air and endeavoured to roll the rider from his seat.

Moleskin saved himself in time. One hand closed like a trap on the tuft which told of an ancient crest, his legs were a festoon round the animal, and in later days, Moleskin, telling of the purchase he held, vowed that his heels met under Saw Bones' belly.

For a while raged a rough and tumble, the rider clinging, the ridden trying to throw. While he had grip of the mane, the night went well for Moleskin, for he who could grip and hold a live salmon between finger and thumb, had always housing when there was something to grip. But at some period axle-grease had fallen on the horse's mane. The tuft Moleskin gripped was slippery, his fingers came away.

The combat now entered on a desperate stage. The animal raised itself on its hind legs, stood in air, and heaved to one side. Moleskin righted himself by slewing in the opposite direction; Saw Bones reversed, but Moleskin kept equipoise by balancing himself in relation to his steed.

'Try!' he yelled, righting himself on a perilous inclination from the level. 'Try! But ye'll sweat blood at the tryin' if that's all ye can do. Dammit!' – he braced himself for the next heave – 'ye're as good as beat already.'

Looking to the ground the rider could see the shadow of the struggle; the horse turning round, the rider gyrating and forming part of the shade that turned upon an axis within its own figure. Moleskin had one startling thought of a feather glued to a flywheel in the threshing mills of hell. But sight-seeing and thought were not within his province at that moment. His legs had lost hold, but his hand gripped something hairy and held.

His position was now quite unorthodox, he was looking in the wrong direction and held the tail.

The figure of a man showed in the near distance, and Moleskin slipped to the ground.

'What the . . . capers are you up to?' came the voice of Macready.

'Found this effigy down at the shacks,' Moleskin explained.

'Was takin' him back to the stable.'

'Ridin' him?' was Macready's polite inquiry.

'Trainin' him to box!' said Moleskin savagely.

'Landed ye one?' asked Macready, coming near. His voice was charged with consideration. 'And he has his bit in his mouth, too. Did he put it in himself?' he inquired, caustically.

'Must have been left in when he was tied up,' said Moleskin.

'I tied him,' said Macready, examining the reins. 'And I took his reins away to patch 'em up. Here, Moleskin, what's up? Tryin' to run down to Dunrobin to get a bottle?'

'That's it,' said Moleskin, glad of any excuse. 'But he's spirited,' he added.

'Spirited!' Macready exclaimed. 'You're the second man that's gone on his back. The first got shell-shock!'

'Any quiet ones in?' asked Moleskin.

'You're in a hurry to get the drink, aren't you?' Macready inquired.

'I am that,' Moleskin lied.

'Then walk,' was Macready's advice.

The joke, though stale, had the occasion to flavour it, and Macready, having made a hit, which in telling would lighten many a future evening, became generous.

'The other beasts ain't no bong, most o' em,' he confessed. 'But there's Jock, not a bad old stager. He always has his crock at the Dunrobin Whistle, and he'll get there quicker than he'll come back. Take him, Moleskin, and I'll be waitin' for a sup when you return. But the place ain't worth livin' in since the whisky merchant skedaddled. I ain't much o' a hand at it!'

'He's all right,' said the mounted Moleskin, when he rode away on Jock, the horse that liked his crock at the Dunrobin Whistle.

The deep night sky was perfectly clear, the million stars sparkling coldly. The moon stood aloft, apparently immovable, and underneath were the cobalt-blue mountains, their contour clearly defined in the night's rarefied atmosphere. The moor was utterly deserted, not even a drunken reveller returning from Dunrobin was to be met on the long uneven cart track.

Moleskin's horse did the journey at a steady canter, and knowing his way, needed not the guidance of the rider. The moor round him was practically level, altering little in contour, but much in colour. In places it was covered with heather, but neighbouring these tracts were dark fields of bog bereft of vegetation. Pools abounded which, under the light of the moon, took the colour of polished bronze.

At eight o'clock Moleskin skirted Dunrobin, which movement caused Jock to sink into a slush of drear depression. He who had cantered now crawled, and did the rest of the journey at a pace that was funereal.

Moleskin rode a mile beyond the village, dismounted and tied Jock to a tree. The rest of the journey was done on foot. Fifteen minutes' brisk walk brought Dunsore Farm within sight.

'Now for the cookies,' said Moleskin. 'Three ways o' gettin' 'em. Pinch 'em, bum 'em, or beg 'em. I'll try pinchin' for a start!'

CHAPTER 12

THE CONCEALED BED

She would not yesterday. She will today.
Not strange, my son. 'Tis a woman's way –
As her fishing season has its rise and fall,
Better a sprat than no fish at all.

– *From* Wayside Proverbs.

Dunsore Farm, the farm of Duncan MacWhapple, and many another MacWhapple, all of worthy stock, who had only lost tenure of the holding when losing tenure of another, that of which Death holds the title-deeds, was brilliantly lit up on the evening when Moleskin came to the place. It was really lit up for a visitor, who was not an escaped convict.

A lady was coming to the place, a Miss Smith, and a real lady, too, as Jessie, the wife of the farmer, strove to impress upon her two servants, Euphemia and Bessie. The old housewife had been in a flurry all day, something out of the normal, for in the ordinary course of life she was quite calm, quite cheerful and always brimming over with good nature. She was a good worker, up early, down late, milked a cow with the best of them and – never talked scandal.

In the summer when the Highlands were peopled by the city-bred, she kept women boarders, 'not ladies', but in what this definition abounded none could determine. However, the home she provided was such a good one that her same boarders came year after year, and generally in the summer time, of course.

But now a visitor was coming in the winter, and this visitor was a 'lady'. Why the term 'lady' was applied in this particular case it was impossible to say. She was coming from London, a not entirely novel happening, for other visitors had come from there before. She was coming in the winter, but on more than one occasion boarders came to Dunsore for the Christmas season.

Perhaps it was because Doctor Taylor, the young country physician who engaged the room for Miss Smith, replied to Mrs MacWhapple's question: 'Is she genteel?' with: 'Yes, Mrs MacWhapple, more than merely. She's a thoroughbred.' There was no getting beyond that, of course. The doctor's word was something to stand on in the parish of Dunrobin.

Being 'a thoroughbred', Mrs MacWhapple must make the house worthy of her coming guest. She resurrected *The Book of Manners* from the linen chest that reeked with mothball, and re-read ancient tenets on etiquette, read them to Euphemia and Betty, directions regarding transport of dishes, shutting and opening of doors, and correct laying of a table.

One point worried the good wife a little. She and her good man always sat at table with their guests, and MacWhapple had porridge twice daily and loved the dish. A paragraph of the volume dealt with the vulgar habit of noisy mastication. The good man masticated noisily, but . . . well, everything except that was all right and Mr and Mrs MacWhapple went to Dunrobin station to meet their visitor, leaving instructions to the servants that the house should be lighted up against their return.

Euphemia, the elder of the two servants, and named Femy, for short, went too, on her own, just to have a first peep at the lady. She was not yet back. Betty, plump and pleasant, was in the living-room of Dunsore farmhouse at the moment of Moleskin's arrival.

'Such goin's on!' she was saying, holding her arms akimbo and fixing a critical look on the fire. 'I don't know what's comin' o'er folk. And the fol-the-dols old Jessie put on to go out. Frills and furbelows.' She made a face at the lamp that stood on the mantelpiece. 'Must see that there's plenty o' fresh air in the room!'

With a snort of disgust she went to the window and opened it, then made her way to the kitchen, humming a song as she went. Immediately the clatter of tin and delf could be heard from the apartment to rear.

At that moment Moleskin Joe came to the window. For a second he looked furtively in, then shoved his foot over the window sill and surveyed the room. As if finding everything to his satisfaction, he drew up a second leg, pivoted round on the window sill and dropped himself to the floor.

'Posh!' he exclaimed, sticking his hands under his belt and making a studied survey of the apartment. His eyes rested longingly on the table and its ornaments. Lifting a scone he smelt it, put it in his pocket and reached for another. 'Not very big,' he remarked. 'But the very tack for Cunnin' Isaacs. The way some coves stuff their bellies and the way others haven't a bite. It's enough to make a man a Bolshy. I wonder how much I could flog this for?' he asked, putting a spoon in his pocket. 'Hell!'

Hushed exasperation was in his voice as he looked towards the window. Outside in the moonlight the silhouette of the girl Betty could be distinguished. Her back was towards the window, her eyes staring into the distance as if looking for somebody. Pocketing another spoon, Moleskin went cautiously towards the door leading to the kitchen. As his hand rested on the knob a sound was heard outside the door at which he stood. Coming quietly back he slipped under the table. The second servant entered – Femy, a middle-aged woman with a shawl round her shoulders.

'Where are you, Betty?' she called, coming towards the table and surreptitiously gazing at its appointments.

'Here, Femy,' was Betty's reply from outside. 'Am lookin' to see if there's any signs o' them comin'.'

'Aye, it's like you,' said Femy crossly. 'Standin' out there, when there's so much to do!'

'I'm in!' said Betty, shoving one leg over the window sill.

'You're not,' was Femy's answer, catching the leg and thrusting it back. 'What are doors for? Come in by the front!'

Femy surveyed the table again, the empty plates and the places where the scones should be.

'Hey, lassie!'

'Aye?' inquired Betty, coming in by the door.

'Where are the scones?'

'I put them on the plates.'

'Well, look at the plates and tell me what you see!' Femy's voice was asperse and firm.

'It's that damned cat again!' exclaimed the surprised Betty.

'And the spoons! Did the cat eat *them*?' asked Femy.

'What's wrong with them?'

'Nothin'. Only they're not there!'

'Not there!' said the girl in pained surprise. 'And I'm certain I put them down!'

'You're goin' dotty, lassie,' said Femy, shortly. 'Lay the spoons down and get the cookies in!'

Betty did as she was directed and rearranged the table under the direction of the elder woman.

'And tell me, did you see her?' Betty inquired.

'Aye, didn't I.' There was a world of meaning in Femy's voice. 'And the whole countryside was waitin' at the station. First class she came by, too. Such a waste of money!'

'And you got a sight o' her!'

'I saw her.' There was dramatic intensity in Femy's tones.

'And what was she like?' Betty was bristling with curiosity.

'I wouldn't go as far as to say that she was beautiful,' said the judicious Femy. 'But for all that, she is a comely wee lass.'

'And what kind o' clothes has she on her?'

'Good! But with her fur coat off, there's a lot of her showin'. Aye, this Miss Smith looks flighty. And what she is to Doctor Taylor, I don't know. Why is he bringin' her here?'

'For a holiday, he said,' Betty remarked.

'A holiday in the winter!' Femy's upturned nose showed disproof of this statement.

'There's more in this than meets the eye.'

Bending to assort the tablecloth, Femy noticed a boot on the floor, and a portion of leg attached to the boot. Her thumb turned to the wall at her back.

'Wipe down them cobwebs, Betty,' she ordered, looking at the place which her thumb indicated.

'Cobwebs!' said Betty indignantly. 'I wiped the wall down twice this day.'

'Do what you're told.' As she spoke, Femy went towards the fireplace and pulled down a fowling-piece which hung there. Holding the weapon at firing position, she aimed at the legs under the table. 'Come out!' she ordered in a loud voice.

The legs did not move. Betty saw and uttered a shriek.

'It's a man! Ooh!'

'Come out!' Femy's voice was imperative. 'We see that you're there!'

Moleskin dragged himself out lazily, got to his feet and went towards Femy, quite undismayed by the hard determined look in her eyes.

'Put your two hands over your head!' commanded the woman.

'What for?' inquired Moleskin. His voice was entirely free from guile.

'Because, if you don't, I'll shoot you!'

The innocence of the man had entirely confused her.

'It's not loaded,' said Moleskin, indifferently.

'If you get what's in that you'll be a dead man!' said Betty. Her hand was on the knob of the door, and being in a position of vantage felt that it was safe to say something.

'There would be three deaths then,' said the man casually. 'I'd be murdered and the two of you would be hung.'

'Well, we'd chance it,' said Femy stubbornly.

'It's the wrong end you're pointin' at me,' said Moleskin.

Femy looked down at the weapon, and immediately Moleskin's hand shot out and fastened on the fowling-piece. With a dexterous turn he twisted it out of her hands. Betty shrieked, and ran into the kitchen. Femy, terror-stricken, gazed at the man, who fixed a look of interest on the weapon.

'Always get the tip of the foresight in line with the V of the backsight,' he said, placing the butt-end of the weapon on the floor and gazing at Femy. He was rehearsing army instructions for rifle practice. 'But for women it's different. They've to place the muzzle against the target, shut their eyes and pull the trigger with both hands. Here's your five-point-nine and hang it on the wall!'

He handed the weapon to Femy, who, viewing the action with suspicion, made no effort to catch the weapon.

'What did you do to it?' she asked.

'Nothin',' said the man. 'But, if you want to murder me I'll load the thing for you.'

Betty, who had been a listener and realising that the man was not as dangerous as she had anticipated, returned from the kitchen.

'And I suppose it was you that took the scone I blamed the cat for?' she asked.

'I'm the cat,' said Moleskin, placing the weapon against the table and taking two scones from his pocket.

'Aye! And the spoons?' asked the valiant Betty.

'These them?' Moleskin produced the spoons.

'Now off with you!' said Femy. 'Put the spoons on the table and keep the scones.'

'Thanks for buckshee!' said Moleskin, pocketing the cookies. 'Are these', he asked, putting the spoons on the table, 'silver?'

'No,' said Femy. 'Be off with you!'

'I'm off!' Moleskin went towards the window.

'Not that way!' Femy shrieked. 'Go out through the kitchen. Have ye never been in a house before?'

'Never had a roof of my own,' said Moleskin simply. 'If ye want to find me, my address is Number One, The Open Air. I carry all my property in my pocket and that burden has never given me a sore back.'

'Take him out through the kitchen,' Femy advised Betty.

'Can't. Tam Wilson's there,' said Betty.

'The polisman!' Femy snorted. 'Between polismen, postmen and poachers you make a big fool o' yourself.'

'A polisman?' Moleskin inquired. 'One?'

'Aye, one,' Femy informed him.

'One polisman can never stop me!' said he, taking a step towards the door.

'And if it's found out that we're feedin' navvies when the master's away, what will be said?' Femy took position in front of Moleskin. 'You're one o' the Glencorrie men, aren't you?'

'I'm one o' the mob,' said Moleskin.

'Well, if I can say anything of you men, from what I've seen, you'll not say "No" to a wee drop?' Femy remarked.

'There's no record of me ever being such a fool.' Moleskin was sure of this conviction.

'Femy!' Betty exclaimed, aghast.

'Even navvies, and them such thieves, must live!' said the warm-hearted Femy. 'Never be too hard on anybody. That's what I say.' She half-filled a glass from the bottle on the table. 'Take this, good man. My father was a navvy!'

Moleskin took the glass, surveyed it with the air of one who is a judge, and drained it to the last dribble.

'Ha'a, h'm!' he grunted with relish.

'Now, hop it!' the woman ordered.

''Twas a nice sup, woman, a nice sup!' said Moleskin, handing her the glass. 'And may you never be without it when you want it, and never want it when you are without it. And if ever you're down on the dead-end, think of this and it will give you comfort: There's a good time comin' though we may never live to see it!'

'I suppose you'll be a married man like most navvies,' said Femy, with a laugh. 'And you don't know where your wife is?'

'I'm not married,' said Moleskin. 'But I've the nicest boy

you ever saw. Cunnin' Isaacs, I call him. Least that's what he calls himself. Not more than the height of my knee. And he likes the wee cookies.' Moleskin touched his pocket.

'A wee laddie, did you say?' asked Betty. 'And not married?'

'I'm not married, but I've got him,' said Moleskin. 'Just came into the shack one night like a stray puppy-dog! And he hasn't got nobody now but us, and we're keepin' it low, not tellin' anybody.'

'But why are you tellin' me?' asked Femy.

'Well, to judge by what you've done, you wouldn't split on us,' said Moleskin. 'And he does like cookies,' he added, with a grin that went to the hearts of both his listeners.

'Ah! I see,' said Femy with an understanding smile. 'Here, open your pockets!'

Moleskin did so and Femy filled his pouches with the desired eatables.

'Thanks very much, good woman,' said Moleskin when the filling was finished. 'Now I'm off to Glencorrie.'

He went to the door, but again Femy's bulky form obstructed him. Outside was to be heard the rattle of wheels.

'You cannot go that way!' said the woman. 'You'll run into them! Go out by the kitchen!'

'But Tam Wilson!' said Betty helplessly. 'He's in there!'

'Why didn't you clear out sooner?' groaned Femy, wringing her hands. 'What are we to do – what are we to do?'

'Put him under the bed,' Betty suggested.

Femy rushed to the curtains that were hung on the wall at the back of the room. Drawing these aside she disclosed a recess containing a bed.

'Get in under here!' she called to Moleskin.

Moleskin did so and stretched himself out on the floor.

'Now, keep quiet as a mouse,' Femy ordered. 'When they've had their supper I'll let you out. And the next time you come here, it's the polisman I'll set after ye.'

The curtains were drawn together and Moleskin was hidden.

'There, they're comin',' he could hear the breathless Femy saying. 'What a house for them! What a house! Go to the door, Betty! When they rap, open wide and stand stiff as a poker, till they pass you by. Then shut the door without bangin' it. Don't speak till you're spoken to. That's what the auld woman got from her *Book o' Manners*. There they are! Run to the door!'

Moleskin wormed his way to the slit in the curtain and looked into the room. He was just in time to see Femy bolt into the kitchen as if her very life depended on it. Betty was at the door, her hand on the knob, her position one of strained attention. A hand could be heard fumbling outside, then the door burst open so briskly that Betty stumbled back a few paces, almost losing her balance. A woman well past middle age, dressed in bonnet and cloak, entered.

'You said that you'd give a genteel rap, m'm,' said Betty in a hurt voice.

'So I did!' said the woman, who was Betty's mistress. She was apparently in great good humour. 'But don't mind about that! She is very genteel, but the nicest, simplest soul you ever met. Just wait till you see her! Come in, lassie, come in!' she called, looking over her shoulder.

A girl whose age might be about twenty-five entered and came to a halt when she stepped across the threshold. Moleskin had a clear view of her. 'A good-lookin' wench!' he thought to himself. His statement was a general one, without detail, but true as it was impulsive.

Miss Smith was of middle height, slim and lithe, with a wealth of brown hair, which fell in ringlets over her ears. Her eyes, liquid and dark, had in them a strange wistfulness, which somehow seemed to point to the fact that she was entering on some strange adventure, the results of which she feared. Moleskin, in some curious way, had a sudden feeling of pity for the girl.

'This is Betty, Miss Smith,' said the mistress, pointing to the servant. 'A brave worker, Betty, and a good lass under a cow!'

'Under a cow!' repeated Miss Smith. She was apparently mystified. 'Did it hurt?'

Betty smiled. The incident of being under a cow had had no appreciable effects.

'You're all right now,' said Miss Smith, shaking the girl's hand. 'I'm pleased to meet you!'

'And I'm pleased to ken yerself, m'm,' replied Betty, rising nobly to the occasion.

'Now, come along and see your bedroom, Miss Smith,' said the old lady, conducting the stranger to the room on the right.

Betty's eyes followed them until the pair were out of sight.

'Whist!' she whispered as Femy came in. 'I saw her. She's

better than I thought. "I'm pleased to meet ye" she said to me, and "I'm pleased to meet you, m'm!" said I.'

'M'm! And her not buckled,' Femy spoke in tones of withering scorn.

'That doesn't matter!' said Betty pertly. 'She soon will be. Doctor Taylor hasn't taken her here for nothin'.'

'Here, they're comin',' said Femy as a noise was heard at the door. She ran to the curtain and spoke through the slit. 'You're to keep quiet, navvy!'

'Doggo as a bag o' cement!' came the voice from the recess.

Farmer MacWhapple and Doctor Taylor entered.

'This is splendid,' Dr Taylor remarked, rubbing his hands gleefully. 'Miss Smith will be quite at home here.'

'Ah, if she only came in the summer,' said the old man. 'Summer here is lovely. And she's only staying for one week?'

'Just a week,' answered the doctor. 'She's run down a bit, and the air will brace her up.'

'But it's always rainin',' said the old man. 'You know that yourself. The folk are born with umbrellas in this quarter. Ha! ha!'

'Aye, it's necessary!' laughed the doctor.

'But in the summer it's grand!' said the old man. 'Last summer we had four here every week, but it's the first time we ever had visitors at this time o' the year.'

Mrs MacWhapple and Miss Smith returned.

'Now sit down and make yerself at home,' said the kindly mistress. 'Femy and Betty will attend to you. Ting that bell, when you want anything. It's a lonely place you've come to, and I often ask Doctor Taylor, how can he, a young man, come to such an out-of-the-way corner. Nobody ever comes to hereabouts – only the navvies.'

'Wild unchristian savages they are,' said the old man. 'Escaped convicts, whisky makers, thieves and vagabonds.'

'Who makes this whisky?' asked Miss Smith, with a show of interest.

'Nobody knows,' said the old man. 'I think they all take a hand at the making. There was one fellow called Moleskin Joe, that was thought to make it. He got sent to prison six weeks ago, and the polis thought it would stop then. But no; it went on just the same as ever.'

'This man, Moleskin Joe, is he in prison now?' asked Miss Smith. She cast a meaning glance at the doctor as she put the question.

'Not now,' said the old man. 'He's got out.'

'Now, we'll leave them to their supper,' said Mrs MacWhapple to her husband. 'Miss Smith will be hungry after her journey.'

The farmer and his wife left the room. The table was a circular one. Miss Smith and the doctor sat side by side and facing the eye that looked through the slit in the curtain. Betty brought soup and placed it on the table in front of the pair.

The doctor put his spoon in the soup, stirred it mechanically and looked at the woman.

'You're very quiet, Marjorie,' he said in a half-bantering tone. 'Afraid?'

'Yes,' was her simple answer.

He put his arm around her shoulder and looked into her eyes.

'May I kiss you?' he asked.

'Yes, if you want to.' Her lips trembled as if she were on the point of tears. The man drew his hand from her shoulder.

'Marjorie!' His voice contained an accusation.

'Yes, I understand you,' she said. 'But you promised –'

'I know I promised, but Marjorie!' He caught her hand.

'You must not, Dick; it's not right.' The girl drew her hand away.

'Fie, Madame Propriety!' laughed the doctor in loving reproach.

'I know that I am awfully conventional,' said Marjorie. 'But to one who has been brought up like me, ritual is almost as powerful as passion.'

'More powerful.'

'Perhaps.'

'Marjorie!' The doctor drew himself up to his full height.

Marjorie looked at him, trembling, then with a strength almost stronger than woman's she clasped his shoulders and flung herself on his breast.

'Forgive me, Dick, forgive me!' she sobbed. 'I didn't mean that. I'm wicked.'

'Wicked, you little silly!' mumbled the doctor, kissing her hair. 'What wicked things have you ever done?'

'It's not what I have done, but what I am doing,' said the woman.

'The next thing you'll tell me is that you love him,' the doctor remarked.

'But I married him,' Marjorie made answer. 'Of my own free will.'

'And loved him?' the doctor insisted.

'I thought I did. He was going out to the trenches then, to die, maybe!'

'Oh, everybody's going to die, sometime or another,' said the doctor. 'I'm going to die, but I don't put that forward as an inducement when wanting your love.'

'But it seemed so near then,' faltered Marjorie.

'You're a strange soul.' The doctor spoke bitterly. 'A declaration of love needs a deathbed scene to make it palatable to you!'

'Please, don't, Dick!' The girl's voice was supplicating. 'You know I do love you – but it's hard, so very hard.'

'Love shouldn't require an effort!' said the doctor.

'But there's such a thing as duty.'

'And the law of duty which says that a contract between two is to be carried out by two.' The doctor's voice rose a little. 'But when one breaks the contract that contract stands no longer. Now, there's the marriage contract to which you were a party –'

'But has it been broken? Whist! –'

Betty came in with the second course.

'Broken, from the very start,' said the doctor, when the servant had withdrawn. 'In the very first place this man, who is your husband, introduced himself as the son of Sir Mortimer Davis, who had been killed in a motor accident in Italy. Sir Mortimer was a widower and had one child – a boy. Malcolm Davis, or Tom Jones, as he calls himself now, claimed to be that child. I have made inquiries. Sir Mortimer did exist, was killed in an accident – but the child died three months before. Davis insisted that the child did not die, that he was the child, taken in charge by an Italian peasant.'

He looked hard at the girl, who was silent.

'He got the idea from a film – American sob stuff,' snorted the doctor. 'I have brought you here to see the father of your husband. He, as you will see tomorrow, is a ganger at this contract job, a good hardworking old man who has given every penny of his earnings to get his son an education, that son who married you, and bigamously married another girl some eighteen months afterwards.'

'So you've insisted.' The girl breathed short and there was

anguish in the eyes which she fixed on the doctor. She apparently alluded to the man's last statement.

'And you don't believe?' he asked.

'But it's so hard!' she pleaded. 'Maybe you've made a mistake.'

'You speak as if you wish I had made a mistake,' said the doctor, his voice rising a little. 'And after all I've done. Not that you're not worth it, Marjorie. When I first met you in the hospital at Abbeville, when I saw you there in your nurse's uniform, so wonderful, I wanted to fly away with you somewhere, and then I found out that you were married to – to –'

He came to a sudden halt. The thought that another man had possessed her, had slept with her, jarred upon the doctor's nerves.

'It makes me mad to think of him, to think that –' He caught her hands, hardly daring to breathe the jealous thought. Moleskin, watching, thought of Sheila, and a feeling of jealousy against somebody unknown surged in his heart. 'Tell me?' asked the doctor, 'how long did he live with you? No, don't tell me. I cannot stand it. He was your husband. That is enough. He had you first. You understand.'

'I understand,' said the woman, suddenly realising his meaning. 'But was I to know!'

'Of course, you weren't to know,' said the man. 'I'm not blaming you. I took you for what you were. I asked no more . . . I ask no more, but it is denied me, that which I ask. Have I not given proof of it? I've spent the time that I should have devoted to my studies, making inquiries, tracking down a man. I have given up a practice in the city to come to this hole, where I've seen myself travelling thirty miles one night to help a man into the world, and thirty miles on the same night in an opposite direction to prevent a man going out. And my recompense for this has been fifteen shillings.'

'Poor Dick!' said the woman, pressing his hair with her hand.

'So there,' he resumed. 'I've sacrificed my time, my practice and, perhaps, my patients.'

'Your patients?' she asked, gazing mistily at the man.

'Well, if I have not, I've almost done so. And, by God, it's worth it, if the thought of what I've done will gain me what another gained by doing nothing whatever, not even dying!'

'You are so cynical!' she sobbed.

'Cynicism is all that is left to one who has made himself cheap,' said the doctor bitterly. 'I have made myself cheap, Marjorie. I've gone to the navvy shacks, have made myself friendly with Ganger Davis, just to find out everything about his son. The ganger likes me, Marjorie, takes me for a gentleman, one who can appreciate his son. And I' – his voice rose – 'I'm a Paul Pry, a Peeping Tom. But you don't believe me yet. But tomorrow I will introduce you to old Davis, and he'll show you his son's photograph.'

'I believe it now,' sobbed the girl. 'I believed it always.'

'And you'll be certain,' said the doctor, 'when I show you your husband's mistress, a girl called Sheila Cannon, who is at present in Markonar Workhouse. What is this?'

One of the curtains of the recess came down with a rip, and before the doctor's words were well uttered it heaved towards the table, wheeled towards the door, turned the knob and made its way outside. Thunderstruck, the doctor and Miss Smith stared at the phenomenon. Both had a hazy impression of a pair of legs moving beneath the curtain. Something dropped to the floor. The doctor got to his feet and lifted that which dropped.

'A scone!' he said.

CHAPTER 13

VISITORS

Three things strong and a house is blest!
The table, the fire and the hand to a guest.

– *From* Wayside Proverbs.

Ten o'clock of the next day saw Windy Corner in a state of great disorganisation, which set in shortly after Moleskin's departure. Digger Marley and others had set themselves down to a game of cards, banker the game. Sid the Slogger, by right of a deft turn-up, became banker and won much money. He was in luck's way and kept there until the moment when the Moocher's arm swept across the table and the heavy fist attached to that arm landed heavily on the Slogger's ear. This rather startling action was the impulsive manner of bringing a certain fact to the notice of the gamblers.

In a pack of cards there is only one ace of hearts. The Moocher was served this ace, and according to all rules of mathematics, no other player should have that card at that moment. And the Slogger had that card!

The trouble might have blown over if it were only a dispute between two. But it was a dispute in which all were concerned. Each player wanted his money back. If he got what he wanted others said that he had gotten too much, and the row started between two spread to others. Implements were used in combat, bunks were torn apart, the stove overturned, and because he protested against such wholesale destruction, Ganger Billy got an ear thickened.

Things might have sobered down in their ordinary way if Ganger Macready had not come in at that moment bearing two jars of mountain dew destined for his own shack. Passing, he heard the uproar and was curious to see what it was all about.

The time was unlucky. Impulse led to thoughtless action. Fighting is a drouthy business and in a second Macready was surrounded, his bag collared, the jars uncorked, and the billy-cans filled.

At ten o'clock the next morning all who had drunk were asleep, some on the floor, a number in the ashes and a few outside in the open.

Cunning Isaacs was afoot and interested. He had seen the latter stages of the fighting and was so much excited that he had slept very little afterwards. If he slept he might have missed something! At the present moment he was working very hard, crooning to himself as he wrought, making a waterworks. To the unknown, a certain litter on the floor, an old boot, a pair of bottom-worn trousers, a muffler, a pair of knee-straps, and something that might have been taken for a scarecrow, would probably mean nothing whatever, but to Isaacs this litter meant all in all to his handiwork.

'What's he up to, Moleskin?' asked Sclatterguff, pointing at the youngster. The old man was seated on a wood-block, caressing his ear. He, too, had been well in the wars.

'That's the waterworks that he's making,' said Joe.

'And what are the old trousers for?'

'That's the piping.'

'And the boot?'

'The pay-box.'

'The scarecrow?'

'That's you. Don't you see the family likeness?' Moleskin inquired. 'Here, Carroty, listen.'

'Listen to what?' Carroty inquired.

'Where's the Ganger?'

'I don't know,' said Carroty. 'He's historical.'

'He's what?'

'All nerves, half off his nob, vulgally speaking,' Carroty explained. 'He gave me sixpence too much when paying me last Saturday, and when the Ganger does that there's something wrong. I suppose it's that gentleman son o' his!'

'Where's the gentleman now, d'ye know?' asked Moleskin.

'Mystery,' said Carroty. 'Goin' to the dogs, I bet. It never does to try and make a navvy a gentleman. The wild duck's egg is never tame. The breed that's brought up on a muck shovel will never know the prise o' a silver spoon.'

'Have you ever seen him?' Moleskin queried.

'Once when he was a nipper, about that size.' Carroty pointed at the busy Isaacs. 'Like him he was too, but all kids are like one another. Here he comes, storming like an explosion!'

The Ganger came in.

'Are you hell-smelts gettin' up this day?' he shouted. 'Do you want to work? Slogger! Moocher! The whole damned lot of you, come on! Get up!'

Half an hour's shoving, punching, and pushing wakened the men into sour sobriety and another half-hour was required to get them out to their work.

'Susan Saunders is here,' the Ganger informed Moleskin when the shack was emptied of all except Moleskin, Isaacs, Sclatterguff and himself.

'What the devil is she wanting?' Moleskin inquired.

'Followin' the waterworks,' said the old man. 'Got the sack wherever she was working, and footed it here to do our washing.'

'Washing!' Carroty exclaimed. 'Who wants washing done here with that ancient. And there's only one shirt per individual. When I was a young man in my first job I had two shirts. I washed one, hung it out to dry and never saw it again.'

'We all must pay for our wisdom,' remarked the Ganger. 'And she'll do washin' for them when they're boozed. And they'll pay for it!'

'They always do,' said Sclatterguff.

'Where's she stoppin'?' asked Moleskin.

''Bout half a mile away, on the other side of the glen, in that old hut that's used by the shepherds in the summer.'

'Know the place,' said Joe. 'I must go over and see her, me and Isaacs.'

'Already?' asked Sclatterguff, winking.

'Well, I'm going out to my work,' said the Ganger. 'And you, Carroty, clear up the mess here, nail the bunks together, patch the blankets and make yourself useful, or by Heaven, if you don't I'll give you the freedom of the world without a character.'

The three went out, leaving Sclatterguff alone. The old man immediately set himself to work repairing the damage of the previous evening. He had righted the stove, lit a fire, when he became aware of a noise at the door. He looked round.

'Who the devil's this?'

Slow wonderment would occasion Sclatterguff at that moment to invoke the Deity, but surprise being sudden, the devil had premier place in ejaculation. There was occasion for surprise. A woman stood at the door, a handsome, well-dressed woman – a lady. The man, hypnotised, gazed at her, rubbing his hands against the legs of his trousers as if in a crude effort to make himself presentable.

A man made his appearance behind her. He was Doctor Taylor, the country physician. Sclatterguff had seen this man before, and knew him to be a great friend of Ganger Davis.

'Nobody in?' asked the doctor.

'I'm here, sir,' the navvy told him.

'Oh, yes,' said the man. 'Is Ganger Davis in here?'

'He's down at the works, sir,' said Sclatterguff. 'I'll run and get him for you, sir.'

'No, no, don't trouble,' said the doctor. 'I'll go and find him myself. And you, Marjorie, just stay here and warm yourself until I come back. I'll not be more than ten minutes.'

He went away, leaving the woman. Carroty looked at her gingerly.

'Come and sit down,' he said. He felt very awkward. 'It's not what one would call much of a place for a lady. I'll just get a bit of a fire to conflagarate in the stove. What's in it is nearly extinguished.'

'It's really very kind of you to go to so much trouble,' said the woman, seating herself by the stove.

Carroty brought a murderous clasp-knife from his pocket, felt its edge with his finger, and looked at the visitor.

'Know what I'm goin' to do?' he asked.

'I'm afraid I don't,' said the woman, visibly shrinking.

'Considering as how I've got you here all to myself, so to speak, what would you expect me to do?' As he spoke he commenced sharpening the knife on his forearm. 'Sharp,' he added, 'sharp as a razor!'

'What are you going to do?' asked the woman, in a hoarse, terrified whisper.

'I'm goin' to make ye a pot o' steamin' hot tea,' Carroty informed her. 'In a silver teapot,' he added, triumphantly.

He pulled a bunk-board from its position, cut several splinters from it and threw them into the stove. The woman was reassured.

'But you're ruining the furniture,' she said. 'And I don't need any tea.'

'Not in a silver teapot?' Carroty remonstrated, with more than a shade of reproach in his manner. 'You've got ter. Lucky you've come when the inmates are out o' the shack.'

'How many stay here?' asked the woman looking round the apartment.

'Eighty at a pinch.'

'And are they all out?

'Aye. Some workin', some gettin' rid of their money.'

'How?'

'Crookin' their elbows and tossin' a pot,' said Sclatterguff, raising an imaginary beaker to his mouth. 'Most o' 'em are very good at it. Now, I'll make ye a slosh o' tea.'

He brought the silver-plated teapot from a corner, filled it with water and placed it on the stove.

'A beautiful teapot,' remarked the woman tactfully. She had noticed that Carroty laid great value on the article.

'Grand teapot.' Carroty purred like a cat to the compliment. 'Got it from my father!' said the old liar.

'Indeed!'

'Aye, lady.' He tickled the fire as he spoke. 'Class, my pergeniters. Money and land. But you wouldn't think that to look at *me*, would ye?'

'Well, I don't know,' said the woman good-humouredly.

'Well, my downfall was, well, what's many another's –'

'Women?' asked the visitor, who was understanding her host.

'Well, I was young, you know, but 'twas never that.' He was in a confidential mood. 'Strong waters, that's what was my downfall. Dryin' glasses without usin' a towel, as the sayin' has it.' He lifted the pot from the stove. 'If a man's fond o' women this ain't the place for him.'

'There are no married men here?' she inquired.

'Scores,' said Carroty, dropping condensed milk from a tin into the pannikin.

'And their wives, where are they?'

'The Lord knows!'

'But how sad!' the woman exclaimed. 'Not knowing where their wives are.'

'Mark my words, lady; there is one thing that would be sadder, and that would be, the wives knowin' where the men are. Now put this down yer gullet.' He handed the pannikin of tea to the woman.

'Thanks very much. It's beautiful,' she said, taking a sip, and trying to look as if she liked it. 'And who owns these shacks, the contractors?' she inquired, obviously making conversation.

'No, no,' said Carroty. 'It's like this, you see; it's a sort of private enterprise. The men with the money, like our Ganger, buys a hut, bed and beddin' and a stove, and charges us so much a night.'

'Oh, yes,' said the woman, sipping from the pannikin. 'This hut belongs to a man with money, and you pay for lodging here!'

'That hits the nail,' said Carroty. 'Ganger Billy's the man that has this establishment.'

'Ganger Billy,' the woman said. She sipped again, but it must be confessed that there was little appreciable diminution of the liquid in the pannikin. 'Is it he, I wonder, who is such a great friend of Dr Taylor. Mr Davis is his name?'

'That's it,' said Carroty. 'Old Ganger Davis.'

'And he often talks to Dr Taylor about his son.'

'Whose son?'

'Mr Davis's son.' The woman's face flushed for some reason, and she took three sips in succession. Carroty fixed a queer stare on her.

'So the Ganger has a son?' inquired Carroty, who immediately drew in his horns. There is a certain amount of suspicion in the manner in which the illiterate look upon the better educated members of society. Why had this woman come? he argued mentally. There were such individuals as women detectives (and he thought of the illicit distillers), as women members of the Society for Prevention of Cruelty to Children (and his eyes turned to the bunk in which Isaacs had slept). Better keep a close mouth!

'You don't know his son?' the woman inquired.

'Never heard of him,' said Carroty.

'Possibly you're a stranger here?' she inquired.

'I may be,' said Carroty. His voice was cold and it took little discrimination to make it evident that he did not desire to be questioned further.

The woman realised that she was proceeding too far. Outside could be heard the sound of the doctor's voice. He was speaking to some workers.

'I admire your caution,' she laughed. 'It's dangerous to be positive on any subject. But you make beautiful tea,' she added, as the door was shoved inwards and Taylor appeared.

'Oh, you're all right, Marjorie,' he said, going to the woman. 'Making yourself at home, too,' he laughed.

'Yes, thanks to my friend here!' She nodded to Sclatterguff. 'A most beautiful cup of tea!'

'It's very good of you,' said the doctor, putting his hand in his pocket and stretching the hand when withdrawn to Sclatterguff. But he, who was the son of a rich man, shook his head in refusal of the proffered tip, and went out, his head held very high, his pose that of a man who has got in some way a bit of his own back.

'Most remarkable!' laughed the doctor.

'Says his father was class,' Marjorie remarked. 'And a very rich man.'

'And living up to it. We all have our little illusions, I suppose.' The doctor's face grew suddenly serious, and he clasped the woman's hand.

'You must not,' she entreated, gently pulling her hand away from his.

'Did you ask him anything about it, Marjorie?' the doctor inquired. He alluded to Sclatterguff.

'I did,' Marjorie replied. 'But he says that Mr Davis has no son.'

'Oh, yes,' said the doctor, as if finding something to coincide with an opinion already formed. 'They are suspicious. There, listen!' He held up his hand to ensure silence. From outside came the sound of a voice raised in anger.

'Now, you doss-house toads, get down to it and finish that maggoty scaffolding,' the great Davis was shouting to his workers.

'That is he, Marjorie,' said the doctor. 'He's coming in.'

Ganger Billy came in at that moment. He was grumbling incoherently in his beard, but seeing the two visitors he came to a dead stop and stared at them.

'My friend, Miss Smith, who has come with me,' said the doctor to the old man.

'Well, 'tain't much o' a place to take her to; is it, doctor?' asked the Ganger, removing his hat, and putting the clay which he smoked in his pocket.

'Oh, it might be worse. Anyhow, it's always the fate of pioneers to live in places like this and take the rough with the smooth.'

'The smooth and the rough don't blend here, doctor.' The

Ganger wiped a form with his hat as he spoke. 'Now, sit down here both of you and make yourselves at home.'

Marjorie, who had risen when he entered, sat down again and cast a sidelong glance at the old man.

'Have one of these, Ganger,' said the doctor, holding out his cigar case.

'Well, I'll not say no,' remarked the old man. 'I never smoke them myself, miss,' he informed the woman. 'But I keep them for my laddie. He's a gentleman, been to college he has, and he likes a cigar, a good one like this.'

He took the cigar and wrapped it in the old red muffler. There were two there now.

'When did you hear from him last?' asked the doctor.

'Not so very long ago.' The old man sat down, his tongue ready for narration. 'But he's very busy. And the letters he sends me. Swell letters, miss. "Dear Pater!" he always starts. Pater! I didn't know what that meant for a long time, and then Father Nolan, he's the priest here, told me 'twas Dad, in Latin. But somehow, miss, I'd rather him call me Dad. It's more homely.'

There was something in the wistful old voice that made Marjorie draw out her handkerchief and flick her eyes, which had suddenly taken on a strange brilliance.

'Is the smoke goin' into your eyes, miss?' the Ganger inquired solicitously.

'Yes, it – it is.' There was a catch in the woman's voice.

'Come and sit on this side of the fire, then,' advised the Ganger, forsaking his seat. 'The draught is pullin' the smoke your way.'

Marjorie faltered a moment, then took the seat which the Ganger had vacated. Taylor could see her lower lip held by her teeth as if the woman were trying to stem a surge of rising emotion. He contracted his brows and a line formed between them like a note of exclamation.

'That's better, ain't it?' inquired the Ganger, looking at Marjorie.

She feigned a cough.

'Much better, thank you!' she choked.

'And what was your son's regiment?' asked the doctor. 'I've such a bad memory . . . I forget.'

Speaking, he bent forward and drew a match along the stove. Stooping, he lit a cigar. His whole movement was awkward, as if he were doing something utterly detestable.

'Holmshires,' the Ganger replied.

'Captain, wasn't he?'

'Ought to have been, if there was fair play,' said the old man. 'And grand he looked in his uniform. Maybe you'd like to see his photo, miss? This is him – my boy.'

He took a packet from his pocket, brought forth a photograph and handed it to the woman. She looked at it.

'That is he,' said the doctor. To the old man the remark was an assertion, to the woman a question. Marjorie nodded.

'Aye! And if you saw him marchin' at the head of his men you would say it was a grand sight,' said the Ganger. Adoration was in his eyes as he looked at the photograph before returning it to its wrappings.

'And he hasn't been here since the job started?' Taylor asked.

'Well, you see, he's so busy day and night at the parm – parma – It's two long words and I can never get my tongue round them.'

'The pharmaceutical laboratory,' the doctor helped.

'That's it, that's it,' said the Ganger jubilantly. 'And aren't they long words! That's where he has his job, miss, or his profession as he calls it.'

'Yes.' The doctor buttoned his coat. 'We're going now, Ganger. Miss Smith, who has just come up from London, is stopping here at Dunsore Farm for a short holiday. And possibly we'll run up again some evening and have another talk.'

'It's not much of a place to come to,' remarked the old man. 'Always rainin'. When children are born here, they come into the world with umbrellas.'

CHAPTER 14

THE ANCIENT

There's a handful of meal in the barrel and a little oil in the cruse,
We wear out our thin-soled sandals; they tan for the next year's shoes.
And whet their axe on the grindstone, while ours hang blunt on the wall,
And willingly shapen the roof-tree, while ours is ready to fall.
The old fleece rots on the wether, the new fleece whirls in the loom.
They weave the cloth for the bridal, we fashion the shroud for the tomb
Who followed the path as we found it from dawn to decline of day –
Till the great world lies behind us, before us the lampless way.

– *From* Growing Old.

Susan Saunders was in high good spirits, as she well should be. On the previous night she had come to Glencorrie, without a penny in her pocket and without a boot on her feet, and reported to Ganger Billy.

'It's old Susan Saunders!' exclaimed the Ganger on seeing her.

'It's me, Ganger,' said she. 'And not so old on it as all that. Any chance of me gettin' a job as washer-up?'

'There's no one here that wants anything washed, and there's no place where you can wash,' said the old man. 'You should have give up that work years ago.'

'The washin' I do can be done easy.' The old woman nodded wisely as she spoke. 'All that I want is a shake-down, a fire, a kettle, and a roof over my head. There's a bit of a house across on the other side of the brae and I can put up there. Give me a bit to eat, a bit of wood for my fire, a blanket or two, and may the de'il fly away with me if you'll ever be sorry for it, Ganger Billy.'

'I'll see about it,' said the Ganger.

'Now and at once?'

'Now and at once.'

He got a few men to tidy the ancient two-roomed shepherd's cabin which stood on the face of the Glencorrie brae, lay a bunk, set a fire, and make the place a fitting abode for the ancient washerwoman.

Report had many stories concerning Susan. She had been married twice; her first husband drowned himself, the second had drunk himself to death. Her age was something over fifty, but despite her years she was still strong and wiry. A day's walking, barefooted, caused her no concern; a day's washing, when there was washing to do, was as nothing in her eyes. She liked a drink, not too much at a time. A little often, was her rule of life.

When Moleskin came to her cabin she was singing the song given above. He waited outside until the story was completed and then shoved open the door. She was sitting by a blazing fire, a billy of tea in her hand. Moleskin looked at her, she returned his gaze and then her eyes rested on Isaacs.

'That your bairn?' she inquired.

'Not mine, Susan,' said Moleskin.

'Are you certain he's not yours,' queried the woman, still eyeing the boy. 'Anyway he's a brave nipper,' she went on without waiting for an answer. 'Now, wee laddie, tell me what's your name?'

'Cunnin' Ithaacs,' was the child's answer.

'What would you say to a wee sup of tea, Cunnin' Isaacs?' she queried.

'T'anks,' said the child.

'Now, if I asked you which would you like best, a wee sup or a big sup, what would you say?'

'Big thup,' was the prompt answer.

'If I ask you to come on my knee and have a big thup will you come, my wee laddie?' asked the old woman.

Isaacs nodded, went towards her, but nearing her he hesitated for a second and looked back at Moleskin Joe.

'Very well, if you're afraid of me don't come,' said the old woman, handing the billy-can towards him. 'Put this into your tummy, for I suppose you'll be like all laddies, gab and guts like a young crow. Take it. I'm not goin' to ate you up.'

'He's always frightened of strangers,' pleaded Moleskin.

'Well, flatten me out, if you're not a catch!' exclaimed the woman. The look that she fixed on Moleskin was filled with contempt. 'You ain't his daddy, and the de'il out o' hell wouldn't call you his mummy. What are you? His wet-nurse?'

For the first time Moleskin felt that his position in regard to Isaacs was ambiguous, equivocal. If a man had asked him his rights he could have answered readily, but with a woman it was different. He stammered some reply to the washerwoman, blushed, and became silent.

'A cradle-snatcher,' was her comment. 'And his clothes!' she added, looking at the boy. 'Who made them for you?'

'Daddy Joe,' said the youngster.

'Who's Daddy Joe?'

'Me,' said Moleskin, going to the assistance of the youngster, who was becoming confused under this questioning. 'I'm Daddy Joe, if you want to know. But I'm not his daddy. My name's Moleskin.'

'I thought I knew you,' said the ancient. 'Gawr, if it ain't a long time since I saw you, ask me another. Put your mit there, Joe!'

She rose to her feet, held out a skinny hand towards him. Moleskin clasped it in his, and looked down at her from his great height.

'You haven't changed much, Joe,' she remarked. 'Hermiston; wasn't that where I saw you last? Hermiston! Ah! a good while since, that, Joe. Six years. They don't show anywhere except on the corners of your eyes. Wasn't it there that you pulled wee Sheila Cannon out o' the water?'

'There,' said Moleskin. 'Do you know where she is now?'

'Haven't seen her since then,' the woman told him. 'Don't know where she went to at all. And Sally Jaup – dead! Me. Well, I'm livin' still and ready for the washin' when it comes. And you!' she looked at Isaacs, who was rapidly emptying the billy-can that the old woman placed on the floor. 'Come here and tell me all about yourself.'

She sat down, with the youngster on her lap. He still held on to his billy, supping mightily.

'Who is he?' she asked, looking up at Joe, and Joe told the story of the youth's coming, dwelling at some length on the helplessness of the little nipper, with some heat on the various pretensions of the men who wanted to take part in the caring of the youth, and with the utmost diffidence on the means used in tailoring him. 'But we couldn't do any more for the cuss,' was his final assertion.

That the old washerwoman kissed Isaacs at various stages of the narrative was vouched for by Moleskin afterwards, and can be accepted as fact, seeing that the assertion profited him in no way; but that there were tears in her eyes when Joe's tale came to an end cannot be accepted by even the most credulous of those worthy people who hold that there is a certain amount of good in the worst creature.

'Your eyes are runnin', Susan,' said Joe, when the narrative was completed.

'It's the smoke, damn it!' said the woman looking at Isaacs. 'Smoke goin' into your eyes, wee dearie?'

'Oo vewy good. Me like oo!' crowed the child. 'Like oo; like Daddy Joe, like Tom Moosher –'

'Cut that out!' Moleskin growled.

'And like tea and cookies.'

'The first thing to do,' said Susan, looking at Joe, 'is to find out who he is, the second thing to find out is who is his mummy and to find out where she's slipped to. Maybe she's come here, and the polis caught her and took her away. They were about here at the time, weren't they, the devil roast them!'

'They were here,' said Joe.

'If she's a woman at all, it would be hard for her to leave this wee dearie,' Susan went on. 'Some women, anyway; what are they?' She was silent for a moment. 'I'll tell you what I'll do, Moleskin. I'll keep the laddie here for a couple of days and find out everything.'

'But I've found out as much as anybody can find out!' was Moleskin's indignant outburst.

'As much as a man can find out,' said Susan. 'But if I begin, I'll start where you've left off. And it's no place to have him with them cadgers in the shacks. It's a sin to have him with them, boozin' and fightin' and swearin' and –'

'I know that,' said Joe. 'But I've kept the place in order since he's come to it.'

'You must let him stay with me, if it's only for one night,' pleaded the old woman. 'It's me that should take care of him when there's no other woman about the place. I know I'm not what you might call a . . Well, Joe, say that you'll leave him with me for the night?'

'All right, he can stay with you till the mornin', but only on one condition.'

'What's that?'

'That there ain't no washin', the washin' that you do!'

'I'm a decent woman when it's a kid like that,' said Susan in a righteous tone. 'And now, dearie, you're to stay here and I'll get the best of everything for you, sweets and jam –'

'And cookies?' asked the child.

'A bagful.'

'Daddy Joe, cookies too?'

'Aye, laddie. And I'll give you a big knife and a whistle.'

'Jam, too?'

'Aye, dearie, a big pot.'

'A big pot, Daddy Joe,' said the youngster gleefully.

'You're not to spoil him, Susan.' Moleskin's voice was dictatorial. He was already regretting having yielded to her wishes. 'It's easy spoilin' them at that age.'

He went to the door, stopped there for a moment, as if considering something, then came back to the middle of the room.

'Have a decko at the nipper, Susan!' he ordered, and the woman obeyed. 'Like anybody you've ever seen?' he inquired.

'Nobody as I can call to mind,' said the woman. 'But at his age all kids are as like as two spits.'

'Nothin' that puts you in mind o' Sheila Cannon in the cut of his face?'

'Can't see anything as makes me think it's her bairn,' said the woman. 'What puts that in your head?'

'Nothing much to go by. Only that she's a married woman –'

'Indeed!' exclaimed the washerwoman. 'And who is the man?'

'Malcolm Davis.'

'The Ganger's boy?'

'Aye.'

'And him a gentleman!' The washerwoman sighed, as if regretting the depths to which gentility had fallen.

'But if he was the Almighty, she's too good for him!' snorted Moleskin. 'Have you ever set eyes on Malcolm Davis? I never have.'

'Long ago I saw him,' said the woman, 'and him only a nipper at the time. But the swell that he was! "Thank you, Mrs Saunders!" "How dee do, Mrs Saunders!" Starched collars, gold studs, silk hankies, gloves! Never saw a to-do like it in my natural. Did his old daddy ever shovel muck? Was his mummy ever anything better than a plain, common servant lassie? To look at him you would think he was the son of a king.'

'Was he red-headed?' Moleskin asked.

'Carroty,' said the woman.

'He ain't a nigger.' Moleskin pointed at the youngster. 'Not a nigger by a long chalk.'

'Cunnin' Ithaacs no niggah,' laughed the youngster, running from the washerwoman's lap and seizing Moleskin's leg. 'But me like white hoss, big white hoss, and me ride. Gee-gee! Gee-gee!'

'Right, my bucko!' roared Moleskin, lifting the child in air and holding him far above his head.

'Daddy Joe, more up!' chortled the kicking youngster.

'For God's sake, Joe, don't let him fall!' said the old woman, getting to her feet. 'Let him come down at once, at once, Joe. You don't know nothing about kiddies!'

'You know nothin' about my arms! Eh, Ikey, my boy, eh Ikey!' Joe stood on tiptoes, laughing louder than the child which he bore.

'Joe, you big ugly devil, you, you'll let him fall. For God's sake take him down!' There was agony in the voice and tears in the red-rimmed eyes of the old trollop. Moleskin brought the child to the ground.

'Now, Ikey, I want you to do something for me, like a good nipper. See that bush!' Moleskin pointed through the open door at a stunted fir which stood on an atoll twenty perches away. 'See it?'

The youngster nodded.

'If you run as hard as you can, run round that bush and come back here, I'll give you a penny,' said Moleskin.

'And oo give me big knife, too?' asked the budding opportunist, looking at Saunders.

'I'll give you the big knife, dearie.'

'And jam?'

'And jam.'

'What tricks are you up to, now?' the woman asked Moleskin when the child had departed.

'I want to speak to you,' said the man, 'about Sheila Cannon. She's in Markonar Workhouse. It was her that took the nipper here the other night, when she was lookin' for her man. I s'pose she fell or something, over the rocks, maybe, and the polis took her there. Nobody in the place saw her either comin' or goin', and Ganger Billy doesn't know that his son is married to her. And if that ain't her nipper – he's round the bush now! – I don't know whose nipper he is. What am I to do with him, Susan Saunders?'

'Take him to his mummy,' said the woman.

'If I go to Markonar in broad daylight, I'll get run in,' said Moleskin. 'And Malcolm Davis, the boy's daddy, is here.'

'What is he doin' here?' asked Saunders.

'Makin' whisky,' Moleskin told her. 'Has been makin' it for the last six months. And he got me into the lock-up, and I'm goin' to burst his head as soon as I meet him, and I've got the wee nipper and I'd burst anybody's head that would say a bad word to the damned cuss, and I like Sheila Cannon better'n any damned thing in God's world. I'd let her cut me to pieces and be happy. I'd –' he was silent for a moment; the intensity of feeling contorted his features – 'I'd murder anyone that'd stand between her and me. And it's the devil's own stew whatever way you look at it, Susan Saunders,' he concluded, as Cunning Isaacs, out of breath and red of face, entered the cabin.

CHAPTER 15

SHEILA CANNON

I weep thro' all the lonely night,
And pray and pray upon my knees,
That maybe with the morrow's light
He'll come back – with the morrow's light –
For Mary, Mother, hears and sees.

– *From* Mater Dolorosa.

The evening settled on Glencorrie. The moorland, which the short-lived sunshine had done little to thaw, was hardening again. The day's work ended, the tools of labour were stored away, and Windy Corner settled down to its games of chance and orgy of drunkenness. Now that Cunning Isaacs was away, the navvies would have peace in the place; they could do whatever they liked, swear, drink, fight, and give expression to their vital life force in whatever manner they liked best. They did like the nipper, of course – damned if they didn't; but after all, men are men, whatever way one looks at it. And life only comes once!

'Only once,' said Sclatterguff, with a heavy sigh, as he did the rounds of the shack with a jar and a pannikin. 'He's a damned fool, the man that dies before his time.'

'If I was a young man last night some of you would die before your time,' growled Ganger Billy. 'See the damned shack, and the way you've left it! Broke to smithereens, the whole place, and all on account of the cadger that makes this whisky. And you, Moleskin – you came out of quod to kill the fellow, Jones, or whatever the devil you call him – and what have you done? Nothin'! You're afraid of him – that's what it is! Afraid of him to the bottom of your guts!'

'I ain't afraid.' Moleskin, who sat on the corner of a bunk, spoke with the voice of one intensely weary.

'You're a drawn out fool, Moleskin,' said the Ganger, rising to his full height and looking down on Moleskin. 'Gawr! If they haven't made an ass of you, ask me another!'

'Spec they have,' was Moleskin's admission.

'Who makes this tipple, that that dried whelp is serving out?' asked the Ganger, pointing a finger of scorn at Sclatterguff. 'Eh, who makes it, Moleskin?'

'Tom Jones,' said Moleskin in the same spiritless voice.

'And you were goin' to twist his thrapple?' screeched the Ganger. 'Bash his head in! . . . Gawr, Moleskin, you couldn't bash in the head of a louse! None of you could!' His red eyes took in the whole compartment. 'Fill up your dirty bellies, wreck everything! But face a man, not one of you could! But this night' – his voice became cold, hard, and precise – 'the polis are comin' here, and I'm goin' to give them the wink, and let them know where this beautiful Tom Jones is carryin' on. And maybe half a dozen more of you will go with him, when he's taken off. Twenty pounds it'll cost me to make up the damage and ruin you caused last night!'

Moleskin got to his feet, and as he did so the Ganger gripped a pick-shaft and stood waiting. Despite his years, the old man would do battle with the youngest.

'You can try all you damned will, Joe!' he snarled. 'But you'll have to walk on me stiff before you can crow over me. Come on, and do your damnedest!'

'Don't be afraid, Ganger,' said Moleskin, sitting down again.

'I'm not,' said the unbowed Ganger.

'Historical!' mumbled Sclatterguff.

'Have you ever seen this bloke, Jones?' Moleskin inquired.

'Will see him this night for the first time when he's handcuffed out o' Glencorrie,' said the Ganger.

Windy Corner rose in arms at that moment. They were not to be denied their booze, the men roared. And it was not Tom Jones who made it. Macready was the distiller, and a good fist he made of the job! And now that Cunning Isaacs was no longer in Windy Corner, there was no sense in keeping sober any longer. Shove round the tipple, Carroty! The devil take the Ganger – and the devil will soon have him if he trucks with the police!

Moleskin Joe got to his feet again, and looked at the gamblers, who were of little interest to him at that moment. In fact, he was filled with a certain contempt for them, for their stupid little deceits, guiles and trickeries. Trying to make him believe that Jones had gone, while the man was still in the neighbourhood! He knew it all along. He knew more than most of them knew. With one word he could break an old man's heart that very moment, but he forbore to speak the word. The Ganger had evidently given information to the police, a mean crime in navvydom, but there was something to be said in favour of the old man. His property had been damaged on the previous evening, and those who had a hand in the wanton destruction were not prepared to use the same hand in repayment. And now he was going to give his son, his gentleman son, up to the police!

'Ganger, put that pick down and don't be a fool,' said Joe. 'They did kick up a shindy last night, but it could be worse!'

'Well, what the hell do you, that never had a penny, call worse?' asked the old man.

'It's not me to say anything about what I have or haven't, but I once had two hundred quid in my pocket, and it was pinched. Did I go to the polis about it?' asked Moleskin.

'What did you do?' inquired the Ganger. His hand was still on his pick-shaft.

'I dished out a few black eyes,' said Moleskin.

'Did that get you your money back?'

'Not that time,' said Moleskin in the equable voice of one who recited ancient history. 'The black eyes wasn't given to 'em as pinched. But 'twas better'n goin' to the polis . . . Now, Ganger, as man to man, I ask you not to have any truck with the polis. I know they're hangin' about the place. Some new hands as have come here, four to Macready's shack, two engineers, and one other bloke as is on the steam crane knows no more about navvyin' or engineerin' than a finger doctor knows about it. Polis in plain clothes, that's what they are. You know that, Ganger?'

'Well?'

'I hope you haven't tipped 'em the wink.'

'I don't say I did, but if I did, what about it?' asked the old man.

'Nothin', bar this,' said Moleskin. 'If you did, it's dirty and the dirt will come back slop in your face. I'll not throw it, and these blokes here (they'll be drunk in a minute) will not throw it, but when it comes, you'll not forget it for the rest of your natural. That's a word of warnin', Ganger. Take it for what it's worth, and chew it if you can't smoke it.'

With these words Moleskin made his way out into the night, conscious of a great emptiness which nothing could fill. Leaving the shack he thought of going to see Isaacs again; in fact, he had filled his pocket with cookies in the early part of the evening and these were intended for the boy's supper.

But now with the cool night air beating against his forehead he asked himself why he should go. It would serve no purpose. The best thing to do was to forget the boy, forget all that had occurred in the last month, in the last year, in the last six years.

But how could that be done? Memories, dreams, feelings had burned into the very essence of his being, rooted themselves in and were part of his life, more than that even. They were his whole intimate existence. They were the man himself, and would be until the day that he was no more.

He had known life, red and sordid, but never came to him a moment like this. On the previous night he had not slept a wink, that day he had not eaten. All was confusion, perplexity, mystification. There were no straight issues now as in the days when the sudden impulse led to swift action in wild out-of-the-way places up and down the world, in doss-houses, ditches, boozers, and tramp-steamers, in seaports where the moral codes were slack, and passions hot as the climates that nourished them, where the sudden blow was response to the chiding word, where the sharp knife-dig followed many a brawl and argument.

How free and simple this plain and primitive life had been! Moleskin thought as he walked the bank of the reservoir. Far better it was than this muddle of worry. And a woman was at the bottom of it all; a woman, an ancient kiss, a marriage, and child! Life had been smooth sailing before he tumbled end-on upon this outfit! Well, to say the least of it, strike him stiff, if it wasn't funny!

He had come to Windy Corner, an escaped convict, but a man with a purpose, and one straight road lay in front of him. He was going to thrash Jones, 'kill him' was his remark at the time, but there are moments when extreme anger is extravagant.

Then Isaacs came. His way cut across Moleskin's, obscuring all objective. Then came the conversation overheard at Dunsore.

All certainty was lost, an entirely new measure of facts arose and subjugated the man. He was lost. What was he to do?

He walked across the spongy wastes, knowing not where he was going. Overhead the stars winked mockingly, and the moon, standing high, had taken on a deathly pallor. Round the man was a desert, bleak and blank, having neither the movement of life nor the essence of death, that movement by which man lives and that essence which makes time palpable. Human history, living or dead, had no place in the bleak highlands, where even natural history had rested in its labour.

He asked himself questions, still walking at a steady pace and taking no heed of where he was going. Before he met Sheila Cannon (he still called the woman by her maiden name) at Hermiston he saw his path, had his road clear in front of him, his customary jobs and customary dissipations. Even when in the army, life was easy for the man, the job had its limits, its regulations, but these, for the time, were bearable enough. The routine and discipline had in them movement and a measure of change. Above all there was little necessity for thought. There were no problems.

But here he was confounded. The future leading into darkness, standing in air like an uncompleted sap, bristled with difficulties. What was to be done?

Sheila was married! How could one get beyond that? He loved her! But what was the use? And the boy, 'the damned wee nipper!' was hers. And Malcolm Davis! As he thought of him, Moleskin ground his teeth. 'I could twist his dirty thrapple,' said the man.

He found himself near Saunders' cabin. All the time his steps had been in that direction, though the whole journey was done instinctively, governed by no cohesive reasoning. To find himself there did not surprise Moleskin. His was the position of a dreamer in an untoward position who takes no cognisance of the train of events that led up to it.

He stopped a moment at the door of the miserable shieling. How hopeless it looked. Even at night when the moonlight tones rough edges, when the slimy rock shows a lustre it never bears in the raw day, when a filthy puddle gleams as if gold were hidden in its clammy depths, when no outline is ruggedly defined, no depth without mystery, no prospect without allurement, Susan Saunders' cabin showed a sordid housing for a human being.

Its one four-paned window was without three of its panes, the squares in which the glass was once set were stuffed with rags. The door was open; a naphtha lamp hung from the roof, a fire blazed on the hearth. Round the lamp and fire a thick vapour, drawn from the damp floor, walls and roof, curled, blocking out all objectives.

Standing at the open door, Moleskin gazed into the intensified fog. Somebody was seated by the fire, somebody who was neither the washerwoman nor child. The person was a young woman, wearing a shawl which hung round her shoulders. Her face, white and timid, was turned towards Moleskin.

Hypnotised he took a step towards her. He had seen such a face, such a figure, somewhere before. The woman's dark brown wavy hair, starred with the congealed vapour of the room, circled a face fair and sweet to look upon.

Although overcast with brooding sorrow, there was in her look and posture, in the lines of her body to which poor clothes seemed to add charm, in her oval countenance, soft large eyes, full lips and delicately rounded chin, a grace which Watts' 'Fata Morgana' would have attained in repose, and grief and anxiety added a certain dignity to the grace already there.

The woman was Sheila Cannon. Resting on her lap and nestling in against her shoulder, was the child, Cunning Isaacs. The boy was asleep.

The man and woman gazed at one another for a full minute without speaking, and for some reason or another, Moleskin took off his cap and put it in his pocket.

'Sheila Cannon, isn't it?' he asked, without coming nearer.

'It's me, Joe,' said the woman.

'I was just comin' by, and seein' the light, I thought to myself, I'd just come in, and I didn't expect to see anybody, and I'm off now. No offence meant, but you see, I was only passin', so to speak. Goodnight to you!'

After speaking thus, Moleskin pulled the cap from his pocket, and stepped backwards.

'And is that all you've got to say to me, Joe?' she inquired in a whisper.

'Well, you see, I'm goin' on a night-shift, and they're waitin' for me to come at once,' the big man explained. 'And it was to see Susan Saunders that I came here. Where is she?'

'Joe!'

'Aye?' He took an undecided step towards the speaker, then

stopped. 'Anything I can do for you at all? . . . If there's anyone as says anything against you, tell me his name.'

Having made this straightforward assertion, and drawn a deep breath, he felt more at his ease. Sheila cast a look, half beseechment, half fear, at Moleskin. He saw her lips quiver and at that moment felt that he wanted her more than ever.

'I know you would, Joe,' she said. 'You've done everything for me. If it wasn't for you, I wouldn't be here this night, and if it wasn't for you, maybe, my wee Malcolm wouldn't be safe this very minute.' She kissed the sleeping child. 'Joe,' she inquired, 'why won't you come and shake hands? I would come to you, if I wasn't nursing him. And I've put a long journey past me, miles and miles of road and hill, Joe. But you're backward, like you always were.'

'Course, you've done a long journey,' said the man, awkwardly catching the woman's delicate hand in his mighty paw. 'And I didn't expect to find you here at all. Are you in trouble, Sheila Cannon?'

'Not in trouble now,' she said, with a bright smile. 'But I was in sore trouble, Joe. I came up here long ago, maybe it's not so long, but it seemed years, and I fell into a brook and there was a fog and it was the polis that got me, and when I came to, I was in Markonar 'firmary. Malcolm wasn't with me, and when I asked the sister for him she said I was wanderin' in my head. And so I stole away and got here this night.'

'Walked all the way from Markonar?' asked Moleskin. He still held the woman's hand.

'Not all the way,' said Sheila. 'I got two lifts on carts and then on a motor-car with a gentleman and a lady. A sweet lady, Joe, and she was so kind. And now I've Malcolm, and Susan Saunders was tellin' me how good you were to the boy. How is it that some people are so good, Joe?'

'Don't know,' said Moleskin. 'Haven't met them, the ones that's so good as all that!'

'But the lady, Joe,' said the girl. 'I never met her afore and she wanted to know if I was in trouble and when I told her that I was, she wanted to help me. And then yourself, see all that you done for me?'

'What did I do?'

'You'll not be sayin' that you've forgot the Hermiston Waterworks, Joe?' asked the woman.

'Not me to forget it,' said the man in the unsteady voice of one who was boiling within. 'I've never forgot it. But, maybe, you did, forgot words you spoke as soon as you spoke 'em. It's a long while since that and you were only eighteen, but you don't look a bit older now.'

'But the heart is older,' said the girl very sadly.

'Your face and head give the lie to it: not one wrinkle, not one white hair.' He dropped her hand and looked at her. 'But you're cryin',' he said.

'I'm not at all,' she answered, her words a choking gasp.

'It's a funny thing us meetin' in this way,' said the man. 'I didn't think I'd meet you again. And it's on the books that we'll not cross each other no more. But now that I've the chance I want to tell you somethin', Sheila, somethin' that if I had had the learnin' in my head and a smart twist o' the tongue, I'd have told you years ago, when the water burst at Hermiston. You remember it, don't you?'

'Will I ever forget it?' asked the girl.

''Twas in the evening,' said the man, reminiscently, 'and you were takin' supper to your father. But, maybe, it's not the same to you as it was to me. And do you know why?'

'I'm sure I don't.'

'Well, I'll tell you, Sheila, leavin' all aside, the breakin' o' the breastworks and the wee bit o' help that I gave you –'

'If it wasn't for yerself, I wouldn't be here now,' said the girl.

'Well, I'll grant you that if you like.' The glance he fixed on her was so steady that her eyelids fell. 'What always comes to my mind when I think of it, Sheila, was you on the banks o' the cuttin' when the waters were runnin' loose like the mills of hell, puttin' your two wee arms round me shoulders, and your lips very close to mine and sayin', "Moleskin Joe, you're the best man in the world!" And you kissed me. But you've forgot it all, as I said, for why should you keep it in mind? You were eighteen, and who wants to die at eighteen. Life at that age is worth a kiss on the grubbiest face. And you would forget it afterwards. You did forget it!'

'I did not!' Sheila's eyes gleamed with a strange light. A blue mistiness seemed to settle round her hair, and in the tremulous light of the guttering naphtha lamp her face had taken on a deathly pallor.

'Even if you did another maybe didn't,' said the man. 'I didn't. And often it is since that evenin' and me in many a place, often in a doss-house, with fightin' goin' on, maybe, and I would rest on my bunk thinkin' of wee Sheila – and maybe, it would be in quod with a plank under me and the jailer at the door, that you would often come to me in a sort o' a dream, and, maybe, it would be in the trenches with Jerry's scrap-iron tearin' at the parapet, and I would think, in my own way, of a kiss that I once got, and didn't give back because I was a rough rung of a man, that was no hand with the women and had no soft talk to hold them.'

'It's not everyone like yourself, Moleskin Joe, that would go lonely long without a woman and havin' talk like that to hold her!' said the girl with a coy smile.

Moleskin suddenly became self-conscious.

'I have been talkin' through my hat,' he said, with an awkward laugh, shaking a little as if his passionate outburst had robbed him of energy. 'It's years ago that I ought to have said that. But I've said it to myself often since then, gettin' into trainin' so to speak, to be able to say it to you when I met you. And if a man can't do a job well after years of trainin' he'll never be able to do it! Sheila!' he reached forward and caught her hands. 'Sheila, I love you better than anything in this world, up and down, or out of it!'

A rapturous smile spread over Sheila's face, but died away almost as soon as it came. She pulled her hands away and looked up at Moleskin, and her eyes became suddenly moist.

'Oh, it's terrible, Joe, it's terrible to hear you speak like that. You mustn't, you mustn't!' she sobbed piteously.

'But I will!' Moleskin's voice was tempestuous. 'I lost you once. You went away then, and I looked up and down, padded the hoof from doss-house to doss-house, on the look out, but never lucky. Then a war broke out, and 'twas come and fight for your country. All the country I had was under my finger-nails, but I went to fight. Then I had a look round again, when the row was over, but the world's a big stretch, and you're not much size after all. And maybe you didn't want me, anyway,' he concluded sadly.

'I did want you, Joe,' sobbed the girl. 'I did want you – badly. That's the terrible thing.'

'Is that the truth, Sheila?' asked Joe, wondering.

'True as death, Joe. Don't ask me anything more, but leave me. Now, Joe, please.'

'Leave you on your own?' asked the man.

'On my own!'

'You've nobody with you?'

'Him,' said the girl after a moment's hesitation. She pointed at the child.

'Then I'll stay with you!' said Moleskin, reaching out his hands to hers again.

'You mustn't, Joe. Please don't!'

'But you've said –'

'Don't think evil of me, Joe, even if I've said what I've never confessed to any soul before, hardly to my own,' the girl pleaded. 'I love you, Joe, God forgive me, I've always loved you since that night years ago, and maybe before that. That's why I don't want to be with you now.' She paused and her dark liquid eyes looked up at his. Her voice was strained with anguish. 'It's too late. It's all over now, all over!'

'Why should it be all over?' asked the man. 'Come with me! Let the two of us go together. I want you, Sheila, more than anything in this world. Let us set off, together –'

'Don't speak like that, Joe,' she entreated. 'I cannot come. There's a reason –'

'Don't tell me the reason,' said Joe, sullenly. 'I don't want to hear. You are married. But *my* Sheila is not married! If she is I don't want to hear about it. I've only once seen a woman – a slip of a girl – with man's eyes, and I don't want her to be anything but what I've made her out to be. Maybe you aren't her –'

Moleskin stopped dead in his utterances, as a noise was heard outside, and he turned a startled face to the door.

'There's someone comin',' said the girl. 'You must go away now, Joe.' She held out her hand to him. 'God be good to you in everything and everywhere!'

'In everything; in murder?' asked the man, catching Sheila's hand in both his own.

'God help us! what are you sayin'?'

'Everywhere: on the gallows?'

Sheila shrank under the intensity of his gaze.

'You look scared,' said Moleskin harshly. 'I've come here, not expectin' to meet you. I've come to kill a man. And then, when one kills a man,' he spoke slowly as if taking pleasure in the words, 'he is a murderer, and you know what happens. He dances on the air, wearing a new cravat, a thin one, thinner than your arms, but every bit as tight!'

As he spoke he put his hand on her hair, and looked down at her, at the delicate contour of her chin, at the whiteness showing through the V-shaped opening of her blouse, at her tumbled breasts and the child sleeping on her knees.

He wanted to say a great deal to her at that moment, to tell her of his life, his adventures and sorrows, the jealousy that tortured him, his love, his desire for a kiss, for a million kisses.

'Joe, you must go. There's somebody comin',' she said suddenly. 'It's Susan, I think.'

'All right, I'm off, Sheila! But once – will ye?'

'What?' she asked, looking up at him.

'Just the same as at Hermiston,' he muttered thickly, and without waiting for her reply he bent down and kissed her full on her lips.

The next moment he was gone.

CHAPTER 16

THE PRIEST

And they that love Him shall be filled with the Law.

On that evening Father Nolan came to Glencorrie on one of his periodic visits. The gig hired at Dunrobin came as far as the mear of Glencorrie. When there the driver refused to come any further.

'If I take the pony downhill on this road and in this frost it'll be a broken leg for't and a broken neck for one of us,' said the driver.

'And quite unnecessary when I can walk,' said the good-humoured priest.

He took his way across the braes of Glencorrie. The night was sharp, bracing, and good for walking. Under his feet the ground was hard, slippery on the slopes and firm as iron on the levels. In the distance a star-flecked leaden blue expanse told of the waterworks. Now and again a breeze rose from nowhere, flipped him coldly on the face and passed.

After a while Susan Saunders' cabin rose out of the night, the light within showing a yellow smudge on the darkness. A workman came round the gable end of the cabin, puffing a pipe and spitting.

'Somebody living here?' asked the priest.

'Aye, Father Nolan,' was the answer. 'Ole Susan has come back again. Thought she had kicked it, I did, but she didn't. The worse they are, the longer they live.'

The man trudged down the brae. Father Nolan went to the cabin door, and almost collided with a mighty-boned individual coming out.

'Up to her old tricks,' the priest muttered, looking in. 'Are you in there, Susan Saunders?' he called through the smoke.

'Who's that?' asked a frightened voice.

'I heard Susan Saunders was here,' the priest replied. 'But that's not her voice. Who are you?' He could see a woman seated at the fire.

'Sheila Davis, Father Nolan.'

'Eh!' the man exclaimed, coming in. 'Sheila Davis. Of all people in the world, you! What are you doing here, child? In this place!'

He was now beside her, looking down at the woman and child. The mother's hand was resting on the child's curls. The red fire grinned impishly against a sooty background.

'Won't you sit down, Father?' Sheila asked. 'We haven't any chairs, but there's a wood-stump. Just pull it in to the heat.'

The priest sat down, stretched his legs to the fire, all the time keeping his eyes on Sheila and Isaacs. The man's face was tanned brown, deep wrinkles showed in a forehead beaded with sweat.

'Now, my child, come tell me all about it,' he said, wiping his forehead with a mighty palm. 'The last I saw of you was in Carlisle, and I told you that I would see your husband if I could. I saw him, as I've told you in my letter, when I sent you the little sum of money that I had some difficulty in getting.'

'I never got a letter at all,' said the woman.

'Didn't get my letter!' Nolan exclaimed. 'Then, if you hadn't the money, how did you get here?'

'Walked. I couldn't pay the rent, and there was no work to be had –'

'My poor child!' exclaimed the priest.

'It's poor wee Malcolm more than poor me,' said Sheila, bending over her child and kissing it. 'But he's a grand wee fellow. Never would cry at all. And you've seen my man?' she inquired.

'I have that,' Nolan told her. 'He has been hard on you, the way that he's left you, but if you can let him see you now, with the little child, he'll come to you again, and the three of you will settle down together, forgetting all the past and be as happy as the flowers in May. He didn't know his own mind at the time he left you. That was the army. It spoilt a lot of young men. But now they're settling down, and when I bring the two of you together tomorrow –'

'I don't want to see him again!' said Sheila.

'But you've come to look for him!' A look almost of bewilderment showed on the face of the priest. 'And now you don't want to see him! I don't understand.'

'I hate him, Father, I hate him!' said the girl, in a sudden burst of anger.

'My child – !'

'I don't want him, Father.' She bent her head and spoke in a low, almost inaudible voice. A thousand facets of light gleamed from the tears that filled her eyes, and she looked very beautiful at that moment.

'But you surely have not forgotten how kind he was to you when you were married. You were happy together. You've told me so yourself. You've had trouble like all poor mortals. When worry comes you've got to put your trust in God, my child,' said the priest. 'And He will see in His own good time that your husband comes back.'

'God's good time is very slow in comin',' said Sheila with a bitter laugh. 'Even if my man does come to me crying and repentant, will he cry off the years that are standing against him? Will his tears blot out our days of hunger and hardships. No, God Himself can't blot out the past!' the woman exclaimed, rising to an ecstasy of passion. 'For myself, I can forgive him, but for the child never.'

The priest felt embarrassed and gazed from under his brows at Sheila. There was a moment of tension, and the night breeze could be heard beating against the open door.

'Father?' Sheila spoke in a whisper.

'Yes, my child.'

'Another man has asked me to go with him, and' – there was a momentary pause – 'and I'm goin'.'

'Another man!' The priest fixed a stern look on the woman. 'And who is this other man?'

He was more at ease now. Here was something definite, more palpable than the fluctuating emotions of discarded love, that play of light and shade, changeable as the colour of polished copper in sunlight.

'Moleskin Joe.'

'Moleskin Joe!' the priest exclaimed. 'Well, child, it was Providence that brought me here tonight to save you from that man, from sin, my child! Moleskin Joe! Well, of all men –'

He was silent for a moment.

'I know him. I've seen him here. He has just gone out, hasn't he?'

Sheila nodded.

'I know him; saw him in France,' the priest continued reminiscently. 'Yes, yes. A bad Christian, but a good fighter.'

'Fighter, Father?' Sheila asked the question mechanically.

'Fighter,' said Father Nolan. 'I saw him fighting. We got into a scrape where the Cross was of no avail, and, God forgive me, I had to use a bayonet.'

'Wasn't it a sin, Father, for you to use a bay'net?' asked Sheila. Despite the simplicity of her outlook, she was quick to work an advantageous moment to her own purpose. 'If *you* sinned, how do you expect –'

'But you don't understand, my child,' said the priest. ''Twas different with me. The occasion, the circumstances, a matter of life and death – and one does not think!'

'If one doesn't think, it's no sin!'

'Well, my child, it all happened on the spur of the moment. It could not be avoided.'

'Can love be avoided?' asked Sheila.

'Oh, that's another matter!'

'Why?' Sheila asked warmly.

'Another matter – for you, my child!' The priest got to his feet. 'In the first place you are a married woman. That is generally enough to keep any woman straight, it doesn't matter what her creed is. But, as you know, marriage in our Holy Church is not only a contract – it is a sacrament! You have to be faithful in thought, word and act, my child. If not, mortal sin, and you know the penalty!'

'But, Father, will you speak as yourself to myself, not as a priest?' asked the woman. 'Am I doin' wrong? It's not all my fault. He has been hard, bitter! Thrown me aside and hasn't given me a penny piece for years. I've had to starve, work my fingers to the bone. In health I've had worry always, in sickness no consolation. Is it a sin, Father, to look for a little happiness?'

'Not at all, if it's not evil happiness. But the greater happiness is that of the next world which will be yours if you bear your troubles with a brave heart and noble spirit. We all have our crosses, some heavier –'

The priest suddenly realised the hollowness of the stock phrases when he looked at Sheila. Irony showed in her eyes. Possibly he had made a mistake, wrongly suspecting that Sheila discovered the artificiality of his argument when he himself became aware of it.

'You're still speakin' as the priest, Father,' she said.

'When it is a matter of your own immortal soul I will speak as a priest.' He was over-emphatic. 'I have got to justify myself before God and I cannot say to you: "Go your own way! Marry a dozen men, if you want to. Be a bigamist, which is wrong in the eyes of the earthly law and means prison; be an adulteress, which is wrong in the eyes of God, and means damnation!" Then you have your son. Is he nothing to you –'

'He's everything to me!' She looked down, shuddering, and buried her face in her hands.

'Then, if you do love him,' said the priest, 'you've got to act so that when he comes to the years of discretion, he will say that you were everything to him that a mother should be. Forbear, my child, forbear. It is not too late, even now, but you've got to go no further. Remember 'tis not the length of the step that counts at the start, but the direction . . . Malcolm Davis is your husband. You are bound to him, not for so long as it suits your convenience, but till death, my child, till death' – he struck the table with his fist – 'for good or bad, for better or worse. That is the letter of the law, the law of God . . . And are you not a Catholic, my child?'

'Maybe I would be happier if I wasn't,' she said.

The girl was a fervid Catholic. Her moral outlook and religious ideals were those of a million other girls of the same faith, which has as its groundwork, submission to mandate and belief in miracles. Progress had not confounded Sheila, old ideas, termed new, were to her unknown. Her creed was a simple one, and the articles of her faith were as barriers of steel which she would not dare to break. The earnest, simple, self-sacrificing woman had, up to then, accepted them with unquestioning assurance.

But at that moment she felt as if her long spell of passive endurance had come to an abrupt termination. Sitting motionless, her hands clasped round her child, she felt tired, languid, indifferent and a little defiant. She did not want to talk any more.

'And who has this place?' asked Father Nolan. 'This cabin was not occupied when I was here before.' He had done his duty as far as lay in his power, and was now ready for conversation on general subjects.

'Susan Saunders,' Sheila told him.

'So old Susan is living yet?' he inquired. 'It's years since I saw the poor soul. And, my child, she's not what one would call a very good companion for you.'

'Of course, she's not good,' Sheila spoke angrily. 'Worse than Moleskin Joe is, if it comes to that. When I came in here this night, Father, without a home, with nothin', she says, "That's for you!"' Sheila pointed to the shakedown huddled against the wall. '"But where will you sleep?" I asks her. "I'll go to the navvies and they'll give me blankets," and out she goes, barefooted, and she'll be back in a wee while. And it's a cold night out, barefooted. Moleskin's not much good either. He one time was nearly drowned savin' me at Hermiston. But, maybe, his life wasn't worth much, nor mine, if it comes to that! Father, it's a lot you, maybe, know about sins and rules and laws, but I'm thinkin' that you know very little about people at all.'

The momentarily rebellious slave became suddenly conscious of what she was saying, and stopped terror stricken. Gentle, meek-spirited, she had never dared to question authority before, and now, with the feeling of resentment suddenly checked, a dimness came over her eyes, her temples throbbed, her hands fell white and limp over her child.

'Leave me, Father,' she whispered. 'Come tomorrow again, any time afore you go away!'

'Right, my child, I'm going,' said the priest. 'But you're looking pale. Have a sip of water! Is there a cup? No. Yes, here's a tin!'

Lifting a tin from the fireside he poured out some water from a jar in the corner and gave it to the woman. She drank.

'What am I to do?' she whispered. 'Have I to go to him?'

'Well, well, well!' mumbled the priest. 'It's your duty, of course, but – but – we'll talk about it tomorrow when you're feeling better. I'm going along to the shacks and I'll send Susan here if I meet her. It's time for you to be in bed, my child!'

When the priest had gone, she kissed her child, kissed his eyes, his cheeks, his ears, the tip of his little nose. She would like to wake him, but forbore doing so. And it was Moleskin Joe who had made the little suit. Susan Saunders had informed her of the fact. And through that suit, Sheila seemed to get possession of the tailor, to absorb him without being aware of it. She could see the navvy's big clumsy hands sewing the seams together – with a packing needle. She could see his eyes fixed on the work, his gestures, his patient handling. Perhaps he knew that the child was hers.

And he loved her! He said things such as no man had ever said to her before, or if they were said they had never such an effect on the woman. There was something about him so intense, so primitively passionate, that she was carried away. The moment he entered she divined his passion in the way that women can. His agitation on seeing her, the awkward withdrawal, the precipitate avowal, the kiss, all told of an over-powering love.

Through the one pane that remained in the window she gazed out into the night. A few stars could be seen, set in a sky darkly blue. Fancies formed in her mind, images of the man who had stolen her heart, not at that particular moment, not when he rescued her from the torrent years ago, but when she was ever so little, a mere lass of fifteen or sixteen.

At that time he was her hero. He was the great, the all-powerful hero round whom the young romantic girl wove dreams and built visions. He was the great adventurer, one who sailed out into unknown lands. A deep sadness was hers when he had gone, and this, coupled with an ardent longing for his return, kept her in a fever of waiting. Then she detested everything, the eternal changing from job to job, the eternal labour in rude shacks, the tittle-tattle of her women friends, the whole sordid round of her existence.

When Moleskin came back, strong, mighty and sure of himself, her life brightened up again. Something surged up in her bosom, and swept over her like the wings of a million flying birds. She recollected the days at Hermiston, his return from the southern seas. He was then the same as ever towards her. He said she was good-looking, but upon saying this he looked confused, as if he had committed himself. Then he hurried away and showed no desire to speak to her again.

She recalled the night when she kissed him. That event of the remote past came to her mind now, as if it were something that occurred only a few hours before. How often she regretted that kiss. It made her cheap in her own opinion. But now, knowing that it was something that brightened up the man's life for years afterwards, she felt consoled. He had confessed it to her. If she had only known at the time, she thought.

'I'm not doin' wrong in thinking like this,' she whispered to herself, half-fearfully, half-defiantly. 'He has been cruel to me, bitterly cruel.' She alluded to her husband. 'If he did not want me he ought to have writ me one letter and told me. Then

I would be free. But to leave me to meself for years the way he did. When I think of the way I cried, the way I suffered! And not a word from him, not a line, nothin'.'

Shaking with sobs she looked down at the child, caught him in her arms and covered his face with kisses. He woke up.

'Mummy!' he spoke sleepily.

'Yes, my wee dear of the world?' She folded him in her arms. 'My own ever and always!'

'Daddy Joe, Mummy?'

'Daddy Joe 'way,' she whispered.

'Comin' 'gain white hoss, Mummy?'

His mother kissed him and he was conscious of tears falling on his face.

'Mummy kwyin', me kwy too!' said the child.

The mother pressed the little one in a closer embrace.

CHAPTER 17

IN THE NIGHT

The witch sits down, a ghoul at her throat,
And over the tarn the goblins call –
The spider has spun its web on the wall,
Waits for its prey and wearies not.

– *From* Choses du Soir.

Malcolm Davies had at last decided to leave Glencorrie for good. The place was becoming uncomfortable in more senses than one. Police in plain clothes, working as navvies, might at any moment swoop down upon him. Contractors, engineers and gang foremen, putting their heads together, were determined to put a stop to the liquor traffic. Even Ganger Davis had avowed his intention of helping the police.

And to add to these, certain indiscretions of his own youth were marshalling themselves against him. His legal wife was in the neighbourhood. He had seen her that morning leaving Windy Corner. One thing he did not know, however – Sheila Cannon's visit. He believed her to be still in Carlisle. Father Nolan's visit was a week overdue. The priest knew the cave and there was no reason why he should not come to it again.

It would be better to clear out now, go to London and start business as a bookmaker. Having at the present moment some two thousand pounds in hand, Malcolm, viewing the theory of Chances and Recurrences from a new angle, was bent on making a fresh start and becoming wealthy. The future spread out in front of him, auspicious, golden-hued, the dream of Alnaschar.

The time was nine o'clock in the evening. He stood in the cave where the darkness was bundled, intensified. On the floor the dying embers of the distillery fire gleamed like glow-worms. Two jars of whisky stood at the man's feet, waiting for Sclatterguff who would come directly and take them away.

The sound of somebody approaching was heard. Davis walked quietly backwards into the dim obscurity of the cave, treading his way softly through the opacity, his ears strained for sound. He could hear the cumbrous scrambling of the one who was nearing the entrance, the slippery shuffle of feet losing and regaining purchase of the wet stones which filled the alley outside.

Suddenly a lighted peat fell through the structure that rimmed the fire and a shower of brilliant sparks rose in the blackness. Davis had a momentary view of the place, the wet walls, the glaucous floor, the thin stream of water falling from the roof and glistening like a silver snake. Thus for a moment and the darkness settled again. Davis still continued his journey, one hand stretched into the gloom that he was piercing. His fingers touched a rock, he felt his way round it and stopped when the entrance of the cave was lost to his view.

A man came in, stood for a moment near the fire, and lit a pipe. Davis peeped round the corner of his hiding place, but not before the match was extinguished. All that he could see was the pipe glowing and the visitor stooping down, gathering wooden blocks from the floor and throwing them into the fire.

In a moment they were ablaze and the watcher was again able to take stock of his surroundings, of the dark cavern with its black corners, serrated projections, gloomy roof, glistening floor. The man who had just entered was visible. He was the ancient Sclatterguff, who had come for the nightly allowance. Until quite recently, Davis hid himself when the old man visited the cave. The jars were then placed by the fire, Sclatterguff carried them away, but before leaving, placed the money on the floor. Now, however, the distiller showed himself when the buyer made his appearance. To Sclatterguff, who did not recognise him as the Ganger's son, he was 'Tom Jones'.

'So it's you, Carroty?'

Davis came from the darkness like a wraith, giving Sclatterguff the impression of a spectre, forming itself from the gloom. The old man sprang two feet in air at the sight of the apparition.

'God! what were you hidin' there for?' he faltered. 'I thought it was old Nick. And my 'eart!' he said, striking his breast. 'I'm all a-shake, with the polis here, there and everywhere.'

'I thought you weren't coming tonight,' laughed Davis.

'What kept you?'

'I'm the only man in Glencorrie that would come up here,' said the old man. 'It's the polis, dozens o' 'em, and all in plain clothes.'

'Looking for me?' asked Davis.

'Well, they don't say as much. Butter wouldn't melt in their mouths by the look o' them. But these new men that have come here within the last five days, nobody trusts them,' said Sclatterguff shaking his head. 'One fellow came the day 'fore yesterday and he had two shirts. That was a bad sign. No navvy ever has two shirts, so he was tipped into the water.'

'Drowned?' asked Davis.

'No, he could swim.' There was a tinge of regret in Sclatterguff's voice. 'But the worst of it is, that some of the men are sidin' with the polis. That's what navvies never done 'fore this. Trade Union, that's the cause of it all. I saw the time when you looked for a job all that a ganger wanted to see was the spread o' your mit and the width o' your shoulders. Now, it's your Union ticket they look at, damn them.'

'Well, there are your two jars, Carroty,' said Davis.

'The same charge?' asked Sclatterguff. 'Seein' that you're rollin' in money, shouldn't you give me an extra dollar for comin'?'

'Good God, man, isn't it cheap enough!' laughed Davis. 'I work eighteen hours a day, and expenses have gone up 50 per cent.'

'But look at my risk,' said Sclatterguff. 'Goin' down to the glen, *I* may run into the polis. Say a dollar for myself?' he pleaded, taking some money from his pocket.

How Davis would have answered this proposal was never known, for at that moment a hand fell on his shoulder and gripped. Davis turned and found himself looking into a strange face, and behind that face were two others, three in all.

'Tom Jones?' asked the owner of the gripping hand.

By a deft turn Davis freed himself and shot out, mixing with Sclatterguff, who, having recognised three of the 'new hands' in the faces blossoming from the obscurity, was as eager as Davis to make his escape. Together the two men stumbled down the defile, slipping over stones, tumbling against boulders. The money which Sclatterguff held fell to the ground and clattered against the rocks, but the old man stopped not to pick it up.

A figure rose from the ground and gripped Davis, but with

the despairing strength of a man thoroughly frightened, he closed with the figure, rolled with it down the defile, broke free and took to his heels again.

The first shock over, his mind brightened immediately, and he considered the situation as he ran. He had to get out of the valley and the only exit was the fissure in which Moleskin Joe had been trapped weeks before. It was the only way to get out. The combe, safe enough in the darkness, was a trap in daylight. He had to get out, and what a fool he was not to have gone on the previous evening, he thought as he ran. Behind him he could hear the shouting of those who followed.

He came to the fissure. The moon shining through looked him full in the face, and gleamed evilly on the icicles which hung from the sharp-edged projections of the pass. The man's eyes sought the ground looking for the snare. But there was none. He shot through into the freedom of the moonlit night.

From the thalweg of Glencorrie upwards on the opposite side the gloom lay thickly. In that obscurity there was sanctuary, in which he could hide himself for hours. Towards dawn he would make his way southwards to freedom. So he argued with himself as he ran. He could hear the pursuers following, but this gave him no trouble now. Davis was a good sprinter.

He crossed the one bridge that spanned the outlet of the reservoir and rose towards the shacks. Once beyond these he was free. Even as it was, he now considered himself out of danger. The bridge was some fifty yards to rear and the pursuers had not reached it yet.

Passing Windy Corner he sobered his pace to a walk. The place was lighted up, but within all was silent as if nobody lived there. They were waiting for the whisky, he thought, and smiled wryly. It would be a long wait. In the adjacent shacks a greater liveliness manifested itself. He could see moving forms in the lighted doorways, hear the sounds of swearing and singing and smell the odour of frying meat.

Two men came towards him, navvies, one with his cap pulled down over his eyes and both smoking.

'Night!' he said passing.

'Tipple here yet?' asked one, Tom the Moocher.

'Dunno,' answered Davis.

'Here, who're yer?' asked the second man, Sid the Slogger, stopping and facing Davis. 'Don't know your voice!'

'Don't know me, matey?' asked Davis with a laugh.

'Don't, but damned soon will,' said the Slogger, and as a preliminary to the acquiring of this knowledge, fastened upon the coat collar of the runaway.

'Glue yerself to'm!' advised the Moocher, and coupling council with action, fastened himself on to the distiller. 'We don't want the damned job run by the polis.'

'I'm not a policeman!' blurted Davis.

'Who're ye, then?' asked the Slogger, holding fast while waiting the reply.

'What's the damned good o' askin' them what they are!' the Moocher growled. 'They're any damned thing if they get off with it. In with you here, and we'll see the cut o' your face!'

Having spoken, the Moocher, aided by Sid the Slogger, shoved Malcolm Davis towards the naphtha-lighted shack that was known as Windy Corner.

From the outside Ganger Davis was watching them. All that evening the old man was in a state of high nervous tension. He had given the police information regarding the cave. He knew where it was although he had never been in the place. In their drunken moments the men had been unwise and spoken foolishly. The Ganger had taken stock of their conversations, and reported the talk as he heard it to the officials of the law.

'And why the hell shouldn't I,' he told himself. 'Another drunk fortnight and every damned penny I've made, my shack, my blankets, my bunks, will be gone. I trust they hang this cadger, Jones, when they lay their paws on him, the devil's whelp!'

And this was the night! A few of the police had gone to the cave in the afternoon. Jones, not in residence then, was out seeing to the delivery of the stores. The carters still brought the various ingredients to Glencorrie, depositing them in some secret dump on the uplands, and from there Jones transferred them to the distillery.

Possibly he was in the hands of the police now.

The Ganger was on tenterhooks, waiting for news. He had been to the engineers' headquarters. The engineers were in the know, but up to the present they had heard nothing.

'But he'll not slip them,' they told the old man. 'It's the proper night for chasing a man.'

'Aye,' said the Ganger. 'There's a good moon, and if he does slip they can follow him for miles. Maybe they've heard somethin' at Windy Corner.'

He dawdled across the slope towards his shack. As he drew near, he could see Windy Corner, plastered silver where the moon shone on the ice already formed there. The shadow of the building sloped off at an obtuse angle, and the light from the doorway formed a square in the night's greyness. The moment was one of quiet; the sound of running water leaving the reservoir intensified the silence.

Somebody crossed the lighted doorway, walking easily. In some dim way the Ganger fancied that he recognised the figure, but made no effort to place it. He heard it questioned by the Slogger.

'The damned Slogger!' muttered the old man. 'He's drunk again!'

'We don't want the damned job run by the polis!' came the voice of the Moocher, who was now scuffling with the stranger.

'And he's boozed too!' said the Ganger. 'Thank God, it'll all stop tonight!'

The Moocher and Slogger hustled the stranger towards the entrance of the shack. The scuffling silhouettes showed against the lighted door.

'Is it to be wreckage and rain again this night?' asked the Ganger dolefully, bearing down upon the trio like a fox stalking its prey.

CHAPTER 18

HUSBAND AND WIFE

Where no hedge is the possession will be laid waste,
And he that hath no wife will mourn
As he wandereth up and down.

For who will trust a nimble robber
That skippeth from city to city?

Even so who shall trust a man
That hath no nest,
And lodgeth wheresoever he findeth himself at nightfall?

– *From* The Son of Sirach.

Had Doctor Taylor a patient for every square mile under his charge, his practice would be a large one; even if all his patients paid sufficient to get him petrol for his car and the merest fee for his professional assistance he might be able to save a little.

As it was, he worked hard for little or no remuneration. He was the Gideon Gray of a later age, differing from Scott's surgeon in that he drove a car instead of riding a horse. His field of duty was much the same, a country of moors, mountains, lochs and rivers, untraversed by roads in many directions.

What Gray accomplished on horseback, Taylor accomplished in his small three-seater. Beyond the fact that it was got cheaply there was no reason why his car should be a three-seater. If it seated one only it would do quite as well, for he drove it himself.

When, on the afternoon following his visit to Windy Corner, he was informed that his services were required some leagues away in the moors beyond Glencorrie, Doctor Taylor brought out his trusty car, which, climbing a hill, skirting a precipice where the slightest aberration would fling it into space, or ploughing a swamp, had in it the aptitude of a mule, tight-rope walker and steam plough.

'May I come with you?' asked Marjorie.

'If you desire,' he told the woman. 'The road is all right as far as Glencorrie, particularly if the frost holds. Afterwards it is mostly moorland with bundles of faggots for bridges, hills that take a tank to climb going up, a grapnel to hold coming down, and roads – footpaths that change with the weather. No, I think you had better not come.'

'But I would like to come,' said Marjorie.

'Very well,' said the doctor, after a moment's thought. 'It is freezing hard already and we'll have the moon coming back.'

On the temporary cart track leading to Glencorrie they saw in front a woman going in their direction, Sheila Cannon walking very slowly, as if extremely weary.

'I didn't think that many women came this way, Dick,' said Marjorie.

'There are always a few to be found about these places,' the doctor replied. 'But they are not always the best of the sex.'

'We must give her a lift on the car,' said Marjorie. 'She looks very tired.'

'H'm!' The doctor's snort was non-committal. 'If I know anything of these she'll feel more at home walking. And then your clothes, Marjorie!'

The road was difficult at this point. The car crawled, and the strange woman stood by the roadside until it passed. Marjorie's eyes rested on her when passing and noticed the woman's poor garb and the sad expression on her face. The wayfarer was young and extremely good-looking.

'Poor soul!' she whispered to the doctor. 'We must give her a lift.'

The car came to a halt.

'Are you going far?' Marjorie called back.

'Glencorrie,' was the answer of the woman.

'Come along, and we'll take you part of the way.'

'Thank you kindly. It's very good of you,' she said clambering into the car with a weary sigh of gratitude.

'Do you live about here?' asked the doctor.

'No, sir. I'm a stranger.'

'But it's no place for a stranger,' said the man. 'You have friends at the works, of course?'

'Yes, I have friends,' said the woman, and was silent. It was evident that she did not want to speak of these friends whoever they were. The doctor started the car again.

'It's cold, isn't it?' asked Marjorie. She wanted to say something more than this mere formality, but did not know exactly what to say.

'It's very cold indeed,' the woman answered. 'But when one's travelling it's not so bad. It's only when a person sits down.'

'Yes, it's cold then,' was Marjorie's comment. 'Your father works up there?' She noticed that the woman wore no wedding ring.

'No, lady, I've no father. He's dead, God rest him! It's my man, workin' at the waterworks, that I'm goin' to see.' The poor woman's glance was so frank and confiding that Marjorie could have kissed her. If she could only help her in some way, thought the city-bred woman.

'Have you walked far?' she inquired.

'A good way, indeed.'

'Will you be staying for a long while at Glencorrie?'

'Maybe I will and maybe I won't,' said the woman. 'It all depends on one thing and another.'

When the car turned at right angles to the glen, she got off.

'You haven't so very far to go now,' said the doctor. 'Two miles will get you to the works. There are not many women there.'

'When you're coming back again, through Dunrobin, if you come that way, call at Dunsore Farm. It's near the village. I will be very glad if you come in and have a cup of tea with me,' said Marjorie. 'Ask for Miss Smith. That is my name. And yours is?'

'Sheila Davis.'

'Eh!' was the doctor's involuntary exclamation. 'You were up here before?'

Sheila blushed and a frightened look came into her eyes.

'I never was at all,' she said nervously. Her eyes got moist; she rubbed them with her hand. 'Thanks to you for the lift,' she said to the doctor. 'And yerself, too, lady, thank ye!'

Without another word Sheila took the cart track to the glen. In the near distance the track was clearly defined, but further along it became indistinct, and ultimately in the far distance, where the first plateau stopped and the ground sloped to a second, the track merged into the waste and twilight and could not be followed further by the eyes that followed Sheila Davis.

'It is she?' whispered Marjorie.

'Of course it is,' said the doctor. 'To her, as to ourselves, he is a curse!'

The car started again. The twilight thickened and the stars came out in the deep sky. The hills stood up sharply against the horizon, and from afar came the gathering sound of the sea.

'Where has she come from?' Marjorie inquired.

'Markonar Infirmary,' said the doctor.

'She looks very ill. Possibly she has stolen away, and walked the whole journey. Some men are lucky,' he added bitterly. 'She trusts and even yet you cannot bear to distrust.' He was silent for a moment. 'On the way back we'll call at Glencorrie and see what is to be seen,' he continued. 'The police are there in force, in plain clothes, and he will possibly be arrested. He's needed for several misdemeanours. We'll see this out to the bitter finish.'

Later in that evening the pair entered Windy Corner shack. The place, hot and stuffy, with a big fire flaring in the red-hot stove, had not a single soul in residence.

'Now, you warm yourself, Marjorie,' said the doctor. 'I've to attend to the car for a moment.'

He went out. The woman sat down and stretched out her hands to the stove. Outside it had been very cold. Feeling had practically gone from her fingers, her feet were icy. Now with the sudden return of warmth she had a spell of delicious agony. Red-hot wires tickled the nerves of fingers and toes. In a calmer moment she would have worried over her untoward position, but now her whole concern was with her feet and hands. She beat the floor with the first, clapped the latter one against another and with an effort kept herself from shrieking.

Five minutes passed; the nerves had become quiet and the pain had worked itself out. The doctor had not returned. When he did, what was to be done? Nothing possibly would happen. Dick had brought her here, taken her all the way from London to see the husband who had deserted her years ago. The husband was living with another woman, or, at least, had bigamously married another.

She had seen that woman in the early part of that day, and recalled now the wistful pain-drawn face, the large soft eyes so frank and confiding, and felt very sorry for her.

From the night came the sudden sound of scuffling. Struggling figures showed outside the door, reeled sideways, backwards, then, as if directed by some fresh impetus, they heaved through the doorway. There were three of them, all navvies as far as Marjorie could judge. She sprang to her feet in terror.

Malcolm Davis was thrust into the shack, powerless in the arms of his strong-limbed escort. The smoke-laden atmosphere, the jumbled bunks, the closeness and squalor were meet environment for the bedraggled man, with his torn tweed cap, clumsily-tied muffler and dishevelled jacket. In his eyes now was a hunted and frightened look.

After the trio came the Ganger, crouching, open-mouthed. In his eyes, which showed pink in the lamplight, was the mystified look of a lurcher that has accidentally nosed a hedgehog. At the sight of the pair, the hunter and hunted, Marjorie, who had risen from her seat, sank back again upon it, deathly white, her mouth half-open, as if with a suppressed cry of terror.

Malcolm Davis stood for a moment in the centre of the shack and gazed at Marjorie, then turned round to fly, and saw his father. The captors released their hold of the man.

'My laddie!' the father stammered in consternation.

'Malcolm!' Marjorie exclaimed, getting to her feet again.

'You here, Marjorie?' asked Davis. He spoke jerkily while assuming the air of one who, having come to the end of all resources, tries to make the best of the occasion. 'You've arrived in time for the killing, anyhow. The police have been on my heels for weeks, and now they're round the place, dozens of them, and I'm cornered. But it doesn't matter!' he cried exultingly, as if pleased to be done with it all.

'What have you done?' asked Marjorie.

'That's not the question, woman,' said the old man. 'If they're after you, you've got to escape. Now, under one of the bunks, my poor laddie. I'll see that nobody comes in here.'

Lifting a pick-shaft from the floor, he went to the main door and stood there on guard.

'Marjorie!' Malcolm spoke. He came in a few steps, and standing in the centre of the floor, looked at the woman. The Moocher and the Slogger edged towards the door.

'Yes?' Marjorie's reply was icy.

'I heard you were somewhere about,' said the man. 'But where is Doctor Taylor?'

'Doctor Taylor!' she repeated, confused. The Moocher went out. The Slogger waited, interested.

'You need not be afraid,' leered Davis. 'All sin, just as you and I have done –'

'You have no right to speak to me like that,' said the woman coldly.

'No, not as a husband, I'll grant,' was the man's admission. 'But as a lover –'

'Lover!' the woman exclaimed scornfully.

'Yes, as your lover,' said the man calmly. 'A lover that damned his soul for you, a lover that truckled to your state of life, that hid his history, because it was not worthy of your upbringing, who made a history, invented a pedigree, lied, thieved, broke laws, human and divine, because he loved you.'

'Loved me! What about the woman, Sheila?' A new note was in her voice, the note of jealousy.

''Twas an error, Marjorie,' said the man. 'But I strove to hide it. For all men the happiness of the future depends on a hidden past. And it happened at a time when the world was off its head, when all were mad and every sense of responsibility gone.'

The Ganger looked round. The old man's eyes were unnaturally bright, with the brightness of agony.

'Now, laddie, get under a bunk and cover yourself up,' he whispered. 'There's somebody comin'.'

'Let them come!' said Malcolm, sitting down wearily. 'I don't care. I'm utterly sick of running over the hills like a hunted hare!'

The Ganger rushed to a bunk, one near the ground, and turned up the blankets. 'Under this, my laddie!' he ordered hysterically, 'and you'll be safe as the flowers in May. They'll not look here. If they do look they'll have to stoop down, and' – he looked at the weapon which he carried – 'and they'll stoop further than they think!' he shouted.

'I don't mind if they do get hold of me,' said Malcolm nonchalantly.

'Dinna be a fool, laddie,' said the old man tearfully. 'I'll give you the whistle when they're comin' and you just scoot in under the bunk! My own shack, paid for in hard money. They daren't come in, no, they daren't!'

Babbling incoherently, he went back to his original position at the door and waited pick in hand. Even as he took up the position he whistled, and at the same moment called out 'Who's there?'

'You keep your wool on!' came the reply from the night.

'You, Moleskin!' said the Ganger angrily. All men were subject to suspicion. 'What the hell are you hangin' about for?'

'Anybody in?' asked Moleskin.

'Spyin' for the polis?' the Ganger grunted. 'Shunt off. You're not gettin' in here this night!'

'What the devil's up your neck now?' was the gruff inquiry of Moleskin, as he gripped the Ganger's weapon and quietly thrust it aside. He entered, looked at the Slogger, the woman, then his eye rested on Malcolm Davis, and he went towards the latter, came to a stop and confronted the man. Standing upright, white and foolish, the shivering Davis stared blankly at the ex-convict.

'Tom Jones, or Malcolm Davis, or whatever the hell you are, you're about the dirtiest sneakin' cur o' the devil I've ever run against,' raged Moleskin. 'Don't speak to me, but shunt! Your wife, one o' them' – he looked sideways at Marjorie whom he had recognised, and a dark flush overspread his face – 'your wife has asked me to give you a hand and clear you out o' this fix, and 'cos she's asked me, I'm goin' to do't, but shunt 'fore I forget myself. There are no cops on the bridge. Get across it and you'll be safe.'

Moleskin ran to the door at the rear, opened it, came back to the dazed Davis, gripped him by the coat-collar and shoved him out. He closed the door after the man and bolted it.

'All's above board for'm now, if his legs are as clever as his head,' he said to the Ganger.

Things occur in moments of turmoil with astonishing rapidity. Even as Moleskin spoke the door at which the Ganger had been standing was flung open, and a stranger entered. In his hand he carried a revolver. He was a new man who had come to Glencorrie that day, looking for a job.

'Who's this fellow?' he inquired, indicating Moleskin and addressing the Ganger. The Slogger edged out.

'What man?' the Ganger vaguely inquired.

'It's Malcolm Davis!' said the stranger, raising his revolver and covering Moleskin. 'Hands up!'

'Keep your blasted wool on!' Moleskin advised, sticking his hands in his pockets and eyeing the man with an air of amused tolerance.

'Take your hands from your pockets!'

'If you're goin' to shoot, shoot and be damned to you!' Moleskin shouted. 'Maybe I ain't the man you want!'

'Who are you, then?'

'You're the man at the wheel, and it ain't your job to go to the fo'c'sle for dead reckonin',' said Moleskin. His voice was calm, but to Marjorie who watched fascinated, tense alertness was evident in the navvy's bearing.

'Malcolm Davis!' said the Ganger suddenly. 'That's not him, polisman. You're on the wrong hoss this time!'

'A rope!' came a welcome shout from outside. 'Has anyone got a rope in there?'

'That's Sergeant Shirley!' was the stranger's involuntary exclamation, as he brought his revolver down.

'There's no rope here,' said Moleskin sarcastically. 'We could rig up a gallows to oblige you, but we ain't got a rope.'

'A man has fallen in the water under the bridge!' somebody said, speaking near the doorway.

'H'm! they're always fallin' in,' said the Ganger petulantly. 'Let him swim!'

'He's caught in the current. He's drowning,' came the same voice from a distance.

Ganger Billy, followed by the stranger, rushed out. Moleskin looked at the woman, who was on her feet.

'Have you ever seen a drowned man pulled out after gettin' crunched on the rocks?' he asked.

'Never!' Marjorie gasped. 'Is somebody drowned?'

'Dunno, but stay where you are and don't come out until all's over!' he ordered, and with these words he went into the moonlight.

For a moment Marjorie stood with her head sunk forwards as if deep in thought, then went towards the door and looked out. She stood there for a moment shivering. Apparently afraid, she came back and looked through the window. Outside sounds of voices were to be heard, loud at first, but gradually sinking into a confused murmur and dying away.

Leaning against the window, her fur coat toning with the wall, she was practically invisible in the smoky atmosphere. Her head outlined against the window pane was so still that it might have been mistaken for a block roundly carved. The guttering lamp hanging from the roof swayed lazily; a coal fell from the stove and broke on the floor. At the sound the woman turned and found she was not alone. The doctor was in the room behind her.

'Nobody in since I left?' he asked.

'Nobody.' Her voice was a whisper. 'We'll go now, Dick.'

'Well, of all!' he exclaimed. 'If we keep putting it off like this, we'll never arrive at any conclusion. We must speak to the foreman, Davis, and the woman, Sheila. We must get to business at once. I'll go out again and look for the old man.'

'He has been here,' said the woman.

'But you said –'

'And he has been here, too.'

'Who is he?' asked the doctor.

'Hey, Doctor Taylor, you're wanted outside at once!' shouted Digger Marley, rushing into the shack. 'There's – there's –'

'Yes, my man, what is it?'

'There's a bloke as is kickin' it, outside! He fell in and him on the run, and lorblimey! the way that his head was cracked again the rocks is somethin' awful. I've seen many a bashin', but if this ain't –'

The doctor ran to the door, came to a halt there and looked back at the woman who was following him.

'You stay where you are, Marjorie!' he ordered in a peremptory tone.

'But, Dick, listen!' Marjorie remonstrated.

'Do what I say! It's not a sight for your eyes.'

'Very well, Dick,' she responded meekly. 'Who was it?' she faltered, turning to Marley. There was a tense look on her face as she waited his reply.

'Well, 'twas like this, and if I may say so, he's done for,' the Digger answered. 'Have been in the army, I have, and saw things like it more'n once. Used to't like, I am. 'Twas a bloke, and he was runnin' from the cops, the polis, to make my meanin' plain, and he tripped again a rock and down wallop he went into the water. It has a run, the water out there, and it leavin' the dam, beggin' your pardon. Well, one o' us, Moleskin Joe his name, jumped in and tried to pull him out. 'Twas a tough job, but he did it. Not that we didn't give Joe a bit o' a hand. 'Twas a hell o' a job all the same, beggin' your pardon again. To hold on again the rush –'

'Was it one of the workmen who fell in?' Marjorie gasped. 'Was the man who ran from the police one of the workmen?'

'He'd too much in his head to be a navvy,' said Marley. 'He's the son of Ganger Billy. Least that's what some o' them are sayin' outside.'

In certain moments of tragedy time stands still, 'is no more'. A moment such as this was Marjorie's then. In her being was an abnormal deepening of sensation and suspense, akin to that of the swimmer who poises for his first dive, or, perhaps, to that of the condemned one who faces the firing party.

'It is he!' she suddenly shrieked, bursting into tears and running to the door. As she went out she had one fleeting impression of an ancient face, a rusty beard and staring red-rimmed agonised eyes, passing her in the doorway.

The face was that of Ganger Billy. He came escorted by Susan Saunders. The old woman, feeling that something untoward was afoot that evening, had not returned to her shack with the blankets which she had wheedled from the old man. Curiosity, which was stronger than compassion, had not permitted her to leave the locality of Windy Corner.

The Ganger came into the shack feeling his way as if sight had deserted him, and eventually, getting to the form by the stove, sat down there, a huddled and broken man.

'Now, my beauty, what are you doin'?' the managing Susan inquired, looking at Marley, who had not left the room. 'You're worse than the whole lot o' 'em! Is there any drink about? Get it at once and give it to me, you old dodderer!'

Marley fished a billy-can from a corner, left it on the seat beside the washerwoman and withdrew precipitately.

'Now put a drop o' this into you and you'll be all right,' said the woman, lifting the billy-can and holding it towards the Ganger.

The words and the accompanying motion were lost on him.

'I knew it was all over as soon as I saw his face,' he muttered, looking vacantly at Saunders. 'I've seen too many done in in my time not to know death. The doctor didn't need to tell me. Death never tells lies.' He paused a moment and groped in his pocket, as if searching for his habitual pipe. 'My own wee laddie, wee Malcolm!' he muttered.

'Your laddie?' asked Saunders. 'Was it the truth?'

'Aye, my boy,' groaned the Ganger.

'But it was Tom Jones,' said the old woman.

'I don't know why he changed his name,' said the Ganger. 'But he had his reasons. My boy! Malcolm, my boy.'

The voice of a disconsolate king in the forest of Ephraim was the voice now speaking in the navvy shack.

'Aye, Malcolm, my laddie, you look a fine bit of a wee soldier!' the old man rambled, pressing an imaginary head that had location some three feet from the ground. 'All the books you have to read, and I bought them all for you. Now, come and tell your old daddy what you're goin' to be when you're a big man! A gentleman? That's it, my boy, that's it! I'll be Mummy to you and I'll be Daddy to you, and I'll make you a gentleman! . . . The polis after you!' he screeched hysterically. 'Them! When you were an officer they saluted you! Dead! It's a lie, a damned lie!'

He got to his feet, groped again in his pocket, and stared at the old washerwoman without seeing her. She looked at him with a furtive, frightened glance, the tears streaming from her rheumy eyes. Suddenly he staggered backwards against the table and sat down again utterly stricken.

Saunders sprang to her feet, grasped the billy-can, which contained a few dregs of that which was responsible for the tragedy, and held it to the old man's lips.

'Now, put this inside you and it'll buck you up,' she advised him.

'I don't want it, woman, thank you all the same.' The Ganger got to his feet and made for the door. 'I'll not be spoon-fed while I've my grinders. Aye, aye!' He stopped as if considering. 'It's cold out there. Wouldn't let a dog lie out, not even a dog!'

Delirious he went to the door, made his exit and became one with the night.

Moleskin, dripping wet, entered at the same moment, and was immediately followed by two policemen. One was the individual who had been there before.

'Moleskin Joe!' called this fellow. 'We want you, my man.'

Moleskin went backward towards the door on the rear, his eye fixed on the two who advanced upon him.

'You forgot all about this door,' said Moleskin playfully, pointing his thumb over his shoulder at the door behind.

'Have I, indeed?' asked the man. 'I'm not as big a fool as you take me to be!'

'Eh!' was Moleskin's involuntary ejaculation.

He looked round to see a massive individual filling the open door. The moment was one for precipitate action, and the ex-convict was not wanting. He made a sudden rush at his enemy's feet, and as the person stooped to seize him, Moleskin applied a wrestling grip, cross-buttocked the plain clothes policeman and sent him flying over his head into the shack.

'Didn't think o' that'n, did you?' Moleskin inquired looking back from the door.

In the space of a second he had disappeared.

CHAPTER 19

THE JOURNEY

The man's a fool that has pity to spare for a cryin' wench or a barefooted duck.

– *From* Moleskin Joe.

Doctor Taylor's car was making its way along the cart track leading from Glencorrie. Driving was comparatively easy, for the sulcated road, rutted by heavy vehicular traffic, was now hardened by the frost. The doctor drove. Marjorie sat beside him, curled up like a little kitten, part of her face only visible.

For a while there had been silence. In fact, not more than a dozen words had been spoken since the car left Glencorrie, and now some three miles of the journey were completed.

The moon hung high, a few wisps of clouds floated amidst the stars, the wind moaned low across the moor, now and again rising in a shrill dirge and afterwards sinking to a whimper, as if tired of its exertion. A profound melancholy seemed to have settled over everything.

Marjorie, with head a little inclined, was watching the doctor with attentive eyes.

'Should I have left?' she suddenly inquired.

'There was nothing more to be done,' said the doctor. 'You could not stay there all night.'

'But his wife!' began Marjorie. 'And the inquest –'

'You're not in England now, dear one,' said the doctor. 'There is no inquest held here, in Scotland. We've a procurator-fiscal instead of a coroner. He makes inquiries, but the sergeant (Shirley was his name, I believe) will state the case to the procurator for this district (I know him well), and the matter will be set right.'

'But I should not have left,' persisted the woman.

'My dear –' the doctor began. 'Who the devil's this?'

He pulled the car up with a jerk, just as a man who obstructed the way stepped nimbly to one side and gripped the side of the vehicle. Marjorie, who was nerved up to a high state of tension, uttered a shriek.

'What the devil are you up to?' demanded the doctor, looking at the man.

'I hope I've not frightened the lady,' said Moleskin Joe, who was the culprit. 'You see, it's like this, doctor. I wanted to speak to you, but I haven't what you might call the free foot. The polis are chancin' their arm on me, like, and I've a lot to do. You see, it's all because – because – I don't know how to set about tellin' you, but if – Well, if it was man to man it would be easier, not that I mean –'

He looked at the woman and was silent.

'Please go on,' said Marjorie, who saw that he felt awkward in her presence. 'You said tonight that Sheila Davis was a friend to you. And as far as I could gather she was more than a friend to you.'

'Well!' exclaimed the surprised Moleskin. 'I never thought that a woman had so much in her as to see through a thing like that. Old Ganger Billy used to say that a woman starts to learn where a man leaves off and this is the first time I've ever saw truth in it.'

'You're Moleskin Joe?' asked the doctor. There was interest in the man's voice.

'Well, if I am, I don't shout about it,' said he.

'Congratulations!' The doctor caught Moleskin's hand and shook it heartily.

'Co'gratulations!' the mystified Moleskin repeated. 'What! What's that?'

'Surely you've not forgotten what you've just done?' asked the doctor with a laugh.

'Well, we all did our best and if the man' – he looked at Marjorie – 'the gentleman handed in his check for good 'twas nobody's fault.'

''Twas a great pity that his life was not saved, after such a gallant effort,' said the doctor.

'Was it?' asked Moleskin, looking in the doctor's eyes and losing hand-grip.

'Of course it was, my man. A man has only got one life –'

'One's enough sometimes and more than enough. But do you mean what you say?'

The two looked at one another. Marjorie sat back open-eyed and stared at Moleskin.

'Mean what?' asked the doctor nervously.

'Does Sheila Davis know?' As he put the question Moleskin glanced at Marjorie.

'I don't understand you,' said the doctor. 'What are you trying to get at? '

'Sheila Davis has been told nothing,' said Marjorie.

'Well, you know what I'm tryin' to say,' Moleskin endeavoured to explain. 'If she doesn't know, it's all right.'

'You haven't changed since you were in the water?' asked the woman.

'That's nothin',' said the man.

'But you're wet!'

'We always change our duds when we're wet,' said Moleskin with a laugh. 'That is when we've any extra togs, so to speak, but we never have.'

'You've a flask, Dick?' the woman asked the doctor.

He brought a silver flask from his pocket, shook it, although he knew it was almost full, pulled back its cap and handed the flask to Moleskin.

'Have a drink!' he said.

'Don't mind if I do,' said Moleskin, putting it to his lips and drinking. 'Body in it!' he said with relish as he handed it back.

'Well?' The monosyllable was a hint that the conversation might proceed.

'I think a lot o' her, Sheila Davis,' was Moleskin's simple admission.

'Ah! In love with her?' asked Marjorie.

'Put it that way if you like. It's all the same to me. Now I want to ask you a question.' He turned to the doctor. 'Did you mean it when you said it was a pity that Malcolm Davis went for good?'

'Certainly.'

'Well, all that I can say is, that there ain't much for *you* to be sorry about.'

'What do you mean?' asked the doctor angrily.

'Keep your wool on,' said Moleskin quietly. 'I heard what you and her' (he indicated Marjorie by a turn of his thumb) 'was sayin' to each other the other night at Dunsore!'

'Eavesdropping?'

'Eh?' Moleskin was mystified by the word.

'You were listening to something not intended for your ears!' said the doctor, pulling a car-lever. The hint was not lost on Moleskin.

'I'm hangin' on, freezin' to the gadget till I spit out what I'm goin' to say.' Moleskin's hands tightened their grip on the vehicle. 'I went to Dunsore to see if there was any chance of pickin' up grub for a wee nipper that I had, so to speak, that wasn't my own, that was, so to speak, not my own, but was – But you'll know what I mean, m'm?'

He looked at Marjorie. He had placed great reliance on the woman, who had become infallible in his eyes. She knew everything.

'You got the food, not for yourself, but for somebody else. Isn't that what you mean?' asked Marjorie, looking at him.

'That's it, that the show, a straight flush,' said the jubilant Moleskin. 'It's Sheila's nipper that I was chancin' my arm on. He wanted cookies, and I went to Dunsore and got 'em. And then I had to hide when you came in before you were expected. And I heard what you said. That's all. My cards are on the table.'

'Well, what do you want me to do?' asked the doctor.

'It's what I don't want you to do; that's the thing,' said Moleskin. 'You're not to tell Sheila that Malcolm Davis, his right name, is not her husband. That won't hurt you. Don't tell her that I had anything to do with pullin' him out o' the water. If you help me in this, I'll eat out o' your hand, doctor, but if you don't, by God, I'll –'

'We'll do everything that's possible,' said Marjorie.

'Everything,' said the doctor. 'I'll try at once to get her a home somewhere. I've a friend that will see to it. The boy will have a chance of getting a good education –'

'A good education,' said Moleskin doubtfully. 'I can't see how it does much good.' His thoughts were on the father of the child.

'It's not always a failure,' said the doctor. 'And now, what are you going to do?'

'Three months,' was Moleskin's admission.

'Why?' Marjorie gasped.

'Well, it's like this,' said Moleskin, his eyes on the woman. 'I've a great notion of Sheila. My head's in a fog about her. I wouldn't stop at nothin' that she wants, for see, I did all I was able to save Malcolm Davis when I could have twisted his thrapple, the dirty sneakin' cur o' hell. 'Twas done because Sheila wanted him. If he was a live man now, I wouldn't be here, talkin' like this, for three months' hard ain't to my likin'. But I'm chancin' my arm on't. If I do three months, it'll mean a clean sheet and maybe then Sheila will listen to me.'

'But why three months?' asked Marjorie, who did not understand.

'Was in for three, but done a slide,' Moleskin explained. 'So now I'm off!'

His fingers slackened and he withdrew a pace.

'But you're drenched,' said the doctor.

'If you come along with us I'll get you some dry clothes.'

'My duds are dry now, thank you all the same,' said Moleskin, slapping his trousers. Frozen stiff, they stood round his legs firm as wooden cones.

Without another word he moved away. The car lurched forward, jolting over frozen snag and hummie. The doctor's eyes were set on the road in front, his friend sat back in her seat, her mind filled with varying emotions, in which Moleskin Joe and the doctor played a prominent part, perhaps the most prominent part of all being played by the rough uncultured buck-navvy.

Would Dick do as much for her as Moleskin Joe did for Sheila Davis? she asked herself, but was afraid to ask him the question. Still, why should she not inquire? She saw Sheila's eyes again, the long lashes, the magnificent dark-brown hair. 'Yes, I'll ask him,' she whispered desperately. Her hand trembled on his elbow and he bent his head slightly towards her.

'Dick?'

'Yes, my dear.' The car jolted and she pressed her head against his shoulder.

'Would you –' she paused.

'Yes, dearest?'

'Would you – would you mind if I went to the funeral?' was her question.

'Certainly not, my little girl.' He put one arm round her and manipulated the steering wheel with the hand that was free.

She leant against him, shaking with sobs. The tears welled from her eyes, but she found no solace in her weeping.

CHAPTER 20

TWO WOMEN

Then cuddle closer, Heart's Delight,
Ere time brings cark and care,
And catch the fancy born in flame,
Ere it dies out in air!

– *From* Longings.

Barefooted and bent under her burden of blankets, Susan Saunders was on the road back to her cabin. During the excitement at Windy Corner she was not above taking advantage of the occasion, and thieving a pair, she added them to her stock.

It was very cold and clear. Objects in the near distance were quite visible, though further away things lost much of their real semblance and had outlines vague and indefinite. It was a raw and lonely night surely.

But physically and mentally, the rawness and loneliness had little effect on the old woman. Her body, inured to inclemencies of many winters, was proof against cold and bleakness; her mind, not possessing that subtle perception of nature's aspects, was unconcerned with the obscure mysteries of the night. To her the moment was a trifle uncomfortable, nothing more.

'Well, well, people will be dyin', and people will be marryin', and there's not much good in makin' trouble for folk,' she told herself as she neared her cabin. 'After the sickness that was on her, the poor wee dear, I'm not goin' to tell Sheila the way her man died. It'll be a relapse, maybe, if she knows. And the devil's sendin' that he was, he should have died long agone.'

The cabin door was open. The naphtha lamp guttered, the fire was a mere heap of white ashes, the apartment had still the damp, mouldy odour which tells of a place that had not been lived in for a long time. Sheila sat by the fire, the boy lay in the blankets asleep.

'I was frightened, Susan,' said Sheila, looking up at the old woman. 'I thought, maybe, you got lost!'

'Folk like me never get lost,' laughed the old woman, throwing her bundle to the floor. In the misty atmosphere of the cabin she looked very old and worn. 'And how are you feelin' on it now, Sheila, dear?'

'A wee bit tired, Susan, but I'll be all right in the mornin' when I wake up, thanks to yourself and everybody that's been so good to me.'

'And he's sleepin', the wee rascal?' asked the old woman, pointing at Isaacs.

'Aye, indeed, and he's sleepin',' said Sheila. 'Closed his eyes as soon as I put him down. It's grand to have him with me again! Hungry I was for him, Susan, and me with nothin' to look at at all but the walls and the rain fallin' outside against the window panes. And wasn't Moleskin Joe the good man?'

'Nothin' wrong with Joe,' said Susan. 'Rough he may be, and tough he may be, but he has the heart. "Daddy Joe", the nipper calls him.'

'Daddy Joe.' Sheila blushed as she repeated the words. 'Even and him sleepin' he called for Daddy Joe.'

'Well, I don't wonder at it,' said Susan. 'Joe is a good fellow – strong as a horse. That's what I liked in my young days, strong men. The grip they have. But I don't think they're like that nowadays.'

'I'm not so sure,' said Sheila, smiling as if at a happy memory. 'Won't you sit down, Susan?'

'We've all had our experience,' said the old woman as she threw a piece of wood on the fire. 'But there's one thing that we always forget, and fools we are for the same, us women that cannot be young for ever. "Make the best of it while you are young" is what I say, for all of us find, some day, that there is no good to be gained by waterin' last year's crops.' With a sigh the woman gave weight to this ancient aphorism.

'I'm always waterin' last year's crops,' said Sheila sadly.

'More fool you, lass.' Saunders was asperse. 'Keep your eye on the bright side of things, even when you're sitting in the ditch as the saying has it.'

'But if there's no bright side?'

'I know what you are wantin',' said the old woman, sitting down by the side of Sheila, and putting her hand on the young woman's brown head. 'A good cry. That eases the heart.'

'I'm not goin' to cry.' Sheila looked up at Saunders. 'I've done it so often and it has never been any good to me.'

'Then laugh.'

'I can't do that either.'

'Neither hot nor cold,' said the washerwoman. 'That's the fault with folk nowadays. Nobody knows what to do. They're afraid to go one way, afraid to go another. The thing that's right for the soul is wrong for the heart. Balderash I call it. Follow your heart. That's the great secret of the world. That's what makes the birds to sing. Sheila, dear' – the old woman kissed the girl's hair – 'follow your heart. Have Moleskin Joe! He's as good as many and better than most.'

'Who told you about him?' asked the startled Sheila, gazing with fearful eyes at the washerwoman.

'He was sayin' things to me,' said Susan.

'What was he saying?' Sheila asked.

'Just what any man would say if he caught it bad.'

'Caught what?' asked Sheila. 'I don't understand.'

'Caught what we are all lookin' for from the time that we twist the first curl in front of the lookin'-glass, to the time when we will say our prayers, knowin' that the washin' we've hung out to dry is our very last. It's love, the love that all have sometime in their life and what Moleskin Joe has for you!'

Sheila nestled in against the old woman's side, sobbing. Saunders put her arms round the young shoulders.

'Aye, you're cryin', lass,' she said in a tone that was almost one of triumph. ''Twon't hurt, for it never does. Now,' she asked, 'what's to be done about it?'

'About what?' asked Sheila.

'About Moleskin Joe. He loves you. And you love him.'

'I love him! Who said so?' Sheila inquired in a nervous whisper.

'Years ago you had more than a notion of him at Hermiston,' said the old woman. 'On in years I may be, but I wasn't blind, thank you, at the time. I could see you tidy up your hair, and put a finish to your dress whenever you went out and there was a chance of meetin' him. Sally Jaup and me wasn't as blind as you thought us.' Susan looked at the young woman, dropped a wrinkled eyelid slowly, until it rested on her cheek. 'And yourself,' she inquired sharply, 'have you the same notion of him yet?'

Sheila was silent for a moment.

'I have, Susan!' she suddenly exclaimed. 'But what's the use at all? What can I do, anyway?'

'What does your heart tell you?' Saunders inquired.

'It tells me to do something that my faith forbids. In the eyes of God, I'm married, and will be married while my husband's alive.'

'He'd do you good, only in dyin',' said Saunders. 'Years away from you and never sent you one penny to help you! If I only had to do with him! And why have you kept waitin' for him all this time? Why? Why?'

'Him!' Sheila indicated the sleeping child.

'Him! Why him?'

'He's our child,' was the young woman's simple explanation. 'Malcolm's and mine.'

'Malcolm, Malcolm, always Mr Malcolm!' said the old woman brutally. 'My dear child, what do you see in him? He's no good! You are only wastin' your time runnin' after him. It's ten to one that you'll never set eyes on him again. Down at Windy Corner they say that he's skedaddled.'

'But, maybe, I will see him again,' said Sheila. 'And, anyway, he's my husband.'

'It's the way always with girls,' said Susan philosophically. 'They never take advice, but make mistakes and get married, most times to the wrong man, and they are always fools. Now, if you take my advice, ye'll nab Moleskin. With the right woman he'll get on. And you're the right woman. Moleskin likes the nipper. He'll be daddy to him. If the polis are after him, what about it? He'll give them the slip!'

'The police after Moleskin?' asked the girl. 'Why is it at all?'

'Did he not tell you?'

'He didn't.'

'He was supposed to do somethin' that he didn't do, and he got three months' hard,' Saunders told her. 'He escaped and now he's on leg-bail. I'm sorry for poor Joe.'

'Why did they put him in when he didn't do anything?' asked Sheila.

'It's the way of the world,' said the old woman. 'What would get a cat off would hang a buck-navvy . . . He's a good man, Joe, and if that isn't a gentleman any day of the week ask me another. Go with him, take Cunnin' Isaacs, and work out your own salvation, lassie.'

'It's not so easy, Susan.'

'I know what's holdin' you.' The old woman got to her feet. 'It's because your church says that a marriage is sacred. But a marriage like yours is not, never was and never will be, it's a sin against God and woman. Follow your heart, lass, and have courage.'

'I wish I was strong enough to do that. Or, maybe' – she paused in thought – 'maybe, it's stronger not to.'

The old woman looked at the window. In fact, she had been casting surreptitious glances at that quarter of the house for some time and not without reason. Something dark and resembling a tuft of heather had been moving outside the pane, now rising up as if wanting to get higher, and again sinking out of sight, as if afraid of being seen. It did look like a bunch of heather, if heather grew to such magnitude and found purchase like the ivy against the walls of a house.

Now it rose to a higher altitude, and at its base something white showed, and in the whiteness was set a pair of eyes. The old woman moved to the door, stood there for a moment, then went outside. A man withdrew from the window, walking backwards towards the gable wall. Coming to a stop, he beckoned to Susan.

'What do you want, Moleskin Joe?' she asked, going towards him.

'Whist!' he whispered. 'I want to speak to you, Susan.'

'What about?' She also spoke in a whisper.

'I want to have a talk with *her*,' said the man, moving backwards.

'What have you to say to her?' asked Susan following.

'Does she know?' asked Moleskin, coming to a halt. They were now twenty yards distant from the cabin.

'I'ven't told her.'

'She'll be told soon,' said Moleskin. 'There are always people ready to run with bad news. But it won't be so bad if she hears it tomorrow after she's had a good night's sleep.'

'And to think o't!' moaned the woman. 'She's not married at all.'

'She is,' said Moleskin.

'She's not and never was –'

'She was; years ago.'

'That ain't true, Joe,' said Saunders.

'What's true doesn't matter a tinker's damn,' growled Moleskin. 'It's what we believe to be true that matters. Sheila's sure that she was married, and if I get anyone sayin' that she isn't I'll twist his thrapple. To have it that Malcolm was her man is everything to the lass, everything that's straight and above board. And all she done was on account of her nipper. That's why I tried to give Malcolm Davis a leg over. Sheila wanted him, and I done my best.'

'Even the polis say that they never saw a thing like it, the way you jumped in –'

'The first time they ever said a word in my favour,' muttered Moleskin. 'Now, Susan Saunders!'

'Well, Joe?'

'I'm goin' to chance my arm on a three-month stretch,' said Moleskin. 'Seein' as how I gave them the slip, it'll mean that my one month done will go for nothin'. It'll be three, and I'm goin' to give myself up.'

'Don't see why as you oughter,' said Susan.

'It's like this,' Moleskin explained. 'Here's me, not much good anyways or anywhere, only in a scrap and a boozer. And there's her, too good for anything. She's gone through hell for that nipper o' hers; he's all in all to her and because of him she wouldn't slip the painter that tied her to Malcolm Davis. It's more than I can get the hang o' why she ran after him.'

'Thought she was his married wife,' Susan mumbled.

'Take it at that,' Moleskin resumed. 'But if she finds out that he was married to another wench before he met her, it'll break her heart. So I've figured it out this way, Susan. She'll hear that he's kicked it, tomorrow. When he's put into the tipper, take her and the nipper to Doctor Taylor, and he'll get her a place, and Isaacs will go to school. That's what the doctor told me. If she gets away from Glencorrie, she'll be as good as made . . . Is she in here now?' He pointed at the cabin.

'She's there, Moleskin.'

'I would like to have a word with her 'fore I give myself up. On the quiet. I mean by that, with nobody listenin' to what we are sayin'.'

'All right, you go in,' said Susan. 'But don't spend all night over it . . . It's too damned cold for anything! And me without a boot on my feet!'

CHAPTER 21

THE PARTING

And on forever,
Since Fates allow,
Full bosomed One
Of the snow-white brow,
I'll see you, Fair,
As I see you now.
–*From* Dreams.

She sat by the fire, that now burned brightly, and awaited the return of Susan. But Sheila's thoughts were not on the old woman. Sitting there she called up the image of the man who had won her heart, seeing him as he was, kind, simple and intense, strong when dealing with others, but pliable in her hands, ready to yield to her moods and desires.

He had taken possession of her, she realised with a vague uneasiness, taken possession of her for ever. In thought she yielded to him, became one with the great big lover in desires and dreams. For years she had hungered for love and now, as if a floodgate had opened, the tumultuous torrent of passion had swept over her, smothering her in its terrible undisciplined confusion.

'Joe, I want you, I want you,' she whispered, and even as the words left her lips she uttered a cry and started to her feet. Moleskin Joe was standing at the door, outlined against the night, the moonshine and the molten-silvered moor.

'It's yourself, Joe?' she asked, gazing at the man, who stood still, timid and afraid.

'Come to see how you are!' he mumbled. 'And to see if the nipper's well.' He looked at the sleeping child, then at the mother, so pale, fresh and beautiful.

'I can never thank you for bein' so good to him,' she said. 'Sit down and we'll talk. There's a lot of things that we must talk about.'

He sat down, resting his hands on his knees as if ready to spring to his feet in a moment. Sheila looked at him, her deep eyes filled with tears.

'I would listen to you for ever,' said the man in a thick whisper. 'For there never was anybody like you, Sheila.'

'You love me?' she asked gently, and waited, hungry for his answer.

'Love you, Sheila!' was his vehement exclamation. He got to his feet. ' If –'

'Please sit down, Joe,' she said. 'I shouldn't have spoke to you the way I did this evenin'. I am a wicked woman, with no control over me tongue. Wicked, Joe. Wicked!'

'Wicked!' Moleskin exclaimed, laughing. 'Well, if you are wicked, I've never heard or seen a good woman in all my natural.'

'It was wrong of me to speak to you in that way,' she insisted.

'What was wrong in it, lass? Nothin'. I've never been as happy in all my days as I was since then. You told me you loved me and is there anything better in the world?'

'Ours is the wrong kind of love,' said Sheila simply. She was suddenly afraid.

'I'm a blunt barge o' a man, but I see nothin' wrong with it,' Moleskin remarked. 'There can't be.'

'But ours is.' She found solace in self-castigation. 'I'm to blame for it all. If I had only not come at all!'

'Why? What makes it wrong?' he asked huskily.

'Him!' said Sheila, pointing at the child.

'Oh, him!' Moleskin exclaimed. 'Well, it beats me how he can have anything to do with right or wrong.'

'He holds me to my husband.'

'Doesn't look as if the nipper holds him to you,' Moleskin snorted.

'But it's for his sake that I mustn't do wrong, even if I want to,' said the woman.

'Easy job, him, Sheila,' said Moleskin, to whom in his great simplicity everything was quite clear. 'He needn't stop you. I'll work for him. Honest to God I will. I won't ask you to do a hand's turn. I'll not let you work. You're so wee, lass, so wee.

How were you able at all to bear all your hardships?' he asked, and the eyes he fixed on her were full of wonder.

'There's a strength to bear everything,' was Sheila's enigmatic assertion.

'I would be able to help you in everything, and the nipper into the bargain,' said Moleskin. 'Don't you think I would?' he asked.

'I know you would, Joe,' said the woman. 'You'd be a better father to him than ever his own has been. But there's more than that to it, Joe, much more. I don't know much about what they call the law, but I do know this, that after a mother has borne her child, gone through the tortures of hell for it, loved it better than her own life, if she finds a good man willin' to do what its own father ought to have done, the father can come along and say the child is his and take it away and do whatever he likes with it. And I can't lose Cunnin' Isaacs!' she cried, bursting into sobs.

'But catch me lettin' anyone come and put even a finger on him. If you just –'

'Don't, Joe, I ask ye!' she entreated. 'Whatever you say to me I've said to myself over and over a hundred times this night, when you weren't with me. I've beaten myself, cut my heart to tatters!'

'Poor Sheila!' Moleskin whispered. He was again on his feet. 'If it wasn't for the nipper, would you come with me?' he asked. His hand touched her shoulder. 'Give me the straight answer, Sheila.'

'Don't ask me, Joe. Don't, don't!' she entreated.

Moleskin trembled. He pulled his hand away and gazed into her eyes, and a great feeling of pity throbbed through him. The glaring naphtha light slanted across her face and buried itself in the folds of her bosom. He could catch her with one hand and put her in his pocket. So small, so helpless, and he wanted her more than anything in the world! He had come in to tell her something, very simple, but now hardly remembering what it was, he had nothing to say. Again his hand touched her shoulder, and she looked up, half-beseeching, half-trusting. Something quivered on her lips for a moment, quivered and died away.

'Sheila, you do love me?' he asked, suddenly catching her in his arms and kissing her lips.

'I love you, Joe, love you better than anybody in the whole

wide world.' Speaking, she nestled in against him. 'I have never loved anyone only you. You are a big simple dear, but you're not to do this. You mustn't, you mustn't!'

'One more!' he pleaded.

She clasped him impetuously with a force beyond that of a woman's and kissed him.

'Here's one more!' she said, 'and another and another. And now' – she thrust him away from her – 'I hate myself. Go, Joe, go away at once. Leave me! For the sake of everything, leave me! God forgive me! God forgive us both!'

'But what are we to do?' asked Moleskin, gazing helplessly at the woman. 'But we can go away, me and you and Isaacs, and no one will know.'

'One will know,' said Sheila.

'Who?'

'You're not a Catholic, Joe?' she asked.

'Never was anything on the prayer gadget till I got into the army,' said the man. 'Then I was an R.C. Couldn't make fist o' the issue, but I liked the chaplain bloke, Father Nolan, a real corker crossin' the top!'

'Father Nolan?' asked Sheila in surprise. 'Do you know him?'

'Know the fellow!' Moleskin cried, 'I think I do! He comes here once a month to shout the odds. Do you know him?'

'He's the priest that married us.'

'Church of England for me the next war,' said Moleskin, voicing a verdict beyond appeal. 'But why do you ask me if I'm a Catholic, Sheila?'

'Because, if you were, you wouldn't ask me why haven't I the free hand. In the church one is married for life. I gave my word to a man and I'm his till death. It's wrong havin' you here; it's sin, a dark sin.'

'I'm goin' away, Sheila, in two minutes,' said Moleskin in a slow, studied voice. He seemed to have got his bearings at last. He pointed his finger at the blankets which held Isaacs. 'Will I be right in sayin' that if you hadn't him, you'd come with me?'

Her eyes, filled with unfathomed thoughts, looked steadily into his. She wanted to be thoroughly sincere; her nature had always found it difficult to be otherwise, but to be frank at that moment, in answering Moleskin's question as her heart bade her answer it, was a sin in the woman's eyes.

Before her stood the man whom she loved, whom she had always loved, a man of flesh and blood, intense, magnetic. But about him were grouped other figures, shadows without substance; her husband, the priest, her long-dead mother, and a thousand other ghosts, upholders of a fervent faith and the age-long tradition in which her being was moulded. And these called to her across space and time, saying: 'Beware! Go no further!'

'No, Joe, I wouldn't,' she said with a resolute suppression of emotion. 'It's too terrible to think of, God forgive me!'

'If your man would die, before me, would you come to me then?' he asked.

'I would, Joe,' was her simple admission.

'Then I'll wait,' said the diplomat, and a smile showed on his face. 'I'm goin' away for a while, but I'll come back, Sheila, whenever you're free, and then, married or single, saint or sinner, I'll have you if I've to go to the pit of hell to get you. Give me your hand on that, Sheila.'

She caught one hand in both her own. Only the man faced her, the spectres faded into the obscure distance and vanished.

'Say somethin', Sheila! Say you love me. Was there ever anything like this?'

'Never in the whole wide world!' she whispered, kissing him.

Susan, who had been shivering outside the door for the last ten minutes, coughed noisily as a polite preliminary before entering. The two lovers drew themselves apart.

'Dear me! dear me!' said the old woman coming in, beating her hands together. ''Twould freeze the toes off a steam navvy. And you are a pair to leave in the house, with the fire half out. And you, Moleskin, what's the good of you. Mischief always wherever you are, damn you!'

There was a certain good humour in her coarse raillery, and in her eyes a knowing look as if she understood all that had happened in the last few minutes.

'It's always the way when it comes to kissin'!' she laughed, shaking her grey hairs. 'No time for anything else!'

'Susan, I don't know what you mean at all,' said the confused Sheila in a whisper.

'The red on your cheek gives the lie to your tongue,' said the merciless washerwoman. 'Where are *you* off to now?' she asked Moleskin, who was edging towards the door.

'He's goin' away, Susan,' said the young woman, sinking her face in her hands.

'Only three months away 'twill be,' said Moleskin. There was gratitude in the eyes he fixed on Sheila. An extraordinary lightness rose in his breast, a radiance through which joyous thoughts and sensations surged like swallows in a clear sky. 'And the sooner I'm off the sooner I will be back!'

'Then hop it,' commanded the matter-of-fact Susan. 'Don't hang about the door makin' a song about it!'

'I'm off,' said Moleskin. 'Good night, Susan.'

'Is that the way you take yourself off?' snapped the old woman. 'Give her a kiss afore you go. God! the fools that are in it nowadays. Kiss the lassie, dammit! Kiss her!'

She caught Moleskin's arm, pulled the big man towards Sheila.

'Can't do no more!' she said. 'It's never done by proxy. But I'll look the other way!'

'Little Sheila, I love you!' said Moleskin, catching her hands.

'Joe!' she whispered, sinking into his arms.

The old woman poked the fire with a wooden stake, performing the action noisily as if to drown all other sounds. Sparks flew up the chimney, a burning splinter fell on the hearth and she kicked it back with her bare foot.

'Will he ever come back again?'

Susan looked round at the speaker. Moleskin had gone, and Sheila was alone.

'Now into bed with you!' ordered the old woman. 'I'll give you a can of tea as soon as you're lyin' down. Back again, eh? Twelve weeks from now he'll be back with you and in six months the two of you will be married!'

THE END